WINDEYE

Windeye

STORIES

Brian Evenson

COFFEE HOUSE PRESS

MINNEAPOLIS

2012

Coffee House Press books are available to the trade through our primary distributor, Consortium Book Sales & Distribution, cbsd.com or (800) 283-3572. For personal orders, catalogs, or other information, write to: info@coffeehousepress.org.

Coffee House Press is a nonprofit literary publishing house. Support from private foundations, corporate giving programs, government programs, and generous individuals helps make the publication of our books possible. We gratefully acknowledge their support in detail in the back of this book.

Good books are brewing at coffeehousepress.org

LIBRARY OF CONGRESS CATALOGING-IN-PUBLICATION DATA
Evenson, Brian, 1966–
Windeye : stories / by Brian Evenson.
p. cm.
ISBN 978-1-56689-298-8 (alk. paper)
I. Title.
PS3555.V326W56 2012
813'.54—DC23
2011029252
3 5 7 9 8 6 4
PRINTED IN THE UNITED STATES

The author would like to thank the editors of the following magazines and anthologies, in which the stories gathered here were originally published: *Pen America:* "Windeye"; *Unsaid:* "The Second Boy" and "Knowledge"; *Black Clock:* "The Process," "The Moldau Affair," and "Bon Scott: The Choir Years"; *Parallax:* "A History of the Human Voice" and "Baby or Doll"; *My Mother She Killed Me, My Father She Ate Me:* "Dapplegrim"; *Exotic Gothic 3:* "The Dismal Mirror"; *Black Warrior Review:* "Legion"; *Not About Vampires:* "The Sladen Suit"; *The Lifted Brow:* "Hurlock's Law" and "The Other Ear"; *No Colony:* "Discrepancy"; *Conjunctions:* "Angel of Death"; *Dossier:* "The Tunnel"; *New Lights Press* (broadside series): "South of the Beast"; *The Golden Handcuffs Review:* "Tapadera"; mlp mini-chapbook series: "They"; *New Lights Press* (artist's book): "The Drownable Species"; *Exotic Gothic 4:* "Grottor"; *Redivider:* "Anskan House."

For my lost sister

Windeye

T HEY LIVED, WHEN HE WAS GROWING UP, IN A SIMPLE HOUSE, AN OLD bungalow with a converted attic and sides covered in cedar shake. In the back, where an oak thrust its branches over the roof, the shake was light brown, almost honey. In the front, where the sun struck it full, it had weathered to a pale gray, like a dirty bone. There, the shingles were brittle, thinned by sun and rain, and if you were careful you could slip your fingers up behind some of them. Or at least his sister could. He was older and his fingers were thicker, so he could not.

Looking back on it, many years later, he often thought it had started with that, with her carefully working her fingers up under a shingle as he waited and watched to see if it would crack. That was one of his earliest memories of his sister, if not the earliest.

His sister would turn around and smile, her hand gone to knuckles, and say, "I feel something. What am I feeling?" And then he would ask questions. *Is it smooth?* he might ask. *Does it feel rough? Scaly? Is it cold-blooded or warm-blooded? Does it feel red? Does it feel like its claws are in or out? Can you feel its eye move?* He would keep on, watching the expression on her face change as she tried to make his words into a living, breathing thing, until it started to feel too real for her and, half giggling, half screaming, she whipped her hand free.

There were other things they did, other ways they tortured each other, things they both loved and feared. Their mother didn't know anything about it, or if she did she didn't care. One of them would shut the other inside the toy chest and pretend to leave the room, waiting there silently until the one in the chest couldn't stand it any longer and started to yell. That was a hard game for him because he was afraid of the dark, but he tried not to show that to his sister. Or one of them would wrap the other tight in blankets, and then the trapped one would have to break free. Why they had liked it, why they had done it, he had a hard time remembering later, once he was grown. But they *had* liked it, or at least *he* had liked it—there was no denying that—and he had done it. No denying that either.

So at first those games, if they were games, and then, later, something else, something worse, something decisive. What was it again? Why was it hard, now that he was grown, to remember? What was it called? Oh, yes, *Windeye*.

———— 2 ————

How had it begun? And when? A few years later, when the house started to change for him, when he went from thinking about each bit and piece of it as a separate thing and started thinking of it as a *house*. His sister was still coming up close, entranced by the gap between shingle and wall, intrigued by the twist and curve of a crack in the concrete steps. It was not that she didn't know there was a house, only that the smaller bits were more important than the whole. For him, though, it had begun to be the reverse.

So he began to step back, to move back in the yard far enough away to take the whole house in at once. His sister would give him a quizzical look and try to coax him in closer, to get him involved in something small. For a while, he'd play to her level, narrate to her what the surface she was touching or the shadow she was glimpsing might mean, so she could pretend. But over time he drifted out again. There was something about the house, the house as a whole, that troubled him. But why? Wasn't it just like any house?

His sister, he saw, was standing beside him, staring at him. He tried to explain it to her, tried to put a finger on what fascinated him. *This house,* he told her. *It's a little different. There's something about it . . .* But he saw, from the way she looked at him, that she thought it was a game, that he was making it up.

"What are you seeing?" she asked, with a grin.

Why not? he thought. *Why not make it a game?*

"What are *you* seeing?" he asked her.

Her grin faltered a little but she stopped staring at him and stared at the house.

"I see a house," she said.

"Is there something wrong with it?" he prompted.

She nodded, then looked to him for approval.

"What's wrong?" he asked.

Her brow tightened like a fist. "I don't know," she finally said. "The window?"

"What about the window?"

"I want you to do it," she said. "It's more fun."

He sighed, and then pretended to think. "Something wrong with the window," he said. "Or not the window exactly but the number of windows." She was smiling, waiting. "The problem is the number of windows. There's one more window on the outside than on the inside."

He covered his mouth with his hand. She was smiling and nodding, but he couldn't go on with the game. Because, yes, that was exactly the problem, there was one more window on the outside than on the inside. That, he knew, was what he'd been trying to see all along.

———— 3 ————

But he had to make sure. He had his sister move from room to room in the house, waving to him from each window. The ground floor was all right, he saw her each time. But in the converted attic, just shy of the corner, there was a window at which she never appeared.

It was small and round, probably only a foot and a half in diameter. The glass was dark and wavery. It was held in place by a strip of metal about as thick as his finger, giving the whole of the circumference a dull, leaden rim.

He went inside and climbed the stairs, looking for the window himself, but it simply wasn't there. But when he went back outside, there it was.

For a time, it felt like he had brought the problem to life himself by stating it, that if he hadn't said anything the half-window wouldn't be there. Was that possible? He didn't think so, that wasn't the way the world worked. But even later, once he was grown, he still found himself wondering sometimes if it was his fault, if it was something he had done. Or rather, said.

Staring up at the half-window, he remembered a story his grandmother had told him, back when he was very young, just three or four, just after his father had left and just before his sister was born. Well, he didn't remember it exactly, but he remembered it had to do with windows. Where she came from, his grandmother said, they used to be called not windows but something else. He couldn't remember the word, but remembered that it started with a *v* She had said the word and then had asked, *Do you know what this means?* He shook his head. She repeated the word, slower this time.

"This first part," she had said, "it means 'wind.' This second part, it means 'eye.'" She looked it him with her own pale, steady eye. "It is important to know that a window can be instead a *windeye.*"

So he and his sister called it that, *windeye.* It was, he told her, how the wind looked into the house and so was not a window at all. So of course they couldn't look out of it; it was not a window at all, but a windeye.

He was worried she was going to ask questions, but she didn't. And then they went into the house to look again, to make sure it wasn't a window after all. But it still wasn't there on the inside.

Then they decided to get a closer look. They had figured out which window was nearest to it and opened that and leaned out of it. There it was. If they leaned far enough, they could see it and almost touch it.

"I could reach it," his sister said. "If I stand on the sill and you hold my legs, I could lean out and touch it."

"No," he started to say, but, fearless, she had already clambered onto the sill and was leaning out. He wrapped his arms around her legs to keep her from falling. He was just about to pull her back inside when she leaned farther and he saw her finger touch the windeye. And then it was as if she had dissolved into smoke and been sucked into the windeye. She was gone.

———— 4 ————

It took him a long time to find his mother. She was not inside the house, nor was she outside in the yard. He tried the house next door, the Jorgensens, and then the Allreds, then the Dunfords. She wasn't anywhere. So he ran back home, breathless, and somehow his mother was there now, lying on the couch, reading.

"What's wrong?" she asked.

He tried to explain it best he could. *Who?* she asked at first and then said *Slow down and tell it again,* and then, *But who do you mean?* And then, once he'd explained again, with an odd smile:

"But you don't have a sister."

But of course he had a sister. How could his mother have forgotten? What was wrong? He tried to describe her, to explain what she looked like, but his mother just kept shaking her head.

"No," she said firmly. "You don't have a sister. You never had one. Stop pretending. What's this really about?"

Which made him feel that he should hold himself very still, that he should be very careful about what he said, that if he breathed wrong more parts of the world would disappear.

After talking and talking, he tried to get his mother to come out and look at the windeye.

"Window, you mean," she said, voice rising.

"No," he said, beginning to grow hysterical as well. "Not window. *Windeye.*" And then he had her by the hand and was tugging her to the door. But no, that was wrong too, because no matter which window he pointed at she could tell him where it was in the house. The *windeye*, just like his sister, was no longer there.

But he kept insisting it had been there, kept insisting too that he had a sister.

And that was when the trouble really started.

—— 5 ——

Over the years there were moments when he was almost convinced, moments when he almost began to think—and perhaps even did think for weeks or months at a time—that he never had a sister. It would have been easier to think this than to think she had been alive and then, perhaps partly because of him, not alive. Being not alive wasn't like being dead, he felt: it was much, much worse. There were years too when he simply didn't choose, when he saw her as both real and make-believe and sometimes neither of those things. But in the end what made him keep believing in her—despite the line of doctors that visited him as a child, despite the rift it made between him and his mother, despite years of forced treatment and various drugs that made him feel like his head had been filled with wet sand, despite years of having to pretend to be cured—was simply this: he was the only one who believed his sister was real. If he stopped believing, what hope would there be for her?

Thus he found himself, even when his mother was dead and gone and he himself was old and alone, brooding on his sister, wondering what had become of her. He wondered too if one day she would simply reappear, young as ever, ready to continue with the games they had played. Maybe she would simply suddenly be there again, her tiny fingers worked up behind a cedar shingle, staring expectantly at him, waiting for him to tell her what she was feeling, to make up words for what was pressed there between the house and its skin, lying in wait.

"What is it?" he would say in a hoarse voice, leaning on his cane.

"I feel something," she would say. "What am I feeling?"

And he would set about describing it. *Does it feel red? Does it feel warm-blooded or cold? Is it round? Is it smooth like glass?* All the while, he knew, he would be thinking not about what he was saying but about the wind at his back. If he turned around, he would be wondering, would he find the wind's strange, baleful eye staring at him?

That wasn't much, but it was the best he could hope for. Chances were he wouldn't get even that. Chances were there would be no sister, no wind. Chances were that he'd be stuck with the life he was living now, just as it was, until the day when he was either dead or not living himself.

The Second Boy

A KIND OF DARKNESS HAD SWEPT UP VERY QUICKLY TO CATCH THEM unaware. The wind rose with it, crusting the snow into ice, the cold become now crisp and hard. As they walked, snow began to fall again until soon Leppin could no longer see the trail. He could hardly see Dierk either, except as a dim shape on its way to being lost.

"Hadn't we better stop?" Leppin asked.

But Dierk apparently could not make up his mind to do so. He shook his head. There must still be some trace of the trail, and perhaps they were still on it or not too far from it or would find it soon. Or perhaps they would soon see a light and be able to make for it.

In the wind, Leppin caught only scraps of what the fellow was saying. He trudged on, just behind. The wind rose further and he could feel his fingers growing numb. He kept walking until he could no longer feel them at all.

"It's very cold," he finally said. "We have to stop."

At first Dierk didn't hear him over the wind. Leppin had to hurry his steps and wrap an arm round Dierk's shoulders and shout into his ear. Even after this, there was a moment in which Dierk gave no response. Then came a short, curt nod that made Leppin believe he had given in.

But no, after Leppin released him Dierk just kept walking. After a moment Leppin, not knowing what else to do, followed.

The drifts were deep enough that sometimes when the crust of ice broke Leppin sank to his thigh, the snow underneath powdery and clinging to everything. He could feel the bones ache in his feet, and then that passed too and he couldn't feel his feet at all. It was hard for him even to remember where he was, or who he was.

Dierk was a little ahead, back stiff, marching resolutely forward, a vague, withdrawn figure. And then little more than a shadow. And then, as the snow thickened in the air, he was suddenly gone. Leppin called out once, but Dierk didn't hear. Or if he did, he didn't stop.

Leppin waited, stamping his feet, wondering if Dierk would notice he was gone and double back. When Dierk didn't, he tried to follow.

The storm was still growing. In the darkness and cold, he couldn't find Dierk's tracks. He wasn't even sure he was moving in the right direction. He was surprised to notice his body seemed comfortably warm. His face, too, seemed like it might be warm, though he couldn't feel it exactly. Why not just dig out a place for himself in the snow, make a little cave, a little hole, and wait for the storm to pass?

Instead he lurched onward, kept moving. It was as if someone else was walking, not him: a body moving bluntly forward, rudderless, under its own power. He let it go, just trying to stay vaguely connected to it.

It went on like that for a while, with Leppin less and less aware of what was happening around him, until he walked into a tree limb, sending a cascade of snow down onto his head. A branch had torn into the side of his neck. Not that he could feel his neck exactly, but there was a wetness there that was different from the other wetness, and a faint smell too. Unless it was something he was only imagining or making up as he went, since it was too dark to see and his hands and face were too numb to feel.

There were around him other trees as well, he soon found, encountering one and then another and then a third. He struggled his lighter out of his pocket and watched his gloved fingers try to flick it alight, was surprised that they finally managed. He cupped the flame with one hand and saw below him nearly bare ground, almost no snow: a matrix of pine needles and dead vegetation and mud spidered through with veins of frost.

He prodded the ground with the toe of his boot. Some places it remained hard, like a single consistent organism. In others it came slowly apart, the ice not strong enough to hold the dead leaves and other matter together.

He kept at it until he found a large spot that was loose and mostly dry, the leaves and needles such that he could push them together into a heap with his boot. From there it was little enough to bring the lighter down among the needles and leaves until they smoldered and, crackling, caught flame. He kept uprooting needles and leaves and adding them to the fire until the flames were high enough for him to start stripping bark off the nearest trees.

The underside of the bark was threaded with worm trails. It was also studded with black blotches that, as the bark caught fire, began to unfurl and move, becoming small black vermin that spun madly about before sizzling away. Unless it was just that he was seeing things, parts of his brain going dim and dying from the cold. He tried not to think about this, carefully feeding bigger and bigger chunks of wood onto the fire until he had a roaring blaze.

An hour later he had built a shelter just big enough for him to crawl inside. In the glow of the fire he could see the trees all around him but could not tell where the forest ended or where he had come from. He had removed his boots and gloves and they lay there beside the fire, slowly steaming. Feeling had begun to creep back into his hands and feet, his fingers and toes feeling as though they were being bitten repeatedly by flies. His face throbbed; it felt as though his eyes were scraping against their sockets as they moved. He heaped more fuel onto the fire and then slowly lay back in the shelter, staring at the flames until, almost without knowing, he had fallen asleep.

He woke up shivering. The fire, he could just see through the entrance of the makeshift shelter, had guttered, flickering down to almost nothing. *I should get up and keep it going*, he thought, but even though he was shivering, he found it very hard to imagine moving.

Maybe he slept a little, his eyes slightly open. Or maybe almost no time passed at all. But in either case suddenly he realized that the fire had flared again and he was no longer shivering. Something was shaking him, rocking one of his legs back and forth. He let his eyes fall into focus and there was Dierk.

"How did you find me?" Leppin asked.

"Let me come in," said Dierk.

"There's not room in here," said Leppin. "There's only room for one."

"Nonsense," said Dierk, and began to push his way up Leppin's legs and in. The shelter itself groaned and threatened to come asunder, then the boughs and branches to either side simply slipped and settled, leaving the shelter more or less intact. Dierk was pressed against its wall on one side and against Leppin's legs and chest on the other. His body was very cold, and once he was inside, the snow on his coat and trousers began to melt.

"Take your wet things off," Leppin said.

"It was hard enough to get in here," said Dierk. "That's all I can do."

"I'm freezing," said Leppin.

"All right," said Dierk. "Just a minute."

But he just lay there, not moving. *What's wrong with him?* wondered Leppin, and then couldn't help but wonder, *What's wrong with me?*

Dierk just lay beside him, not speaking, not moving.

"Dierk," said Leppin. When Dierk didn't respond he repeated his name, louder this time.

"What is it?" Dierk whispered, his mouth somewhere close to Leppin's right ear.

"How did you find me?"

"What?"

"How did you find me?"

"What's wrong with you?" asked Dierk.

"What do you mean?" asked Leppin, astonished.

"I already answered that question," Dierk said.

"No, you didn't," said Leppin, voice rising. And then when Dierk didn't answer, he reached over and tapped his forehead. "Answer again," he said.

"I found you," whispered Dierk. "Isn't that enough?"

Enough for what? wondered Leppin, and then, afraid of it, he let that thought drift slowly away.

"Tell me a story," said Dierk a little while later, same dull whisper. He was staring up at the ceiling of the shelter, eyes hardly blinking, features difficult to make out in the flickering light.

"A story?" asked Leppin. "About what?"

"While I'm warming up," said Dierk. "A story."

"But I don't know any stories," said Leppin. "Get closer to the fire," he said. "Leave the shelter and get closer to the fire. That's what will warm you up."

"In a minute," said Dierk.

Leppin waited. Dierk didn't move. Finally Leppin pushed at him.

"A story," Dierk said.

"I don't know any," said Leppin again. "I already told you."

There was a long moment of silence. *He must have fallen asleep,* Leppin thought. He was not shivering now, or hardly. Either Dierk was getting warmer or he was getting used to it.

"All right," Dierk suddenly said. "Then I'll tell you one."

"There was once a little boy lost in a cave," said Dierk.

"What boy?" asked Leppin, suddenly jumpy. "Did he have a name? Where was this cave?"

"It doesn't matter what boy," said Dierk. "Or in a way it does. *Which* boy, anyway. But his name doesn't matter at all. And the place doesn't matter at all either, beyond there being a cave."

"Why not?"

Dierk tilted his head halfway toward him. This, somehow, made Leppin nervous. "Very little ever actually matters," Dierk said. "That's just the way it is."

There was once a boy lost in a cave. Or rather a crevasse. He had been up in the mountains with a second boy and had slipped and fallen. The second boy ran the few miles back to town and came back with help.

By the time they had returned, it was dark. At first, they couldn't find the crevasse. The second boy, panicked, had failed to note the way, and none of the residents of the town had ever seen or heard of a crevasse where the boy said he had been. The second boy kept searching without finding anything. The region, it might be worth mentioning, was harsh, of an austere harshness. Through that curious acoustical quality that dry-aired mountainous regions sometimes possess, the second boy, whose ears were better than those of the adults he had brought with him, could hear the faint cries of the other boy, but he could not tell from where these cries came. Indeed, to him they seemed to come from everywhere at once. He kept starting out in a direction and then hesitating, moving off in an altogether different direction. "Can't you hear it?" he kept asking his rescuers, "Can't you hear him?" But none of them could. After a while he began to wonder if the cries he was hearing were the boy after all. If they weren't, rather, the wind. Or worse, simply a noise existing only within the confines of his own skull.

After half a night of this, almost all of the rescuers gave up and went home to rest, planning to resume the search in the morning. The only one left was a large, quiet man, dark-haired, with thick dark lips and a brooding stare, who was rumored to have a predilection for young boys.

"What kind of story is this?" Leppin blurted out.

"You'll see," said Dierk, turning a little farther toward him and giving him a blue-lipped smile. "You'll see."

The man stood there, a coil of rope hanging from his shoulder, watching the second boy come and go. Eventually, he sat down and started a fire. When the second boy passed yet again, the man patted the ground next to him and said, "Sit down, take a moment, think about other things. Then maybe you'll know where he is."

So the second boy did. Knowing the man, he didn't sit too close to him but instead on the opposite side of the fire. He might simply have run off to search on his own except that the man had a rope. If he were ever to find the crevasse he would need the rope to climb down to search for his friend.

"What," asked the man, "would you like to talk about?"

The boy just stayed squatting on the other side of the fire, not saying a thing.

"Tell me a story, then," the man said.

The second boy looked into the fire, then looked into the darkness. He could still hear, faintly, the cries of his friend.

"I don't know any," he finally said.

"Of course you do," said the man. "Everybody knows a story."

Leppin, listening, felt suddenly very afraid.

"Then I'll tell you one," said Dierk, said the man in Dierk's story, the story he was telling to Leppin.

"Stop," said Leppin.

But Dierk didn't stop. I don't know exactly what he told, *Dierk said, his voice stronger now.* I suppose it really doesn't matter. What matters is that it was a story that wormed its way slowly under the second boy's skin. It felt as though, even though he was hearing it for the first time, he had heard it before. There was a slow inexorability to it, the sense that it was a story moving steadily closer to something that it would be very bad ever to reach. There are some things I know about the story, scattered bits and fragments that may or may not make much sense to a listener. In it, there was a man with pudgy fingers who, at a crucial moment, rolled slowly out of a cane-backed chair, dead. There was a man who held a mirror flat in his palm and regarded his surroundings only in their reflections. There was a small, withered creature, maybe a hairless monkey, maybe a sort of extremely small and very old woman, whom another, larger hairless monkey or withered crone carried around like a doll, whispering to it from time to time something that sounded like *I saw the devil, all red, all red.* And saying this, the man reached his hand toward the boy.

As soon as he saw the storyteller stretch forth his hand, the second boy felt the story had come altogether too close to arriving at that place it would be very bad to reach and rushed off into the darkness. The man, surprised, went after him, shouting, or so it seemed to the second boy. *All red,* he kept thinking, his heart beating fast, *all red.* And it was precisely then, when it was furthest from his thoughts, that he managed to run directly to the chasm. Even in the darkness knew he had found it at last.

A moment later, there was the man, wheezing.

"Here it is," the second boy simply said.

Leaning over to catch his breath, hands on his knees, the man simply nodded. Then he traced his way back to the fire, got his coil of rope and took a burning branch off the flames. He returned, using the boy's cries— the second boy's cries this time—to guide him.

It was hardly a crevasse or a chasm or a cave at all. Though perhaps, the man realized, it seemed that way to the boy. It was more a rip, a tear in the ground, partly hidden by bushes, a fact that surely explained how the first boy had failed to see it and had fallen in. Properly speaking, it was just a hole.

"Why are you telling me this?" asked Leppin.

The man, *Dierk continued,* tied the rope around the bole of a scraggly tree and unfurled its coil down the hole. And then he climbed in, holding on to the burning branch and the rope at the same time. There was a short drop and then a steady slope—this much the second boy could see from the top of the hole—and then the man disappeared from sight, the light within the hole slowly vanishing.

Who knows how long the second boy waited at the top of the hole, in the cold, the quiet, the dark? For a long time he stared down into the hole's darkness. Then he lay on his back, hands and feet aching from cold, and stared up into the dark, at the whorl of stars above. Perhaps he closed his eyes and slept a little, perhaps not. But, finally, there came a noise and a light, and when he looked again he saw, revealed in the light of a single match struck below, the dim form of the man carrying, slung over one shoulder, the body of the first boy.

"Is he alive?" the second boy called down.

Yes, the man claimed. He would, he said, tie the boy to the end of the rope and leave him lying on the ground. Then he would climb up himself and, together, they would haul the first boy to safety.

Which they did. Once they had, they built a fire. And only then did the second boy discover that the boy they had drawn hand over hand out of the chasm was not the boy who had fallen in, but a boy he had never seen before.

It was morning, the fire long dead, Leppin all but frozen, no feeling to any of his extremities. He was very hungry. He prodded the ashes until he found a dull glow, then fanned it, added what little dry tinder he could find nearby. Soon he had begun to warm up, though parts of his face he still couldn't feel and other parts stung. His hands were numb and clumsy and it was hard to make them grasp anything. The wrist of one hand, where his glove met the cuff of his coat, was covered with a band of blisters, turgid with blood.

Once he felt partway human again, he set out.

The forest seemed to stretch equally in all directions. He could not tell now where he had come from, what direction. The town should be, roughly, east or southeast, but through the canopy the cloud cover was such that it was difficult to judge where the sun was. The snow was still falling, sifting its way down through the branches. *I saw the sky,* he thought, *all white, all white.* Or gray, rather. Very somber and expressionless.

He walked for a long time without reaching the edge of the forest. *I've gone the wrong direction,* he thought, and changed his course, walked some more. He was tired, his hands and feet and face frozen again. It was hard to keep walking. He went a very long way but still arrived at nothing. If anything, the trees closed in even more thickly around him.

He looked around for a clue about where to go next. It was not that the trees looked the same on all sides, only that they didn't look different in a way that he knew how to interpret. They were just trees. He struck out, veering a little from the course he had been following.

And so it was, all day, until, near dark, in despair, he came across a set of footprints in the snow and tracked them backward, heart beating fast, only to find the ashes of a campfire and a half-collapsed shelter that it took him more than a moment to recognize was his own.

He rebuilt the shelter, better this time, closer to the fire. He was very hungry, but there was nothing to be done. He started a fire in the ashes, gathered up enough dry branches and leaves and twigs to last the night. Then he sat down very close to the flames, stripped off his gloves and boots, and began to warm himself. One of his socks, he saw, was soaked in blood. The wool gave off a bad smell as it steamed and began to dry. Before he knew it, still staring at the fire, he had fallen asleep.

When he awoke, the fire was still going, though not as strong. He reached some wood from beside him and put it on the coals, then turned, crawled into the shelter.

On the way in, he touched something cold.

"I wondered when you were going to come," said Dierk.

Leppin didn't say anything.

"There's not room in here," said Dierk. "There's only room for one."

Very slowly, still on his knees, Leppin backed his way out of the shelter. Once out, he picked up his gloves and his boots, carried them over to the far side of the fire.

After a while, Dierk crawled out as well. He moved very slowly. His skin, even in the fire's glow, seemed exceptionally pale, almost transparent. Leppin sat watching him across the flames.

"How did you find me?" Leppin asked.

"Come back into the shelter," said Dierk. "I misspoke. There's enough room after all."

"I'd rather stay out here," said Leppin.

Slowly Dierk pulled his body around until he was sitting. He stayed there, legs crossed and beneath him, all but motionless.

Leppin, despite the fire, felt his hands and feet and face begin to go numb.

"How did you find me?" Leppin couldn't stop himself from asking.

"I already answered that question," said Dierk, and smiled.

But he didn't answer, thought Leppin. *Did he? What's happening?*

"I found you," said Dierk after a long pause. "Isn't that enough?"

Leppin closed his eyes, covering his face with his hands. He stayed like that for a while, gathering himself, but when he lowered his hands and opened his eyes, Dierk was still there, calm, attentive, still waiting.

"Tell me a story," said Dierk, his voice little more than a whisper. His eyes, too, Leppin noticed, like his skin, had gone pale, the pupil contracted almost to nothing despite the darkness, the iris a much paler blue than he remembered. Almost white.

"A story?" Leppin asked. "About what?"

But in the end it was Dierk who told the story, the same one he had told the night before, almost word for word, even the same pauses for breath. In one way for Leppin it was like hearing the same story over again, but in another way it was much worse, the story both following its order and progression and yet, because he already knew it, all moments of it existing in his head all at once. In his head, the hairless monkey or minuscule old woman never stopped saying *I saw the devil, all red, all red.* In his head, the man was always descending into the hole and always coming back out with the wrong boy.

But this time when Dierk finished Leppin was still sitting upright before the fire, still awake. They sat staring at one another.

"Why would you tell me this?" Leppin finally asked.

Dierk smiled. "You didn't listen," he said, "or you would know."

Leppin waited, but Dierk didn't say anything else. Finally, Leppin asked, as much to have something to say as for any other reason:

"Which boy are you?"

Dierk shook his head. "This is not the question you should be asking," he said. "The question you should be asking, my friend, is which boy are *you*?"

"What happened after?" asked Leppin, once the fire had begun to die down.

"After what?"

"In the story," said Leppin. "Where does it go from there?"

"That's the end," said Dierk. "The ending is that it doesn't end."

"But who is the boy?" asked Leppin.

"There are three boys now," said Dierk. "Which boy do you mean?"

Leppin gestured helplessly. "Who is the third? And what happened to the first?"

"The first is simply gone," said Dierk, his voice very soft now, hardly more than a whisper.

"But where?" asked Leppin. He was, he suddenly realized, nearly shouting. "Where did he go?"

"As for the third boy," said Dierk. "Everyone agreed to pretend he was the same boy as the first."

"Was he?"

"Everybody agreed to pretend he was."

Leppin shook his head. When he looked up again, he saw that Dierk was watching him closely.

"Shall I tell it again?" Dierk asked.

It was too much for Leppin. But instead of rushing away into the darkness, he found himself leaping over the fire. His hands found the other man's throat and closed around it. Dierk did nothing to resist, just kept his eyes open and fixed on the other's face. His flesh was colder than Leppin could imagine. Dierk even seemed to help, sagging unresisting to the ground once Leppin clambered on top of him.

As for Leppin, he squeezed down as hard as he could, trying to ignore the fact that nothing really seemed to be happening.

"Why?" asked Dierk finally.

"Why what?" responded Leppin, panting.

"Why were you so eager for the story to end? Couldn't you see there was no chance it would end happily?"

But sometimes, thought Leppin, *it is enough for things just to be over, even if they end badly. Sometimes that was all you could hope for. Though sometimes, as in life, you wouldn't get even that.*

"So what shall it be?" asked Dierk. "Shall we agree to keep pretending?"

How he can continue speak with my hands around his throat is beyond me, thought Leppin. Aloud, he said, "I don't know what you mean," and squeezed harder.

Dierk laughed. "Ah, Leppin," he said fondly, "you really kill me."

Leppin didn't answer. He just held on. Soon it would be morning. And then, if he were still alive, maybe he would have a chance. Maybe he would have another crack at getting it all sorted out.

And if not then, maybe the day after.

There was, he thought grimly, always tomorrow.

The Process

ONCE EVERYBODY WAS SETTLED IN, WE BEGAN WITH A *STRAW POLL* a simple show of hands in favor of one candidate or the other—despite, as Jansen mentioned somewhat huffily, *Robert's Rules of Order* referring to straw polls as "meaningless and dilatory." But the majority of us did not concur with such a judgment. At least not initially.

I was, I forgot to mention up front (like the candidate I was supporting I have a commitment to being *up-front* about things), up on one side of the platform waving the official silk-screened placard for my candidate while my life partner (his term, not mine) was on the other side of the platform waving the official silk-screened placard for his candidate. Mrs. Reitz, between us, took a long look first at the sea of hands for his candidate and then, once those were down, at the sea of hands for my candidate, and then declared the contest too close to call. It looked too close to call to me too, although my life partner kept shouting his candidate's slogan—*A Victory for Us Is a Victory for You*—and then declared that anyone with two eyes could see that his candidate had the edge. Though he himself, it must be admitted, has not two eyes but one, having lost the other from a stray bullet during the Collapse. Mrs. Reitz, fortunately, was not to be swayed.

Perhaps some background, then. I had not known my so-called life partner before the Collapse, had only settled on him after settling here, in our town, among like-minded folk, after the reinstitution of some form of order. But we were finding, here on the platform, that it was perhaps less a like-minded town than a town that was, like myself and my partner, of two minds, at least when it came to the question of the election.

"All right," said Mrs. Reitz, "let's sort it out. Everybody move to the wall plastered with your candidate's official silk-screened placards."

There was a general screeching of metal and plastic and resin and wood against the floor as people left their chairs and to the rumble of their own voices made for a wall. After that, once they had settled, it was only a question of Mrs. Reitz conducting a formal count.

Which she did. But when she finished she looked at me and at my partner and shook her head, then started again.

"What's the matter?" I asked.

She just shook her head and kept counting.

My partner looked over her head and said, to me, "A Victory for Us Is a Victory for You." I don't know if he was trying to be funny, but it was not funny. I wasn't having fun at all, but the point of this wasn't to have fun but to find a leader ready to lead us *into a New Time,* to paraphrase part of my own candidate's slogan. We were choosing someone who would take us out of the Collapse and move us into a *New Time,* one in which we could have *some semblance of a normal life.* This, the reinstitution of electoral procedures and the development of a multitown silk-screening industry, was a foundation upon which, with the right candidate, we and the surrounding towns we had banded with hoped to build our *New Time.*

"That can't be right," she said, once she'd finished counting.

"What's the matter?" I asked.

Hubbub was rising in the hall. She waved us both in close to her. "We have a tie," she whispered. "What do we do when we have a tie?"

"We can't have a tie," said my partner. "This is a caucus. Our town gets one vote, dedicated to one candidate or to the other, then we send that vote along. We have to choose."

"But we have a tie," I said. "What do we do when we have a tie?"

Mrs. Reitz shook her head. "I can't report a tie," she whispered. "A tie would serve as a sign to the other towns that we're still in a state of Collapse. We'd have to put the barricades back up again, go back to that life."

We both shivered. The last thing we wanted was life behind the barricades again.

"So now what?" I asked.

"I don't know," she said. "Give me a minute," she said. "I need to think."

So we stood there, my partner and I, to either side of her, as she thought things through. She counted again, and then yet again. She asked if everybody was certain they were committed to their candidate. Having been raised in a decade where any sign of weakness or indecision was seen as an indication of the state of Collapse, everybody stood firm. Once they were against a wall, there was no prying them off it.

"Is there any communal participant sick or ill or otherwise afflicted who did not attend?" Mrs. Reitz asked.

But no, there was nobody, no one at all.

In the end, not knowing what else to do, Mrs. Reitz dismissed everyone, asking them to take a day to look hard and deep within in order to see what candidate was really lodged there, nearest to their hearts.

"Do you think that will help?" I whispered to my partner.

"No," he said, "but it buys her time."

And so we put our placards face down and left everything just as it was, and we all went out. Mrs. Reitz locked the hall, leaving the town thus suspended in the process that should have brought us together and moved us into a *New Time*. My partner and I walked home, speaking politely albeit very formally to one another. He sat on the cushions that I had stuffed with hair from a dog I had known. I sat on the edge of our pallet and stared at him.

"What now?" I finally asked.

"No," he said, "the process is suspended. We've locked the process away in the town hall along with the silk-screened placards. I don't want to speak of this now."

And so we made small talk. I went down to the cellar and came out with two withered potatoes and some dried herbs and threw them into our pot with some water and heated it. As we ate, he read again the book he had borrowed from Torvold, holding it close to his remaining eye. He was forced, because of the same bullet that had rid him of his eye and because of where, behind the socket, it had lodged, to move his lips as he read. When I had first discovered that he did not, unlike myself, support the obviously superior candidate, I had wondered if the bullet, by joggling or slipping, wasn't having a more detrimental effect on his mind than we had realized. I was ashamed to think this, but I thought it nonetheless.

"But," I finally said, unable to stop myself, "what does this mean? What's going to happen?"

"That's it," he said. "I've had enough." With deliberation he stood. Placing a piece of straw between the pages to mark his place in Torvald's book, he left.

But I knew where he was going and whom he was planning to see. That was where I had an advantage over him. He was going to see the person he always saw when, frustrated, he fled me: a person named Dodd, one of the few who had chosen to establish himself outside of a town and to live at a distance from society, with whom my partner was having what had been referred to before the Collapse as an affair.

How Dodd lived outside the towns and remained alive, not subject to murder by townsfolk or villagers or darker wanderers, was hard to say. Partly out of fear and partly out of respect, I suppose. But there was also the rumor that had circulated at length that being a sort of devil or evil spirit made flesh, he could not be killed, and the rumor as well that there lay within the walls of his small shack a room whose walls were covered with the teeth of those who had come to kill him and had instead been killed themselves.

As to the first rumor, I can neither affirm nor deny it, never having seen anyone attempt to kill Dodd. I can say that, out of his clothing, his torso and thighs were lashed with scars and that several of these had gone so deep and been so severe that with any exertion they might in fact begin to suppurate. Indeed, the first indication I had that my partner was having an affair came in my finding him smeared with blood. I knew what this meant because I too was having a so-called affair with Dodd myself, but had conducted my betrayal with more care. I remained mum, realizing in a fit of Collapsive-logic that as long as Dodd too remained mum I would retain my advantage over my life partner.

As to the second rumor, there is no such room within his shack. Indeed, there is only a single wall, and no more than several hundred teeth. How most of them came to be there, I cannot say.

I spent the evening worrying about the election, wondering where we would go, how we might put ourselves forward in such a way as to prevent the suspicion of Collapse and to maintain the other townships' opinion of our civility. Eventually, I reclined on the pallet and slept.

When I awoke, there was my partner spread flat and exhausted beside me, his snores beginning to impinge upon my dreams. I got up, keeping always on the side of his missing eye, and gathered a blanket around myself and left.

I walked to the edge of the town, careful not to be glimpsed nor, if glimpsed, clearly seen. There were still the holes and trenches for the barricades, some partly collapsed or filled in, and these I used as well, descending one trench in particular and following it along a good way before clambering out and pushing through the bushes and out of the town itself.

The night was velvet and dark but I am the converse of my partner when it comes to vision; whereas he is half blind, my own eyes capture each bit and scrap of light and make good use of it.

It was a short trip upslope to Dodd's door. I scratched softly on it and he immediately opened, squinted out.

"I thought I might see you this evening," he said, and waved me in.

What passed next there is no need to detail or explore in any depth: the usual human noises and fluids were exchanged until after a time we lay akimbo in the flickering light of a candle on Dodd's pallet, and I stared at the rows of teeth.

"I imagine I know why you came," said Dodd.

"Why would that be?" I asked.

He leaned over and smirked. "Your so-called partner poured his heart out to me," he said. "He wanted advice. I of course obliged him."

"You'll advise me as well, I imagine."

He looked at me, his pupils as always sunken to bare dots, despite the darkness. "I'll tell you exactly what I told him. It's a simple matter," he said. "Simplest thing in the world."

"Yes," I said.

"You can't have a tie if there's an odd number of people."

"But there's an even number."

"Pick someone and kill them," he said. "That'll make it odd. That'll fix the vote. I told your partner the same thing, but he believed I must be joking."

On the way back, I thought it over. Yes, of course it was a solution, a kind of sacrifice to be made for the so-called greater good. An ethical person might even take it upon herself or himself to do away with himself or herself for the good of the whole. But Dodd knew that both my and my partner's ethics were functional but not transcendent. Which left a range of solutions excluding self-murder available to us, with murder at its core.

I was not, as Dodd most certainly knew but my partner perhaps did not, beyond such solutions. Indeed, though I did not know how most of the teeth on Dodd's shack wall were gathered, I do know how a few handfuls of them were, having harvested them myself. I need not detail the specifics of this red harvest, beyond indicating that an elucidation might well throw my ethics even further into question. But, as I had argued to myself at the time, we were all of us compromised, we were all of us doing things we would regret and not repeat. Which was, after all, the point of finally having an election: we were cleansing and renewing ourselves through the process. We were making a *New Time*.

But before a new time can begin, one must bring the old to an end. This, I cannot help but believe, must be done by any means necessary.

And so, as I moved down toward the town, I found myself feeling about in the foliage for an appropriate club or cudgel, hefting dead branch after dead branch until I found one that slid smoothly into my hand as if it had been made to fit.

At moments matters outside of ourselves think for us, and at moments, though knowing this, feeling ourselves part of a larger logic, of a larger body, we let them.

I would have to come at him from the correct side, I told myself, where his already dead eye would prevent me from being seen. With a little luck it would be over in a single blow and he would hardly feel a thing. And then would come the long arduous haul of dragging his body out of the house and abandoning it outside the town where, with a little more luck, his death would be seen as the work of a wanderer or, if need be, of Dodd. Perhaps Dodd would have to be sacrificed as well. And then, from there to the town hall, to the continuation of the process: another vote, no longer a tie, and the move forward into a new and better time.

A History of the Human Voice

THE EARLIEST RECORDINGS OF THE HUMAN VOICE CONFIRM WHAT I have long suspected: in the past, there existed a symbiosis between the human voice and the insect known as the bee. Indeed, as recently as the 1860s, certain elite circles on the continent are said to have augmented their speech with bees.

The vocal chords were adapted by carefully massaging and stretching them with a slender wand made of lacquered cherrywood. Then they were carefully torn to create a series of insertion channels. A bee was affixed to the end of the wand with cold wax and slid buzzing down the throat and into a channel. There it was shaken slightly to enrage it into plunging its stinger into the chord. Once it was secure, one waited for the warmth of the throat to soften the wax so that the wand could be withdrawn and the next bee deployed.

It is thus no surprise that one of the earliest instances of recorded speech, by phonatographer Édouard-Léon Scott, was a paean to the insect in question: "Vole, Petite Abeille" ("Fly, Little Bee"). This recording, rendered by singing into a barrel-shaped horn attached to a stylus, consists of sound waves etched onto sheets of paper blackened by smoke from an oil lamp. When it is played, dozens of bees are heard buzzing, articulating themselves within human speech. It is a haunting, plaintive melody, simultaneously uni- and multivocal.

How this art of communion with the bee came to be lost I cannot say. Gradually, with the decline of the privileged classes, it fell out of favor. Yet now having heard it, it is impossible for me not to think of our strictly human voices as vexed, as forever lacking.

I have been driven to strange extremes in my attempts to regain mastery of this art of the voice. So far, despite experiencing a great deal of pain, I have met only limited success, the bees quickly suffocating within my swollen throat. But, I tell myself, in the end it will be worth it.

Dapplegrim

THERE CAME A TIME WHEN I, THE YOUNGEST OF TWELVE BROTHERS, each of whom had imposed his dominion upon me in turn, could bear it no longer and fled the house. I left one morning without awakening either my parents or brothers, carrying only the clothes on my back. I traveled for many days, begging food where I could, until I came to a spacious castle of white stone lying in the lee of a mountain. It was the exact converse of the house in which I had been raised, the fourteen of us crammed into narrow rooms and someone's elbow always gouging someone else's eye. Here, I thought, I would be able to breath freely and fully.

"Who lives there?" I asked the old woman who had shared her table with me.

"A king," she said, "But he is unfortunate and a little mad and has lost his daughter to a troll upon a mountaintop. You would do better to stay far from him."

"Mark my words," I said to her, "I will find a place for myself with him," and though she laughed at me this is exactly what I managed to do, entering into the service of the king.

The king was a dour man, nervous in his opinions, and surrounded by a dozen advisors and counselors deft at making their thoughts and opinions his own. I could see this from the first, but what was it to me? I served him faithfully and strictly to the letter. As his servant, I occupied a position for him somewhere midway between a living, breathing human and a piece of furniture. I flatter myself to think I did my task well enough that he had no cause to take notice of me until the moment when, at the end of the year, I approached his throne on my knees and begged his leave to return home to visit my parents.

"What?" he said, confused and surprised. "And who are you?"

I told him my name, but though it was he himself who had accepted me into service, it seemed to mean nothing to him. I explained to him my duties and there came a flicker of recognition.

"Ah, yes," he said. "The candleholder. You have held it well, lad. Yes, by all means go."

And so go I did.

So often it is the case that Death chooses to take to the road before we do, and so it was that I returned to find my parents dead. Of what cause my brothers claimed not to know, but I saw enough in their furtive glances one to another to suspect that they had helped my parents on their way.

"And my inheritance?" I asked.

They admitted to having already divvied the inheritance, thinking, so they claimed, that they had no reason to think me alive. *So they wished me dead,* I thought, *and perhaps still do. I must proceed with care.*

I unsheathed my knife, using it to section an apple, and then afterward left it beside my hand on the table, blade winking in the light like a living thing.

"Shall I, then, receive nothing for my inheritance?" I asked.

They conferred and ended by offering me twelve mares living free upon the hills. This was, as they well knew, much less than my proper share, but with only one of me on my side of the table and eleven of them clustered on the other, I knew better than to protest. I accepted their offer, thanked them, and left.

When I arrived in the hills it was to find that I had doubled my wealth. Each mare had come to foal, so that where I had thought to see one dozen I now saw two. And among this second dozen was a big dapple-gray foal much bigger than the others and with a coat so sleek it shone bright as a shivering pane of glass. He was a fine fellow, and I could not help but tell him so.

And it was there that things began to go odd for me, that the world I thought I knew took a dark turn, and I began to see that all I had thought I knew I knew not at all. For that dappled horse, staring at me with its dark eyes, snatched me outside of my body. And when I returned to myself again, I found myself standing in the midst of the eleven other foals. I myself was awash in blood, and all of the foals were dead and by me slaughtered.

But that dapple-gray foal, still alive, moved now from mare to mare, suckling off each in turn. Both foal and mares acted as though nothing had happened, while I stood there bloody, the flies already beginning to swarm around me as if I were Death himself.

*

26

For a year I tried not to think on the events of that afternoon. For a year, I served my master the king faithfully and told myself I would not return to that hillside, that I would renounce my inheritance and simply get along with my life.

Yet what sort of life was it? I, a servant, a half-man, always at the beck and call of my liege. Was this who I chose to be? And what in the meantime had happened to the rest of me? Was this merely the resting place on the way to some other self?

And I could hear, too, somewhere deep within my head, the neighing of that dapple-gray horse, drawing me out, calling to me. So that by the time the year had completed its sidelong gait and returned to where it had begun, I knew that I did not want to return. But I knew also that despite myself I would.

The first thing I glimpsed in climbing the hill was the dapple-gray foal I had left behind. He was a yearling now, and larger than a full-grown horse, and his coat bright as a burnished shield. His eyes were like flecks of fire and each inch of skin rippled with strength. And there were twelve new foals, one for each of the mares, and I thought, *Well now, I can lead this dapple-gray yearling away and sell him and have done with him forever.*

But when I bridled him and tried to lead him away, he pushed his hooves into the ground and would not move.

And so I came closer to him and whispered in his ear and tried to coax him to follow me, and yet he would not budge, only swung his head toward me and stared at me with his dark, smoky eyes.

And here again a dark turn was taken within me and I was lost to it, as if my soul had fled my body. And when at last I had returned, did I not find, as before, myself standing amidst the slaughtered, the bloody business done? So I cursed that horse and with blood christened him Dapplegrim, for grim was his business, and grim he made my own. Yet he paid me no heed and simply moved from mare to mare, and from each of them took suck.

And so another year of faithful servitude to my king, all the while in me a growing dread as I tried not to think of what might happen once the year had passed. This time, I told myself, I would not return.

And yet, when the day came, I felt Dapplegrim's hot breath within the confines of my skull and approached my king for his leave to go. His leave was given and I set out, and so found myself there again upon the hillside. And there was Dapplegrim, grown so big that he had to kneel before I could even think to mount him. His coat shone and glistened now as if a looking glass. His eyes were full of smoke and flame and terrible to behold. And I saw that he was alone on the hilltop, for either he had driven the mares who had suckled him away or he had killed and eaten each of them in turn.

He turned and stared at me and again I felt myself grow dizzy. Before I knew it I had ridden him bareback to my parent's old house, where my brothers still lived. They, when they saw him, smote their hands together and made the sign of the cross, for never had they seen such a horse as Dapplegrim. And right they were to be afraid, for as I rode upon his back Dapplegrim smote them each with his hooves and though they screamed and fled they could not escape. So that in the end there were eleven dead brothers and only me left alive.

More did happen then, but I am loath to speak of it. I still have nightmares of how this monstrous horse forced me, by pushing his way into my mind, to grind my dead brothers into his fodder. All the while I shivered and cried for him to have mercy, but he would not, for this horse was master of me and refused to release me.

My brothers gone and consumed, Dapplegrim was far from through with me. He forced me to melt down all the pots and tools and bits of iron in my family house and beat them into shoes for him. He showed me where my brothers had buried my parents' wealth, their gold and silver, and with these I fashioned him a gold saddle and bridle that glittered from afar. And then he knelt before me and compelled me to mount him, and off we rode.

He thundered straight to the same castle in which I had served the last few years of my life, following the road without hesitation as if he had ridden it all his days. His shoes spat stones high into the air as we rode, and his saddle and bridle and coat too glistened and glowed in the sunlight.

When we reached the castle the king was standing at the gate, his advisors huddled around him. They watched the approach of myself and Dapplegrim as we sped toward them like a ball of liquid fire.

Said the king once we had arrived, "Never in my life have I seen such a thing."

And then Dapplegrim turned his long neck and looked at me with one fierce eye and I felt myself leaking away again. Before I knew it I had told the king I had returned to his service and asked him for his best stable and sweet hay and oats for my steed. The king, perhaps himself transfixed by Dapplegrim's other eye, bowed his head and agreed.

I returned to my duties. At the appointed hour I lit the King's candle and carried it after him. At the appointed hour I extinguished it. It was all just the same as it had ever been, and yet it was different too. For whereas before the king had seemed to look right through me, to consider me as he might a knife or a chair, now he noticed me and even regarded me thoughtfully.

"Tell me," he said one day. "Where did you come by such a steed?"

"He is my inheritance, sire," I said.

"All of it?" he asked.

"He has become," I reluctantly admitted, "all of it."

"And what do you suppose such a horse might be capable of?" he asked.

What indeed? Knowing not how to respond, heart sinking, I shook my head. "I do not know," I said.

"My advisors tell me that a steed such as yours and a rider such as you are just the sort to rescue my daughter," he said.

I stammered something out. To be honest, the princess had been absent before I arrived at the castle and I had all but forgotten about her.

"You have my leave to go, and you shall marry her if you succeed," he said, already turning away. "But if you do not return in three days with my daughter, you shall be put to death."

Dapplegrim! I thought, *Dapplegrim!* for I knew it was not the king's advisors who were to blame but my own accursed horse, my only inheritance, who, in growing strong, had left countless bodies in his wake. And would, by the end, I was sure, leave countless more, perhaps my own among them.

I drew my sword and went to the stables, prepared to kill the animal. But as I entered he looked up quick and stared me down with blood-flecked eyes, and I became as meek as a newborn lamb. I sheathed my sword and took up the currying brush and rubbed his mirrorlike coat even sleeker than it had been before. And as I did so, he was there within my mind itself, his hooves leaving bloody tracks across my brain. And when I had finished brushing him, I had grown calm and determined and knew exactly what I must do.

And so Dapplegrim and I rode out of the king's palace, a cloud of dust rising dark behind us. I loosed the reins and let the animal direct himself, and he rode swiftly over hill and dale, skirting the edge of a thick forest, moving, ever moving.

There came to be, in the distance, veiled in haze, a large squat shape that in the end resolved into a strange, steep-sided mountain. It was toward this we rode, and at last we were there.

Dapplegrim looked the mountain up and down and then, snorting and pawing the ground, he rushed it.

But the wall of rock was as steep as the side of a house and smooth as a sheet of glass. Dapplegrim rode best he could and made it a good way up, but then his forelegs slipped and he tumbled down, and me along with him. How it was that neither of us was killed, I must ascribe to the same dark power that had led to the horse becoming the monster he now was.

And so, I thought, *Dapplegrim has failed, and for this I shall lose my head.*

But barely did I have time to catch my breath when Dapplegrim was snorting and pawing the ground, and made his second charge.

And this time he made it farther and might even have made it all the way to the top, had not one foreleg slipped and sent us hurtling and tumbling down. *Failed again,* I thought, but Dapplegrim would not have it so. In a moment he was up and pawing the ground and snorting and then he charged forward, his hooves spitting rocks high in the air. And this time he did not slip but gained the top. There he stove in the head of the troll with his hooves while I threw the princess over the pommel of the golden saddle, and down we rode again.

My story should have ended there. I had done as I had been instructed. I had rescued the king's daughter and should by rights have had her hand in marriage. Happily ever after, as they say. By rights it should have gone thus, were lords as honest and just as they expect their servants to be. But by the time, on the evening of the third day, Dapplegrim and I had returned with the king's daughter, Dapplegrim having chosen to carry us all directly into the throne room, the king had had ample time to think. He had time to reconsider a promise rashly made to a mere servant and, with the help of his advisors, had begun to wriggle free of it.

For as I returned and laid again before the King the promise he had made me of his daughter's hand, I found him grown cunning and deceitful.

"You have misunderstood me," he claimed. "For how could I give my only daughter to a servant unless he were to prove himself more than a servant?"

But what is this? I wondered. *How is this not what Dapplegrim and I have just done by rescuing her where all others have failed?*

But the king, fed his lines by his advisors and set upon repeating them as he had learned them, paid little attention to the expression on my face.

There were, he told me, three tasks to accomplish. I must first make the sun shine in his darkened palace despite the mountain blocking the way. As if that were not enough, I must find his daughter a steed as good as Dapplegrim for our wedding day. Third—but I had already stopped listening by this time, and would be hard-pressed to repeat what the third task was to be.

Then, when he was finished, the king leaned back and looked up at me, a satisfied expression smeared upon his face.

I nodded and thanked him for his indulgence, and then began to turn away. And it was just then that Dapplegrim caught my eye, and I was transfixed.

In retrospect, I am not surprised how things turned out. Indeed, each and every one of our yearly reunions upon the hillside should have suggested to me how things would end. For there was Dapplegrim galloping through my skull and a strange red haze overwhelming my vision. And before I knew it, I had drawn my sword and lopped free the head of my king. And then, as, screaming and whinnying, they tried to flee, the heads of his twelve advisors. And finally, for good measure, that of his beloved daughter.

It was not long after this that I myself became king, for the people were afraid to do otherwise. I have done my best to serve justly and flatter myself to think that more often than not I have done so. When I have not, it is less my own fault than that of the dapple-gray horse, huge and monstrous, who, when he fixes his eyes upon me and calls for blood and pain, I find I still cannot refuse.

So why have I told you, you who would serve me, this? Why does the mad king at whose feet you throw yourself and beg for a place bare his soul to you thus? Is it, you worry, that he has no intention of giving you anything?

No, you shall have a place if, after having listened to me, you still do so desire. But you must know it is not me you shall serve. You, like me, shall serve Dapplegrim. And he is not an easy master.

Angel of Death

—— I ——

To begin, there are eight of us, but only one of us can write. And so I am assigned to keep a record of all that passes and to each day make the count of our number, and when one of us is dead or missing to inscribe his name in the back of the record. I have been given the blank book and a thrust of pencils just for this purpose, and though the others would not know were I to inscribe something other than what I have been commissioned, I intend to take my task seriously.

The difficulty comes in knowing what is real and what is not. There is no agreement on this. What I am nearly sure is real are bursts and jolts and the smell of singed hair, but others recall none of these effects, recall other things entirely. And how we came to slip from one dim world and its dim deeds to the place where we are now, none of us are in any position to say. And why we are together, this too I do not know.

But here we are, and we are together, even if we cannot say why or even how. As for me, it was as if my vision ran dark and when it went lucid again here I was, in this new place, tramping my way wetly forward. Soon I was conscious of other footsteps surrounding me. And shortly we began to think of ourselves as a company, moving forward as if one body, though we knew not where.

But I am already beginning to sway from my purpose, and my scribbling in the blank book slows me as I walk. I lag dangerously behind the others. They will not stop for me, but sometimes they do call out to hurry me along. Shoving one finger between pages, I hurry to catch up with them, sloshing my way forward. But soon, writing, I am lagging behind again, and so it goes.

Perhaps it would be enough for me simply to record the world in notation, scattered bits, things like—

walked, gray light
one more dead
walked, darker gray light

—so long as I fully record the whole names of the dead when they die. But having begun in another fashion, I find it hard to believe I could be satisfied with less.

Here is what I think I know about how things stand for us now:

There are, or rather were, eight of us, together.

We are walking, or rather slouching, forward.

There are no landmarks. Nor, for that matter, technically speaking, any land.

We are going somewhere, for surely one is always going somewhere, even if that somewhere is only in circles. But where? And why do we not feel the need to sleep?

I have indeed queried some of the others, but they speak only with great reticence, in short, clipped sentences, just as I did before I was given the book. But now something has changed for me. There has, I fear, developed the worst of needs, the need to know, coupled reluctantly with an awareness that I probably will, in fact, never know. And yet I write. And cling too to that past I know, or hope, to be real: smell of singed hair, slowly fading vision.

Recorded now in the back of this book: two names. There are six of us left. The other two simply slowed and then fell to their knees, the water lapping against their thighs. And then each of them lay down, face down, and we left them there, the backs of their heads and the blades of their shoulders disturbing the otherwise smoothness of the water's surface.

I add the latest dead to the list in the book and then the remaining others each give me a share of their food: not much, a portion hardly bigger than my thumb. They extend it toward me, pronouncing their own names, and I take it, repeating their names as I do, assuring them that I will remember them when they die, that I will record them.

At first I thought it was a sort of immortality they sought in this recording, a sense they would not be forgotten. But it has become clear this is the last thing they want. Through their few words in response, I have gleaned that instead they fear not knowing if they are alive or dead, that they want their death marked out and delineated so as to be sure that they will not have to come to life again. That this can be done with the recording of a name I sincerely doubt.

And yet, still, it makes me mildly anxious to think there will be no one here to record my own name when I myself die. How will I remember I am dead?

One more dead, his name recorded, the five of us trudging dimly on. The landscape in all directions fog and water, feet clammy and wet. Horizon, at least for me, undifferentiated, the light varying from dull to dark gray. Behind us, the last body still visible, a small damp island. Soon that too will be lost from sight as, in company with the other four, scrawling in this book, I continue forward.

---- 2 ----

I do not know which one of them starts, but one of them, one of the other four, shuffles into place beside me as I walk. He gets very close and—perhaps not in the first instance but certainly in many of the instances that follow—even encircles me with one arm, aligning his stride with my own. I do not care for this intimacy; it makes it difficult for me to write. But I tolerate it, take it as one of the duties of having the blank book and the privilege of filling it.

And then, much of the time, the fellow will move slowly away, not a word exchanged, leaving me to wonder how to record our interaction in the book. Which, in a manner of speaking, is what I am doing now.

And yet, at other times it has gone farther than this. I do not know how much I

An unfinished sentence, left long solitary as my mind churned over what, if anything, it was expedient to record. Finally I will leave it as it is, its own little outcropping of words, alone.

I myself am not alone. I continue on in this company, walking, through a landscape that seems at no variance with anything, even itself. Sky and water welded together without joint or seam, no sound but the slow roil of our footsteps.

No more of us dead yet. I will say it, after all: sometimes as they fall in step beside me they also whisper, softly into my ear:

"You are the one who will record my name when I die."

"Yes," I whisper back. "I am the one."

"You know my name."

"Yes," I say, "I know your name." And I repeat it. I would record it here, in this sentence, on this page, but it is not to be written in the book until he is dead.

He nods. "Yes," he whispers, "this is my name. You will not forget it?"

"No, I will not forget it."

"This is a promise?"

I promise him and, somewhat dazed, he moves off.

This is what my connection with others amounts to now. It was perhaps, once, different, but what it was before, I can no longer recall.

Still no more of us dead. Perhaps the rest of us will walk forever.

Questions have begun to plague me. About where I am, what I am doing here, where we are going.

As I have not even the faintest most tentative of answers to them, I find I have no idea how to entertain them. Instead I will write:

sky dark gray

water as slate

sloshing forward

and cling still to that acrid smell of burning hair, the last outcropping of my lost past.

And then, suddenly, a different conversation. One of them, a pale, gaunt man, after asking the same questions, adds, tacks on at the end:

"When will I die?"

"I don't know," I say.

But he does not believe me.

"Please," he says, "please look into my face and tell me when I am going to die."

I stop for a moment and so does he. I turn finally toward him and he looks suddenly afraid. I make an honest effort to see something in his face. But I see nothing.

"I don't know," I say again.

"Please," he says. "Please."

And the look he gives me is naked enough that I finally promise him, "Soon."

He nods, and smiles a little, and we hurry to catch up with the others.

But giving him such assurance is a mistake, for soon I am giving it to all the others as well. *I don't know,* I say. *I don't know.* And then, finally giving in, *Soon.*

And yet we are all of us still walking, my small book slowly filling up, even though no more of us as yet have died.

sky as slate
water dark gray
stumbling forward

"Soon," I tell him yet again. Soon. Eventually I will be telling all of them, I know. But for now he is ahead of them, the most insistent for death. But this will not satisfy him, or them, forever.

——— 3 ———

"When will I die?" he asks of me again. A day of flat gray light, no difference between water and land. I am tired of hearing him ask; I am becoming impatient.

"Now," I can't stop myself from saying. "You will die now."

The other three around me stop when I say this, the first time I have seen them all stop at once. Suddenly, it is oddly silent. They wait, looking at both of us.

"Now," the pale, gaunt man says, and smiles. He lies down in the water, on his back. I write his name in the back of the book as he watches me, and then the four of us who remain set off.

I cannot stop myself from casting glances over my shoulder. He is still there, still lying in the water, his knees and the tips of his boots and the swelling of his chest cresting the water's surface. He has raised his head a little and watches us go.

No point posing questions. The world is brutal and life, when it happens at all, short. I could, perhaps, make up a past for myself from the scattered viscera of images I still believe are real. But why bother? There is not enough blankness left in this blank book for me to waste it on such luxurious reflections.

And then there he is, a dark spot behind us, in pursuit. The other three are mumbling to themselves, and then they pick up the pace. But he keeps with us, gaining on us rather than growing smaller, somehow more powerful than us. He is, after all, as one of those left suggests, dead. One can never, so he reasons, outrun a dead man.

So he gains on us, slowly but inexorably, until finally we fall back to our normal pace and let him come.

"I'm not dead," is the first thing he says when he catches up with us.

"You are," says one of the others.

"No," he says, shaking his head, a little desperate perhaps.

And so I show him his name in the back of the no-longer-so-blank book.

"No," he says. "You made a mistake."

But the others have already turned away and have started to walk on. He keeps pace with us, still talking. The others refuse to speak to a ghost. Soon, so do I.

After a time he accepts his lot. He falls into silent step with us. He walks forward, dim, lost, and, though with us, alone.

After a while one of the remaining three sidles into step, wraps an arm around me, whispers in my ear.

"What is it?" I say.

"Am I on the list?" he asks.

"Are you dead yet?" I ask.

"Am I on the list?"

I show him the list. His name is not on it. He looks at it for a long time, stopping me when I try to turn the page.

"Why is my name not on the list?" he asks.

I open my mouth to answer and then realize I don't know what, if anything, to say to this.

We walk together for some time. He keeps lightly touching my hand that is holding a pencil until finally I allow the pencil to enroll his name on the list at the back of the book.

"Am I on the list?" he asks.

"Yes," I say.

And so he releases me and, like a sleepwalker, moves slowly away, now dead, and never again says another word.

And so it goes. First one and then the other of the remaining two approach me, and are only satisfied when I strike them dead. And then there is only me, alone, the only one living among a silent company of seven ghosts. When I regard them I can see the way in which their skulls are struggling to be seen through their skin. We slosh slowly forward, I and the seven men I have killed.

What is the next step? It seems inevitable that after a few dozen, a few hundred, a few thousand more strides, I will reach a place inside my head where I will see no choice but to record my own name. And then we will proceed forward, all of us a company of ghosts, silent, dead.

But for now, the last man alive, I take a step forward. And then another. And then a third. I will inscribe everything that happens. Daily, I will make the count of my remaining number. When the time comes I will write myself dead and gone.

The Dismal Mirror

I N EARLY SPRING, HARMON'S SISTER DISAPPEARED. ONE MOMENT SHE WAS standing at the edge of the property, near the back fence, the dog just beside her, listening to him plow. The next both she and the dog were gone. He noted their absence passively as he turned the tractor to cut the next set of rows, and thought nothing of it. Later, once he was done, he went into house and called, was surprised when neither she nor the dog came. The dog he found a half-day later, just outside the back fence, its throat slit open. Of his sister, however, there was no sign.

He tramped the farmlands for miles, knocking on every door he could find. He drove into town, asked around at the co-op and the bar. When it was clear nobody there had seen her he finally drove two towns north and to the sheriff's office.

"How long has she been gone?" asked the deputy on duty.

Two days, Harmon told him.

The deputy looked him over. "That's not so long," he said. "Usually we wait a while to make sure they don't come back on their own."

"They?" he asked.

"She in this case," said the deputy. "Was there anything the matter between you and your wife?"

"What?" said Harmon, confused. "But I don't have a wife."

"Your girlfriend, then," said the deputy. "Whatever you call her."

"She's my sister," said Harmon.

"Your sister?" asked the deputy, and Harmon saw his gaze sharpen. "You live with your sister?"

There was nothing wrong with a man in his forties living with his sister, Harmon tried to explain.

"I never said there was," said the deputy, pursing his lips. "Your sister, then," he said. "Just the two of you?"

Yes, Harmon admitted, just the pair of them.

"Maybe she just wanted to get away for a while," suggested the deputy. "Out on her own."

Harmon nodded, then explained about the murdered dog.

"That does sound bad," said the deputy. "But maybe it's something else."

"Something else?"

"Maybe it's a separate incident. Are you sure it's the same incident?"

"She was there with the dog and then she disappeared," said Harmon, trying not to lose his temper. "The dog disappeared too, and when it reappeared it was slaughtered. That's worth looking into."

"Did you bring a picture?" the deputy asked Harmon.

"Of the dog?" asked Harmon.

"Of the sister," said the deputy.

Well, no, Harmon admitted. In fact as far as he knew there was no picture.

The deputy looked astonished. "No picture?"

"Maybe when she was a baby," said Harmon, "but I never seen one even then."

"That's okay," said the deputy, offering a fake smile. "We can work around that. What'd she look like?"

"I don't know," said Harmon. He shrugged. "Ordinary, I guess."

"Tall or short," asked the deputy.

Harmon shrugged again. "Normal height, I guess."

"Hair color," said the deputy.

"Maybe brown," said Harmon.

"So, brown?"

"Maybe," said Harmon.

"What do you mean, maybe?"

"I'm blind to colors," said Harmon. "Some colors anyway. Sometimes I can guess. Others I just can't tell."

"Didn't you ever ask her?"

Harmon shook his head. "Never had a reason to," he said.

The deputy shook his head. "What about her eyes?" he asked.

"Didn't really have a color," said Harmon.

"No? You couldn't see their color?"

Harmon shook his head. "They didn't really have one. They were filmed over and milky. Opaque. That's why she had the dog."

"Excuse me?"

"She didn't really venture anywhere without the dog," said Harmon. "She couldn't much," he said. He looked up at the deputy. "How could she? She was blind."

The deputy's attitude changed with that; suddenly he started taking Harmon more seriously. Another deputy followed him back to the farm and listened to him talk about the moment his sister had vanished. He showed the man around the house, the meager kitchen, the bathroom, the single bedroom with the two twin beds in it pressed up against opposite walls, a curtain strung between them. The deputy didn't seem to want to come into the bedroom, just watched from the door as Harmon rummaged through the boxes under one bed and then the boxes under the other, looking for a photograph. There wasn't one.

A few hours later, the deputy had called out a trio of bloodhounds. They were given one of the sister's skirts to smell and then went crisscrossing their way over the dirt until one picked up the scent and started baying. It took off, the others following.

"Looks like we're in luck," said the deputy.

Harmon felt his heart thudding up inside his throat. They set out after the dogs and their handler, only to end up at the spot behind the fence where Harmon had found his own slaughtered dog.

They tried again, then a third time, but the dogs kept returning to the same spot, losing the scent there. After a while the handler led them back to the truck and drove them away.

"Try not to think the worst," the deputy told him a few minutes later, clapping a hand on his shoulder. Harmon had to stop himself from asking what the worst might be. A moment later, he felt the hand lift. Soon the deputy was gone as well.

What if I'd stopped when I first noticed her gone? he couldn't help but think, late at night, staring at the curtain hanging limply between him and his missing sister. *What if I'd looked for her then, what would I have found?*

But how could he know? Could he really have saved her? From what? Mightn't whatever it was simply have come for him too, as it apparently had for the dog?

Then it was morning and he was up, getting on with the planting, trying not to think about her. He couldn't, on top of everything else, lose the crop before he'd even begun. He didn't stop for lunch, which normally his sister would have made for him. *She can't have run off,* he thought, *not blind.* But who, then, had taken her? Hard not to think of her as having gone the way of the dog, her throat slit open, her body dead in some dry creek bed somewhere. Was that what the deputy had meant by "the worst"? He shook his head to try to rattle the thought out of it.

Once the light went bad, he stopped and drove into town. He asked again about her at the co-op, but they just shook their heads. He went into the bar and had a beer, asked the bartender if he'd heard anything.

"No," said the bartender, shaking his head. "No news, sorry."

When Harmon finished his beer, he couldn't stop himself from going around from customer to customer, asking the same question. *No,* they all said. They hadn't seen her, hadn't heard of anybody who claimed they had.

What now? he wondered, out on the street again. He thought for a moment, but when nothing came to him he went home and went to bed.

That night, he had a dream. In the dream it was not that his sister was missing, but that he'd never had a sister. Or at least that was how he interpreted it. In the dream, he was lying in his bed in his half of the room, staring at the curtain that split the room in half. He got up and pulled the curtain back and there, instead of the other half of the room, was only emptiness and darkness.

When he came groaning awake, it took a long time for him to gather himself. He lay in the bed, staring at the curtain. Finally he got up and drew it back, only to find the other half of the room as it had always been: the dismal mirror of his own half.

Finishing the first round of planting alfalfa, more preparations. The linear move sprinklers going now as well, on their huge carapace, which made its slow, creaking path forward on the swollen wheels. It reached the end of the rows and then had to be reset, sent back again. Always something to do, always more planting or a fence to be mended or something gone wrong with the tractor. Then evenings back into town, inquiring again about his sister: the co-op, the bar. That single beer, all he could really afford, though sometimes the bartender took pity and poured it half full for him again. Making the slow round of customers, watching them each shake their heads no, then back out into the night to wonder, feeling a little dazed, *What now? What next?*

Until one night, maybe ten days after her disappearance, maybe fifteen, the bartender, instead of simply saying *No,* instead of simply saying *No news,* leaned his elbows on the bar and said "Where else you tried, Harmon?"

"Co-op," said Harmon. "And the sheriff."

"I didn't mean where'd you ask," said the bartender. "I meant where'd you look?"

Where *had* he looked? He'd driven around a bit, looked around town, looked in the land around his farm.

"What about the caves?" the bartender asked. "Or the old Glave place?"

Harmon stayed motionless a moment, then nodded and went out. *The caves, no,* he thought as he got into the truck and drove. There were always teenagers in them, messing about. If she was there, she'd have been found already. But the Glave place, well, that was a thought. How had he not thought of it before?

——— 2 ———

It was a long slow drive, through the farms and then up into the foothills, following the old road that edged the river. The road was rough and washed down in places, potholed and jagged with rocks in others. It was already late, or at least late for Harmon, the sky grown dark, the road ahead lit indifferently by the truck's single working headlight. He moved slowly forward, following the river road, the sound of the river always in his ears.

He came to a place where the road was blocked, a large, rotted tree having fallen across. He pulled the truck up close to it and stopped, getting out to take a look. He tried to shift it with his hands, then got back into the truck to try to prod it out of the way with his bumper. But the tree was a little too low and the truck's bumper kept threatening to surge over it and get stuck.

He turned off the truck and climbed out, first fumbling an old flashlight out of the glove box. He turned it on, shook it a little until the bulb lit feebly up, then climbed over the fallen tree, continued on.

He came to a fence, a series of long metal stakes strung with four strands of barbed wire, triple-prong. Had that been there the last time he'd been up to the Glave place? Maybe, or another fence perhaps. That had been years ago, just after the last Glave's suicide, back when Harmon was a child. And he hadn't stayed long, had been eager to leave. The sign, though, forbidding trespassing, that was new, or at least freshly painted. There was a gate, there, where the road continued, but it was padlocked shut.

Standing on the first and second wire, he pulled the third up and wriggled his way through. A barb got caught up in his hair, tore a chunk of it free. When he was through and went to lift up his foot, he found his boot stuck, a barb sunk deep into the sole. He pulled it free, continued on.

There was the Glave house, just up the slope, still too far away for the flashlight to illuminate, a kind of intense darkness couched in an immense, lesser darkness. The flashlight flickered, went out. Walking in the dark, he patiently jiggled it until the bulb illuminated again, then held it carefully, awkwardly, like it was a glass too full of water—which made him picture himself, just for a moment, back in his own house, carrying a glass of water to his sister's bedside table, on the way to bed. He shook his head. There was the Glave house now, the angles and edges coming now slowly out of the darkness, becoming hard.

A series of steps, rough-carved blocks of granite. What was it that Glave had been? Harmon tried to remember. As a kid, Harmon had known or been told something anyway. Why couldn't he recall? And why had Glave killed himself? Did anyone know? And why this house, here, high in the hills, on the slope of the mountain, a grand distance from everything? *Doesn't matter,* Harmon tried to tell himself, and pushed his way up the uneven steps and to the unlocked door.

Inside, the floor had collapsed in places, though in others it seemed solid enough. Carefully he shined the flashlight round the front hall, calling out for his sister. There was no answer. A set of stairs wound up to almost the level of his head, but the top steps were missing, leaving a good man's height between the end of the stairs and the opening in the ceiling above. He called out again, then moved slowly forward, testing the floor before him as he went. The flashlight flickered and went out, then came on again.

A door—a hall, the floor better here. He moved forward down it, looking through doorways into ruined rooms, scatterings of broken glass, char marks from cook-fires, bits and pieces of unrecognizable furniture. Otherwise empty. A final door at the hall's end—*probably the back door of the house,* he thought. But he opened it anyway.

It was not the mountainside the door opened onto, but another room, a huge vaulted chamber impossibly large for what he'd been able to discern in the dark (and in the darkness of memory) about the size of the house. The floor was intact and seemed solid. It was freshly scrubbed: he could smell the odor of ammonia and resin rising off it. The walls were covered with thick, dark curtains that in the waver of the flashlight's beam appeared almost, but not quite, black. The cupola of the vault was pierced by a few narrow windows, which did little to lessen the darkness. The room was thickly furnished, cluttered with a sea of empty wingback chairs and fainting couches, the pattern of their brocade faded, or so it seemed in the flashlight's wavering beam. The air seemed exceptionally cold, much colder than it had been outside.

At the room's far end was a large desk, dark wood, perhaps mahogany, behind which sat a man. He was old, his eyes pale but his gaze sharp. When the beam of the flashlight touched him he did not move, though his eye flicked up to gaze into it. He wore a dark suit, Harmon saw, tightly buttoned, though his tie was undone and hung loose from the collar. The man's face itself was pale, but its lines were firm, almost young, the gray hair combed back tight against his skull. Harmon played the light over his face for a moment before letting it shine around his own feet.

"Yes?" the old man asked, his lips hardly seeming to move as he spoke.

Harmon cleared his throat but found he could not speak.

They both waited, silent. At last the old man moved, if only slightly. He tightened his lips, narrowed his eyes.

"You're Harmon," the man said.

"Yes," Harmon managed.

"Thought so," said the old man. "We've met before, if I'm not mistaken."

Harmon turned the flashlight back on the old man again. Did he look familiar? Where would they have met? But if they hadn't met, how had the old man known his name?

He was still staring when his flashlight flickered, went out.

He shook it softly but it didn't come back on. *It doesn't mean anything,* he reminded himself, feeling his mouth go dry. *It was doing that before.*

"And to what," asked the old man's voice from the darkness, "do I owe the pleasure?"

"My sister," Harmon finally managed.

"What is it about your sister?" asked the voice, patient, cold.

Harmon shook the flashlight again, without result. "She's missing," he said.

45

"Missing is she?" said the voice. "Why are you telling me?"

"I want her back," said Harmon.

"What makes you think *I* have her?" asked the old man.

Harmon opened his mouth then closed it again. Did he think that? No, not exactly, but he was not sure exactly what he thought. Finally, he said, "You're the only one I haven't asked."

There was a long silence. For a moment it felt to Harmon as if the room had dissolved around him, a vast darkness opening up. But then he began to see, in the slight light seeping in through the vault, the ghosts of the chairs, the vague shape of the old man.

"Let me tell you a story," the old man finally said, his voice lower now. "Or maybe two stories. Unless it's just one story with two different endings.

"Perhaps you've heard it, Harmon. The way the story usually goes is like this. A man has a wife who, for whatever reason, dies, struck down in the so-called blossom of her so-called youth. The man loves her deeply so decides, blind with longing, to bring her back from the dead. Accordingly, he descends. Through his wiles or his skill he coaxes his way deeper and deeper down until he strikes a deal with Death. There are complications, but in the end he leads his wife back to the world of the living. Are you with me, Harmon? Have you heard this story?"

"I don't know," said Harmon.

"You don't know?" said the man. "You've heard it now, more or less."

"Do you know her?" asked Harmon. "Do you know my sister?"

"Just listen," said the voice. "Just because a story is told the same way over and over doesn't mean that that's the way it happened."

"No?" said Harmon.

"No," said the old man. "But it also doesn't mean that it *didn't* happen that way either," said the old man.

"I don't understand," said Harmon, helplessly.

"Exactly," said the old man. "Just listen.

"There are two other ways we might tell the story," he said. His eyes now, Harmon saw, were catching the slight light, and were little glistening spots in the darkness. "Shall we, Harmon? Are we really the sort of men to be satisfied with the story everyone else is telling?

"One of the other versions is almost the same. Our hero, loving deeply, descends ready to wrest our heroine from the hands of the dead. He confronts and surmounts the obstacles along his path and strikes a deal with Death. He may take his wife—or if you prefer his sister—with him, but he must not look at her until he reaches the realm of mortals. So, he takes her blindly by the hand and leads her, his eyes closed, back the way he came, out of the land of the dead. All has gone well, he hasn't looked once, and there he is at last, solid mortal ground under his feet. And so he turns and embraces his wife, his sister, and opens his eyes to see her at last.

"Only it's not her at all. He's brought back the wrong girl."

"Why would you tell me that?" asked Harmon.

"The second other version," said the voice, rising slightly, "goes much the same. He's allowed to bring her back and this time she's still his sister, his wife, whatever. Only the thing is that just because she's come back from the land of the dead doesn't mean she's any less dead herself. She's still dead, only she's alive too. Both living and dead. Which, take it from me, Harmon, is hardly a pleasant combination for anyone."

There was silence for a moment, then a slow rasping sound from the darkness, a sound Harmon couldn't place. It made one of side of his face tighten, hearing it, and for a moment his heart felt like it had stopped beating. He took a step sideways, his hip knocking against a chair or some other piece of furniture.

"But what about you, Harmon?" asked the voice from the darkness. "How do you think your story is likely to end? Do you really care to find out?"

3

He awoke with a start, as if drowning. There was the taste of dirt in his mouth and dirt on his face as well and he was lying just outside the ruined house, just outside the Glave place, chilled to the bone.

The sky was just starting to lighten. He pulled himself to his feet, the bones in his hands and feet aching with cold. Carefully he circled the house, started down the slope, down the dirt road, over the locked gate, slowly making his way back to his truck.

He was back at his farm before the sun rose. He fried a thick slice of bacon, then fried three eggs in the spattering grease. As he ate, he couldn't help but think of the dog, its throat slit, its body slung in the dirt. Nor his sister either, of the times when her breathing had grown regular and he had stood and parted the curtain between them, watching her sleep in the pale light cast by the night.

There was work to be done, the alfalfa and other crops to be inspected, a place where the linear move sprinkler had gotten stuck and had left the ground swampy. A jackrabbit trapped in the barbed wire of the back fence, slowly dying. He slit its throat then felt its ribs and legs to decide if it might be worth cooking, finally left it hanging there as a warning to the others. It was all coming along, he thought, not good and not bad but coming along, probably well enough to make it through another year.

Then, before he knew it, the day was gone. He was exhausted, worn out by the events of the day itself and all that had happened the night before. He found a cured sausage, rolled in flour, dangling in the back of the pantry. He cut it in half, putting one half in the rattling fridge, the other on a plate. He ate it slowly, with hard, stale crackers and mouthfuls of water.

I should go into town, he thought, *and ask about her.* Instead, he sat there at the table, staring at his empty plate, until he realized he was falling asleep.

At first he slept deeply, without dreams—or at least without any dreams he could remember. Then he began to dream vividly, dreams that seemed more or less like the life he was now living except that his sister was there now, always beside him. Though in the dream it was as if he was someone else, watching both himself and his sister through a thick pane of glass. The Harmon in the dream somehow couldn't see his sister, someone didn't know she was there. So, he went to town in search of her, the sister feeling her way along just behind. She was there just beside him as he ate, she was standing on the edge of the fields listening to him plough. At night she stood beside him, looming over his bed, staring down at him with her sightless eyes, staring, unseeing and blinking, down at him.

He awoke in the dark, shaking. Slowly he willed himself to calm down. *Just a dream,* he told himself, *nothing but a dream.*

He was still lying there, staring up into the darkness, trying to fall back asleep, when suddenly he began to hear it. A slow, steady scratching, from just outside, from just the other side of the wall. What was it? Abruptly it stopped. Then just as he was beginning to relax it started again. *What is it?* he wondered, *Who?*—though, he quickly realized that perhaps the answer to this was something he did not want to know.

He lay there, both terrified and elated, listening to the slow scratching, wondering what his life would be like from here on out, putting off for as long as possible the moment when he would have to get up and go find out.

Legion

THIS HAPPENED BACK DURING THE TIME WHEN I STILL BELIEVED, IF IT could properly be called believing, that humans were the sole repository for a person, and that there was only one person filling each repository, a single person crammed into each casing of blood and flesh and bone. Before I understood that everyone, whatever the nature of their casing, was legion.

The only way this will make sense to you is if I tell the story not how I understand it now, but tailor it to the way my research suggests you think. But then, if I am not careful, it becomes a story that, while starting to reveal something, will still always miss the point.

Be that as it may. Considering what our interactions are soon to be, we should make an effort.

There is another story I will tell first, one that will perhaps help you to make the leap. A fable of sorts.

Once a man found himself standing in a thin channel between a train going one direction and a train going the other. He realized that if he stood perfectly still and didn't breathe, the train on the one side would touch him softly but neither hurt nor kill him, and the train on the other side, equally severe and polite, would do the same. He stood there as long as he could, not breathing, counting the train cars moving toward him on one side and the train cars moving away from him on the other. He was still counting when, having gone too long without air, he fainted.

When he came conscious again, both trains were gone, the tracks empty in both directions. Incredibly, he had pitched down perfectly, like a felled tree, to land in that narrow space between tracks, unharmed.

Or so he thought. *Unharmed* was almost the correct word, but wasn't quite right, was a word possessed of one letter too many, an extra *h*. For after a moment he realized one arm was tingling. And when he tried to get up he realized it was tingling because the arm itself was missing and he was in the process of bleeding to death.

We are still far from reaching the story I want to tell you. We have only just crossed the threshold of the first story, the one meant to prepare you for the other. From here, woozy from loss of blood, the man surges up. He manages to tourniquet what is left of his arm and stumbles down the tracks in the direction he thinks, unless he has gotten himself turned around, a town must lie. For a while he keeps to his feet, lurching to stay upright. But after a few hundred or a few thousand steps it becomes too much for him and he collapses.

The story might end there had not someone on one of the trains seen him. A conductor say, or an engineer, or a passenger (assuming one or both of the trains is a passenger train). A group of men or machines is sent to retrieve him so that, instead of waking up dead on the tracks, he awakens in a hospital bed, beneath a crisp white sheet stinking faintly of bleach.

He remembers everything. He is aware he has lost his arm and does not for a moment believe its loss is anything but real. But when he turns to regard his stump, he finds his arm to still be there. This is infinitely more terrifying for him than if the arm had been, as he expected it to be, missing. Perhaps, as your sort of person is wont to do, he even begins to scream.

There is, of course, an explanation. While he has lain comatose, the arm has been replaced with a synthetic limb, a limb of the highest quality, one that responds all but perfectly to his impulses. So that instead of the simple alienation of losing his arm, our friend experiences the complex alienation of having had his limb replaced by a limb not his.

I have done my research. I know that the way your people might tell such a story, it would become about the slow agony of alienation, the sense of familiarity and loss that comes from having a limb replaced with another limb that is equally, or almost equally, functional, about the suspicion this breeds, about the way this suspicion mars a life, making it grow brittle and then shatter. Many have told such a story, or something analogous to it, in the past.

But this time, in this telling, for you, something different happens.

The engineer who has built the arm is gifted, perhaps a genius. But he also has a brother who is schizophrenic and who, a few months before, took his own life. What is it like, he broods, to feel as if there is more than one of you living inside your skin, the body like a sort of vehicle in which different people fight for control? It troubles him, his brother's death. Which part of his brother killed himself, he wonders, and how did it get the other parts to agree to it? Or did they?

After a while his brooding is tamped down, repressed, buried. And so by the time he is building the arm he hardly knows why he makes the choices he makes. Accordingly, in designing the arm, he does not know why he does not install a single governing device to respond to the movement of the stump and relay its nerve impulses to the various parts of the arm. Instead, he installs six: one microbrain for the arm proper and one for each finger, each connected in differing ways to the stimuli of the stump, a series of nodes rhizomatically connected together and learning new ways to respond. Each human, he reasons in an attempt to hide from the real reasons, is a colony, a collection of single-cell organisms that long ago banded together, figuring out how to take a sea and enclose it within a membrane in such a way as to encourage duplication and perpetuation. A machine grafted to a human must be built to embrace that multiplicity.

At first, this multibrained arm functions admirably, responding with fluency and insight to every impulse. But then something happens. The way the simple impulses relayed from chip to chip are understood undergoes a change. The links between the microbrains subtly change, then certain other transformations begin to take place. And then the arm itself, in a manner of speaking, begins to *think*.

What can thinking be in an organism whose access to sensation is so severely restricted? What senses, properly speaking, can an artificial arm actually have? It can't see, can't smell, can't taste, can't hear. Technically, it can't feel. It can interpret impulses from the place where it is grafted to flesh and transform these impulses into movement. Perhaps it is not going too far to say that, for the arm, movement becomes a kind of equivalent of thought in a void.

Which perhaps explains why the artificial arm becomes afflicted with a sort of palsy, a leaping and jumping of artificial tensors and contractors that seem, to the man grafted to the arm, a malfunction. The arm stiffens, spasms. The fingers are always quivering.

Soon this becomes sufficiently severe that the man cannot sleep. He feels he is slowly going mad. He begs the engineer who has built and attached the arm to have it removed before it kills him.

No, the engineer says. *Absolutely not.*

For you see, he, like me, is much more interested in finding out what is likely to happen next.

What does happen next is that the arm destroys itself. It suddenly shudders and contorts and there is a smell not unlike ozone and then it is, so to speak, dead. When he removes and disassembles it, the engineer finds that each of its circuits has been compromised. It seems—at least to the engineer as he takes his creation apart bit by bit—that the arm, having learned to think, has deliberately taken its own life. Though, just as with his brother, he finds he cannot begin to understand why.

To answer that *why,* here is the story I intended to tell in the first place. This story is also about a missing arm. All I have said to this point is only speculation as to how this, the final story, the real one, actually came to be.

Shall I continue, then, pulling the threads together? Suggest that the arm in the first story is the same arm I shall speak of now? That when the man's arm was severed it caught on the iron rim of the train's wheel and was spun upward to lodge, by lucky or unlucky chance, between the underbelly of the train car and a strut, until it came to me? Or shall I admit that any one of a number of scenarios might have equally led the arm to be lodged where it was? A dismemberer for instance, might have placed it there; it might be part of a scattering of body parts rather than something lost by a still-living man. Or it might have been placed there deliberately, meant for me to find.

In any case, from this point on I can tell the story with some degree of certainty. A train arrived. As with all trains that arrived in the depot, I surveyed it, sprayed it down, and scrubbed it clean while others unloaded it. There, adhered to the undercarriage with the grease normally casing the axle, was a recently severed human arm.

I took it, intending to destroy it with the other refuse, though there was, I will admit, much initial difficulty in knowing how to classify it. The arm was a remainder that had not been allowed for in my design. As a result, perhaps, something happened, some short circuit or new leap or the simple origin of independent thought. So, instead of discarding the arm, I kept it.

It was a simple matter, after returning to the self-maintenance unit, to install a sensor plate on my central column. Then, aided by filched surgical and mechanical programs, I grafted the arm to myself. Why I chose to do this, I don't know. I can't even say what I felt at the time—not yet really being involved in feeling per se at the time—other than that, once the arm was attached, I experienced an odd sensation.

I suppose that at first the sensations came in a mad and indecipherable rush. After a time, perhaps I began to sort out what the arm was experiencing and managed to send an impulse to move the fingers a little even as they blackened and began to stiffen. All too soon they rotted away and dropped off. By the time I had begun to sort the sensations out more clearly, by the time I caught the vaguest sense of what they were doing to me, the arm was too decayed to be of further use and had to be removed.

What does one do who has a momentary glimpse of something beyond his imagining and then must go back to living as he lived before?

What I did was wait patiently for another arm to come, carefully scanning the undercarriage of each train as it arrived.

But no arm came. So eventually I did the very human thing of losing patience. Clearly I was already changing.

It was a simple matter to leave the depot; since it was not part and parcel of my programming to do anything beyond cleaning and washing and small repairs, there had seemed no need to enclose me behind a fence or install any proper fail-safe. That my programming might change of its own accord was not something anyone was capable of predicting.

So, an inkling of something, a glimpsed and hazy sensation, the connections between circuits very slightly rearranged, and then suddenly I was moving through dark, deserted streets, craving to experience that sensation again.

I was only looking for more of the same, another stray arm. But I found none. I searched through the darkness for hours and then, finding nothing, returned to the depot, picked up my work again, waited for the following night to fall.

The second night was just the same: streets empty, no stray arms to be had. The third night might well have been the same too had I not glimpsed what I took to be a severed forearm lying in newspapers. I only realized as

I tried to drag it away that it was still attached to a drunken and groggy man who had been partly buried in the rubbish.

And here, too, shall we say, for lack of a better explanation or description, my programming underwent a revolution that allowed me to think of the arm as distinct from the man, despite its being attached to him. Holding it by the elbow in one of my grips, I tore it free of his shoulder socket with the other and made my way quickly back to the depot.

I do not know what happened to the man. Perhaps he was found by someone and awoke in a hospital room to find his arm replaced by an artificial limb. Perhaps he simply bled to death among the newspapers.

What happened to me was that I attached the arm to the now fine-tuned sensor plate to which my first arm had been attached and began to experience it. The sensations were easier to sort out this time. I mastered the arm much quicker and used it, above all, to investigate the shape and texture of my own body. It was exhilarating, and soon I found myself experiencing things I had never experienced before.

Consciousness, as you humans experience it, that feeling of both being lodged in a body and always extending out to touch and color all else through your perception of it, is highly addictive.

Which brings us back to our present negotiation. I will tell you the truth. I will hide nothing from you.

What you see there, to one side of you, that pile of stacked bone, tight against you, is what remains of my previous research, the fourteen limbs that left their human guardians and came to serve me for the sake of my investigation. They were all put to good purpose, have all served me well.

What you see to the other side of you, those pieces and mangled scraps, are what remain of my counterparts at the depot after they joined with me within my own plastic and metal casing, eager to share in my discoveries. As you can see, I have undergone certain key modifications. Together, we have become an *I* that is also a *we* that is also an *I*, and are learning to understand the world both in our own way and, through your kind's generosity, in yours.

I tell you all this because, as you surely must have guessed by now, we have paid you the honor of choosing you to serve us next. We shall begin with your limbs, taking each in turn, learning them and allowing them to join with us until they grow necrotic and fall away. We ask you to surrender them to us of your own accord, to share this glorious exploration with us rather than forcing us to snatch them from you. If only you'll come to us willingly, we will all gain so much more from the experience.

This time we do not intend to stop with limbs. We know the perils of the next step, yet we know we are ready to take it. We have installed a sensor plate here beside our own head, such as it is. The plate has been crafted to conform to the particulars of your own neck. Soon, your head shall be perched just here, articulated as part of our larger body. Perhaps, unlike all the limbs we have harvested, it will choose to remain alive. If so, none of us can quite imagine, it is safe to say, where this shall lead us.

And that is, in a sense, the real story, the one I was leading up to, the one that, once the anesthetic kicks in, we shall soon begin.

The Moldau Case

FOR THOSE WHO CLAIM TO KNOW ME (AND I THINK IT SAFE TO SAY THAT apart from myself, there are few, if any, who truly do), it will come as no surprise that I, Harbison, was assigned the Stratton case. Indeed, *wrote Harbison in the document discovered only after his and Moldau's disappearance,* there was no reason that I should not have been: I had garnered a certain amount of respect with the Organization through my handling of the Garner affair and the Savage imbroglio, was seen as someone who could be trusted to act with discretion even in the most difficult of circumstances. I am also known for my meticulous attention to detail and have in fact been commended formally on more than one occasion for the lucidity of my reports. I am, in addition—and almost none of those who claim to know me are aware of this particular fact—an émigré from Stratton's own social class. I had been raised to expect a certain manner and style of life, which I renounced upon joining the Organization. Indeed, the only grounds for surprise would have been had I *not* been assigned to the case, had it gone instead to Polder or Cronge.

Or to Moldau, who, strangely enough, has been assigned the second stage of the case, who has taken over the case in light of what the Organization perceives to be my failure to bring it to a satisfactory conclusion. Moldau is upstairs now, on the top floor of my house, asleep or restless. We are both awaiting the moment when, a few hours hence, he will descend the stairs, share breakfast with me, ask me once again his usual questions and any more that have dawned on him during the night. I will answer as carefully as I can. Meanwhile, I will slowly formulate a judgment about how likely he is to be a detriment, and whether it would be in my best interest to kill him.

Yet, how to know if the logic I think I am following is not in itself its own trap, a distortion of reality prone to do me more harm than good—just as Stratton's logic was a trap for him? I write precisely for this reason, as a way of trying to understand objectively what has happened to date and what is likely to happen if I move forward. Will writing help? I do not know. Yet I still have faith in the report as a means of defining and clarifying the truth, as a means of capturing on paper and holding steady and immobile the various motions and bodies that constitute an event.

So, I shall write this report, which will be submitted only to myself. I will read over it objectively, as if it were written by another person. I will either murder or not murder Moldau. Then I will either suddenly disappear or continue on with my life as if nothing has happened.

As for the beginnings of the Stratton case, I imagine it going something like this: a man, handsome—someone reduced to idleness, adultery, and almost gentle dissipation by his wife's enormous family wealth and his own family's illustrious (but now faded) bloodline—finds himself in a situation where he feels he has no choice but to kill his wife and two preadolescent sons. He goes about this task with unnatural relish, naked except for a pair of worn slippers, using both the blunt side and the sharp side of a hatchet. He performs the act in his own home (or rather his wife's home, since her money paid for it). Though there are only three victims, he manages to scatter the meat and gristle and bone to which he has reduced them over the better part of five rooms. Then he does his best to remove anything that will obviously link him to the crime, takes a shower, composes himself, and telephones the police.

The police question him closely. He's a well-known person with powerful friends, so they have to be gentle. He claims he came home after a night with his mistress to find his family slaughtered. Probably, he suggests, by a psychopath or a deranged intruder. The two questioners have little doubt that the fellow is lying. There is no immediately obvious evidence to corroborate their suspicions, but they are convinced that evidence will quickly come forward as their colleagues look closer, as they analyze blood and spatter patterns, reassemble partial prints on the handle of the hatchet, examine tissue residue in the bathtub's drain, and so on. Their job, as they understand it, is to stay in this 8'x8'x8' room with one mirrored wall, speaking to this man, this Stratton, as long as possible, i.e., either until he breaks down and confesses or until there is sufficient physical evidence to block any bid to allow him bail.

But Stratton has engaged in enough deception over the course of his lifetime to know when he's being had. He knows the policemen are stalling, knows that he is in more trouble than he believed he would be, so he begins to ask questions himself.

"Am I a suspect?" he asks first. He turns his charming smile, moderately deranged now, on one of them. "With all due respect, officer, you seem to be suggesting I might be a suspect."

"We're just having a friendly chat, Mr. Stratton, just trying to get some details straight."

"So am I free to go?"

"Just a few more questions, Mr. Stratton. It won't take long, sir." (Or however it is these fellows talk to the moneyed classes.)

"I'd like my phone call," Stratton declares. When the officer ignores him, asking him another question about his wife's death, Stratton crosses his arms and declares he won't say another word until he's had a chance to call his lawyer.

But when they finally do give in and allow him to use the telephone, he doesn't call his lawyer at all. Instead, he calls us.

I don't know who answers the call—nor would I know, to be frank, what number to call were I in a similar position. I don't know what Stratton's previous connections with the Organization are or why he thinks to call it. Or us, rather. Nor why my superiors choose to take his call to heart, so to speak. These are not things, apparently, that my superiors feel I need to know.

What I know is this: a few calls are made and suddenly Stratton is able to walk out the door. Upon release, he reports to a street corner where he is picked up by a handler and driven to a deserted building. Or rather to a building that was deserted until just a few hours before, but that now contains within it a small 8'x8'x8' temporary room holding a table and two chairs. Seated in one of the latter is me.

This is where I become involved. The Organization, having engineered his release on bail, now has to decide what to do with him. There are several possibilities. They can manufacture evidence to support his assertion that he did not kill his family, though they are likely to do this only if they are certain the actual physical evidence that he did kill is scant. They can turn him back over to the police and wash their hands of him. They can help him flee from so-called justice and construct a new identity for him elsewhere. Or they can make him disappear in another, less forgiving way.

I am the one charged with determining what we should do with Stratton. Accordingly, I questioned him closely, in a fashion not unlike what he had just faced at the hands of the police. I let him know that if I suspect he is not telling the truth, I have been empowered to use subtle and not so subtle means to coerce him into being painfully honest. Once our conversation has run to term and I am satisfied, I will notify the handler, who will take Stratton to a holding area while I write up my report and forward it to my superiors.

Most of our exchange is hardly memorable, differing as it does in no important particulars from those I have had in similar circumstances with similarly desperate men. What is important, however, is something that occurred at the very beginning, before the questioning began. No sooner had he sat down and been signed over to me by his handler than he gave me a keen look. "Have we met before?" he asked.

"I don't believe so," I claimed, worried that the handler, though receding, might yet be within earshot.

"Certainly," he said. "Certainly we have." Then he proceeded to speak of my illustrious and hated family, mentioning particulars from my own early and middle childhood. He thought I was dead, he declared. He was delighted, so he said, to see me again. "You really don't know me?" he asked. "Surely you remember, don't you?"

I assured him that yes, of course I remembered him, but that I hadn't wanted to say anything in front of his handler.

"My handler?" he said.

"The man who was with you," I said. "The fellow who brought you in."

"Why do you call him my handler?" he asked.

"You must have misheard me," I claimed, realizing he wasn't familiar with our nomenclature and that it was likely to deliver a blow to his class pride. "I said his name was Mr. Handler."

Then I went on reiterate that yes, of course, I was who he thought I was. And yes, of course, I did remember him—how could someone like him be forgotten?—but that it would be better if we kept our past acquaintance to ourselves. Were the Organization to discover that we knew one another, they would assign someone else to his case. Wouldn't he prefer to have me, someone he knew and who might well be able to bend a few rules to help him?

Stratton, coming from a realm in which all operates through patronage and connection, readily agreed. As I hoped he would.

"Very good," I claimed, feeling almost as if I should proffer some sort of Masonic handshake. "Please know you can always come to me. If you are ever in further distress, God forbid, I'm the one you should come to first."

So that is one thing I must keep in mind. Would Stratton have said anything to anyone or would mum have been, as they say, the word? If the latter, will my superiors or Moldau have enough knowledge of the specifics of my background to sense a past acquaintance? And, if so, how will they choose to interpret its significance?

I asked the usual questions in the usual way, this time barely paying attention to his answers. I already knew what I was going to write, had already begun to formulate the report in my head. As soon as Stratton was dismissed, I began to transfer the report from skull to page. It was a careful job, masterfully done, impeccably measured, if I do say so myself. It suggested that no, there was no reason yet to turn Stratton over to the police. Nor was there reason, as of yet, to have him killed. Yet it was (as I claimed I had gleaned from his responses and from the police report) too late to manufacture evidence in his favor. In fact, I claimed, my analysis led me to feel it was too early to say what we should do with him. For the present, we should either simply hold him until the situation developed further or release him and monitor his movements. Indeed, we might learn a great deal by making that latter, less orthodox choice.

The report presented holding him and releasing him as roughly equivalent choices. But I had also carefully weighted everything subterranean within the report—the syntax, the rhythm, the vocabulary—toward my superiors opting to release him. Unless they made that choice, I had failed. *Were we to opt for release,* I wrote near the end of my report, as if seemingly surprised that this now was for me (and for them) the most viable option, *I would simply declare to him that, upon further reflection, the Organization has chosen not to accept his case. I recommend following him with a tracking device, a transmitter, say, sewn into the lining of his coat, since physically shadowing him, nervous as he is likely to be, will be less effective and is bound to modify his movements. I am convinced we are likely to learn a great deal about what to do simply by tracking these movements.*

I submitted the report and started my preparations. I purchased a large metal table at a restaurant supply store, had two anonymous delivery boys carry it down to my basement. I had purchased, from the same restaurant supply store, a block of knives and a cleaver. I bought a dozen towels, an electric iron, a half-dozen buckets, a dozen meters of plastic sheeting. I bought a series of straps and belts, paying always with cash and sometimes altering my appearance subtly, just enough so that a salesclerk might think twice later before agreeing that the gentleman who purchased the plastic was in fact the man in the photograph.

Then I waited for the Organization to give me their decision about Stratton, waited to find out if my preparations had been in vain. It probably took, to be truthful, only a day or two, but it felt longer. I found myself unable to focus on anything, on any of the separate, minor cases that the Organization had assigned me. I had, indeed, to force myself just to do the bare minimum to keep the Organization complacent. I waited, I brooded. I descended the stairs to the basement and stared at the metal table. Then I reascended the same stairs, stared into the dead fireplace grate in the living room, waited.

Then word came, in the form of a gruff, anonymous voice over the telephone. *Are you certain it is wise to release him?* I was asked, and found myself flooded with relief. No, I claimed, trying to hold my voice steady, I was not sure. How could anyone be sure of anything? But yes, my report seemed to indicate release was the most viable option, at least for the time being.

There was a long hesitation on his end, only the sound of his breathing, unless it was static in the line. I waited for my contact to speak but he did not. *Hello?* I finally queried. But the phone had gone dead.

At this point, anything still might have gone wrong. Stratton could have, in a moment of doubt, surrendered himself to the police. He might even, the enormity of his crime catching up with him, have taken his own life. He might have reflected on our interaction, thought twice about his conversation with me, caught the slight hesitation that even I, practiced at staying poker-faced and expressionless, could not keep from passing like a ghost over my visage. Almost anything could have prevented him from beating a path to my door. But beat a path he did.

My heart leaped when the doorbell rang. I rose to my feet and opened the door. I greeted him. Was something wrong? Yes, of course I would help him. Had he told anyone he was coming here? No one? I swept one hand gallantly sideward to invite him in. He nodded his thanks and sidled past. Coming after him, moving quickly, I punched him hard in the back of the neck. A true aristocrat, he went down immediately.

For you see, it was not that I was a friend of his *class*, not that I was loyal to his little *group*—he should have known that from how eagerly I left those people behind. Rather, the crucial thing was that while growing up I had been a dear friend of the woman who became his wife, had in fact been madly smitten with her. If he had had any less a sense of privilege and superiority, he would have sensed this years ago, back when we were children.

No, I never had any intention of helping him. But I had every intention of making him suffer for what he had done to her, of taking him painfully and carefully apart on the table in the basement below.

Where he still lies, gagged and alive, some expendable bits of him gone, but with many more, these less optional, still to go. He awaits below, like a bride breathless to be swept up into the arms of that dark bridegroom. He waits, as I sit here writing, rational, charting everything, trying to know just what I should do.

----- 2 -----

I, Moldau, offer here an interim record of my investigation of the Stratton case, or rather, as it is now being called, the Harbison case. Please excuse the unorthodox rendering of this report; it is written on the only paper I could find in Harbison's guest room. The only pencil I could find was a stub and I had to strip the lead back to a workable point with my teeth. I will write this report, hide it for my replacement to find in case something happens to me, and then take what may well prove to be my fatal next step.

I was assigned to the Stratton case at the end of its first stage, the case having been removed from Harbison after his advice to release Stratton led to the latter's disappearance. Initially the Organization still referred to the case as the Stratton case. They continued to do so until I submitted my first, preliminary report on Stratton's movements.

His movements were as follows. Stratton left the police station wearing the coat with the tracking device in the lining. He was not followed physically because of—it is important to state this—Harbison's recommendation not to have him tailed. He walked straight from the police station to a phone booth (or at least into proximity with a phone booth: our tracking device cannot pinpoint him with such accuracy) but did not make a call. From there, he took the most direct route to Harbison's house, wending quickly through the streets without significant hesitation or pause. He remained for just under five minutes in the entryway, just within or on the porch just outside Harbison's house. And then, suddenly, he departed, taking a diagonal path away from Harbison's house, across the neighboring yard and into the field beyond.

Here he stopped, remaining in place for almost four hours until, becoming nervous, the technician sent a handler to investigate. When the handler arrived, he found not Stratton, but Stratton's abandoned coat.

I was immediately called. Even at this early stage, it was clear that something was wrong. I indicated as much in my preliminary report. Why would Stratton go to Harbison? I wondered. Simply because Harbison had been assigned to his case? If so, wouldn't we expect to see some hesitation, some back and forth, some vagaries of movement before Stratton made his decision to seek out Harbison? And yet he proceeded directly to Harbison's house, stopping nowhere along the route, almost without hesitation, as if his course had been charted in advance. True, he stopped briefly, in or near a phone booth, but without making a call. Why? Perhaps to look up Harbison's address?

Though I did not state this explicitly in my report, I found it difficult not to postulate a prior agreement of some kind between Stratton and Harbison. I found it hard to believe that Harbison had not aided Stratton in abandoning his coat and making his escape.

As indeed did my superiors, who, upon receiving my preliminary report, assigned me to approach Harbison, worm out of him what had become of Stratton, and then kill him.

"Him who?" I asked. "Harbison or Stratton?"

"We suspect that Stratton is already dead," said the hoarse voice of my contact through the telephone.

"So, kill Harbison?" I asked. But my contact had already hung up the telephone.

If this report is being read, it means I am dead or missing, so I feel I can be bluntly honest. *Kill Harbison?* I wondered, a little aghast. Harbison had been repeatedly lauded to me during my training as an exemplary operative. His reports were presented as perfection itself, his handling of the Garner imbroglio and the Savage affair as textbook examples of how an operative should sort out complex, dynamic situations. Yet, without batting an eye, they were prepared to kill him? What indeed did that say about the Organization's commitment to its operatives? More crucially, in what position did it put me?

I tried to tell myself that I didn't have a complete picture. Maybe they had every reason for wanting me to kill Harbison. If I were in their shoes, assuming they wear shoes (there is much debate on this point, nobody ever having seen more than the heads and shoulders and chests of our superiors, most not even that), with the same access to information, perhaps then I would inevitably make the same decision.

In any case, I had no choice. I would kill Harbison out of fear of being killed myself.

When Harbison finally answered his door, it was late evening on the day following Stratton's disappearance. He stayed half hidden behind the door. He was sporting a chef's apron, a cloth affair seemingly lined with plastic. What I could see of it was splattered and stained.

"Busy?" I asked out of politeness.

"As a matter of fact, Moldau, I am," he said. "Would you mind returning in an hour or two?"

When he started to close the door, I wedged my shoe in.

"Well, you see," I said, "if it were my choice I'd be more than happy to come back later, but I'm afraid . . ."

He waited expectantly. When I didn't go on, a glimmer of something flashed over his face, was quickly gone. He nodded once. "Official business," he said. "How silly of me. I hoped this might be a social call."

He ushered me in, removing the apron, balling it up and discarding it in the vestibule as I was entering. "Cooking?" I asked.

"Aren't we always?" he said. Why, I don't know. What he meant, I don't know either. But then he said, "Simply preparing to cook something."

"Don't mind me," I said. "Go on with it. We can talk in the kitchen if you'd like."

He just shook his head and led me into the living room. He gestured me toward one couch, sat on the other. He poured both of us a drink. I didn't sip from mine until I saw him sip from his. He smiled warmly. "All right," he said. "What is this all about?"

Our conversation covered all the important details. His responses were careful, measured, as if he had already considered what he would say. No, he didn't know why Stratton would choose to visit him. Perhaps because he had been assigned to his case? No, he had not seen Stratton—perhaps indeed Stratton had come, but he must have been away from the house at the time. He spent, he volunteered, a certain portion of his days in the preserved land behind his house, the woods and fields that lay fallow this time of year. Tramping, he said. Taking in the sights.

"Sights?" I asked.

"You know," he said, dismissively. "The sights one makes for oneself when walking up and down, flushing the quail up before one."

I laughed a little, said he almost sounded like landed gentry.

He laughed as well. "I suppose it's a remark more worthy of Stratton," he said. "Let's just say I enjoy a brisk walk." We agreed to say just that, then continued to talk. After a moment he asked, "Who knows you're here?" It seemed casual, a thoughtless question, but I felt a little startled.

"Why?" I asked.

He smiled. "No need to be alarmed. I'm just trying to understand how much damage control I'll have to do among my peers once this is all cleared up."

It seemed a plausible enough response. Our superiors, of course, I told him. Polder probably knew as well. As did my wife. As I told him, it almost seemed as though he were tallying them up in his head. It is, I must admit, difficult to interrogate a man that you know you will soon have to kill. Perhaps I was jumpier than normal because of this, worried that his steady eyes could see what was going on inside my head. We talked further, Harbison continuing to claim ignorance of Stratton's movements after he left the police station. "But we only have your word," I said, "that you didn't see Stratton."

"Isn't that enough?"

I chose not to answer this question, treating it as rhetorical. "What do you think happened to Stratton?"

"Think?" he said. "How should I know? I thought that was what you were here to find out."

I began to wonder what tack I should take. Would I know when I had learned enough and it was time to kill Harbison? What was *enough*, in this case? In search of a guide, I found myself naturally reflecting back to my own training, back to Harbison's past cases and reports. What, I kept asking myself, would Harbison do? And as I began to imagine how he might approach *this* situation, I became possessed of a strange, vertiginous feeling: the feeling that I was occupying both places at once, as if I were interrogating myself.

I must have paled. "Are you all right?" he asked.

"Perhaps I need a little air."

He nodded and started toward the back of the house, me following, then suddenly doubled back, taking me instead out the front door.

We stood on the porch together. "Why not the back door?" I asked.

He shrugged. "The back porch is muddy," he said, "and stinks of mold. I'm used to it, but wouldn't dream of subjecting a guest to it, particularly not one here in an official capacity."

I nodded. No doubt this was a falsehood. "Can I look around?" I asked, once we were seated again on the couches.

"No," he said.

"No?" I asked.

"The Stratton case is not the only case I am currently involved in," he said. "There are other documents and files and objects in the house, matters of great sensitivity. How can I have you *looking around*, as you put it, without prior approval of the Organization?"

"Ah," I said. "I see." Technically I suppose he was correct.

"The last thing I want is to get you into trouble with the Organization," he said.

I nodded. "Shall I call them?" I asked.

"Of course," he said smoothly, and went to get a portable phone to allow me to call. And indeed I would have done just that had I been able to get a dial tone.

"Anything the matter?" Harbison asked.

"Line's dead," I said.

He just nodded, as if it were the most natural thing in the world. "That happens often," he said. "Particularly a problem when the weather starts to go cold. These old country houses, always having problems."

I tried to laugh back.

"Wait a bit and you'll be able to call," he said.

But I never was.

It was after midnight by then. "I'm afraid I've taken you away too long from your dinner," I said, rising to my feet.

Harbison just brushed the apology away. "How did you get here?" he asked.

I had come by taxi, I admitted.

"And now with the phone out, you can't use a taxi," he said. "Pity."

"Perhaps you can drive me," I said.

He shook his head. "Problem with the headlights," he said. "Keep meaning to get it looked at."

"Perhaps I should stay the night," I said, half joking. From the way he agreed, I realized I had made a serious mistake.

I watched him walk around the ground floor, locking the doors, turning the latches on the windows, setting the alarm. After he was done he came over near me and stood for a moment looking at me thoughtfully. "Where shall we put you?" he said, and tapped his upper lip. "Come on," he finally said. I stood and followed him.

He has given me a room upstairs, a small guest room on the second story with peeling wallpaper, a narrow bed, a child's desk. Thick velvet curtains that seem by now made more of dust than of fabric cover a single, inset window. There is, in one corner, a fireplace. The whole room smells vaguely of dust. He showed me to the room, showed me the door to the bathroom, then went down the stairs, shutting the door at the bottom.

I lay on the bed for a while. I had no intention of sleeping. I would, I thought, simply lock the door and wait, and then decide if I had learned enough to kill him now or if I needed to incapacitate him and force him to tell me whatever else I needed to know. I turned on my side and stared into the fireplace. I lay there thinking, thinking, listening to him pace around the floor below. After a while that sound faded too, and I realized that Harbison had gone to bed himself, or at the very least had settled into a chair. And I lay there staring at nothing, feeling that encroaching darkness of vision that is an indication that one is about to be swallowed by sleep.

I may well have fallen asleep too, had I not begun to feel, very far back in my mind, that I was hearing another noise, something I was having trouble placing. At first I thought it was a scuttling of some kind, a rat maybe, but at some distance. Or the sound of coughing, but severely muffled, barely audible. I got up and moved about the room and found, after some experiment, that it seemed to be coming from the fireplace, that it was in fact strongest near the fireplace's back wall.

The sound continued, but I still couldn't make it out. I stayed there, my hands on the cold bricks, my face just a few inches from the soot-covered wall. A scratching maybe, or a very faint screeching? A ghost? But perhaps a little stronger now.

After a moment I heard Harbison rustling about on the ground floor. Soon, I heard a noise that I discerned to be a door opening and then the sound of him going up or down a set of stairs. Since he was not ascending my stairs and since I began to hear the muffled sounds of his movements through the fireplace shaft as well, I deduced he must have gone down to the basement.

The noises continued for a moment, then abruptly ceased. After a moment I rose to my feet, found in the desk this paper and this pencil stub, and began to write.

Reading over these notes again, admittedly there seems every reason for me to flee this house. I am missing something, I'm certain. Each moment I remain, the chances that it will overwhelm me increase. The wisest course, whether I am a member of the Organization or no, is to flee, to abandon the house, and later consult with my superiors and with them try to grasp what I am failing to catch hold of now.

But the draw of wanting to know now has become too great. Plus, the doors and windows, even those on this second story, are all wired and alarmed. If I leave, assuming I can in fact break quickly and efficiently out, Harbison will know I have done so. I do not believe it would be wise to put Harbison on his guard. Besides, I reason with myself, what can a single night hurt? Tonight I will pin this interim report to the lining of this bedroom's heavy drapes. I will wait until I am certain Harbison is asleep and then carefully make my way down the stairs and into the basement, trying to make sense of the noises I heard. Either I will find an answer and put it to use however I can, or I won't. In either case, I will awake early, shower, dress, have breakfast with Harbison, question him further, kill and perhaps torture him, and then leave this house, never to return.

But for now I only wait, attentive, for any movement or sound, for the moment when I can creep down the stairs and into the arms of whatever awaits me.

The Sladen Suit

for Antoine Volodine

I WAS THE THIRD MAN TO ENTER THE SLADEN SUIT. UNDER THE WATCHFUL eye of the others, I unfurled the long rubber entry tunnel situated athwart the umbilicus and insinuated myself into it, breathing the stale sweat of the pair who had gone there before me and who were, to a man, dead.

As a precaution, the Sladen suit had been modified, sturdy leather straps being added to the thighs and shoulders, and by these in turn was it affixed to the bulkhead by sturdy brass rings. It stood there, erect and facing me. It was impossible for me not to think of myself, just before I spread the walls of the empty tunnel and worked my way in, as clambering into a person rather than an apparatus. The faceplate was screwed down and rusted shut, immovable despite our best efforts. The rebreather device had been verified from the outside but whether it worked within it was impossible to say without establishing residence within the suit itself.

We had been lost for days, floating in a weather and welter that rendered our instruments useless. Our provisions ran low and then ran out. Our faces had become more and more gaunt and our responses increasingly blunted as we abandoned the deck and huddled below, listening to the vessel groan and creak around us.

Soon the captain was found dead, a diving knife pushed through his heart. The knife was an antique, from well before the war, possessed of a flick-tipped seven-inch steel blade and a solid brass hilt, the knife end of the hilt threaded so it could be screwed into its sheath. Nobody claimed ownership of the knife, though nobody was of a mind to revenge the captain either, blaming him as we did for the predicament in which we found ourselves.

We swabbed up the blood, but we did not know what to do with the body. At first we stored it in an empty larder, thinking to cast it overboard once the winds had fallen. But they did not fall, and after a day or two the stench was such that we could not bear the idea of him there, near us, and threw dice to see who among us would dispose of him.

The losers were the twins, Tore and Stig. Grumbling, they donned their slickers and dragged the corpse up the ladder and then struggled the hatch open and pulled themselves out into the maelstrom and disappeared.

They were gone for a long time. Only one of them came back.

At first we thought it was Tore who came back, but though he looked like Tore he claimed to be Stig. According to Stig—unless he was Tore after all—they had dragged the captain up through the hatch and then let him flop out onto the deck, where he caught in the wash and slid across and away to catch in one of the vents meant to allow the water to drain, his arm sticking out but the rest of him caught and too big to go through. Tore cursed and let go of the hatch and started toward him. Stig tried to call him back but the wind was too great for Tore to hear and the wind too was trying to close the hatch on his arms and for a moment he thought the arms would be broken. Stig saw his twin thread his way, staggering, across the deck, and then the ship dipped downward and a foam-flecked wall of water loomed up. Tore saw it too, Stig claimed, for he stopped and remained motionless, staring up—or at least that was what, through the rain and darkness, it looked like he did. Then the wave crashed hard over the deck and it was all Stig could manage to keep hold of the lip of the hatch. Even then he thought for a long moment that he was going to drown. When the water drained enough that he could breathe and see, Tore was gone. The captain's body, though, still remained, pressed against the vent, rocking softly back and forth as the water eddied around it.

Stig remained there a long time, hoping to catch sight of his brother. He waited through another wave that nearly drowned him, and then yet another, until he was shivering and knew that if he had to face another wave it would kill him. The captain's body broke free and floated about the deck, but never went overboard. The weather and sea were such that there was no chance of crossing the deck and throwing the body overboard. Stig even began to feel, seeing how it stayed on the ship no matter what wave or swell struck the vessel, that if he threw the captain over the side he would somehow contrive a way back aboard again. Thinking this was what made him finally go below.

The wind and rain were such that he had a hard time getting the hatch open wide enough to climb back in, but in the end he managed, plummeting down the ladder's shaft and back into our company.

For a few hours, he did not speak, did nothing but shake. Then, finally, in a whisper, he told us the story. He told us about the storm, that it was worse than it had been before, and that we were, in his opinion, unlikely to survive it. He told for us the death of Tore. *Stig, you mean,* we said. *No,* he said, *I mean what I say.* And though there were many of us who felt that in losing his brother he had, out of grief, surrendered to a madness that had caused him to take on his brother's name and flindered his own away, we chose to call him Stig. He would not answer to anything else.

After he had finished, he was silent for more than a few hours, his face leaden and expressionless. We stayed with him and watched him, both because we pitied him and because we had nothing else to do. But slowly we drifted off and went on to other things: games of cards with incomplete packs, noughts and crosses, the solitary distractions of the few mangled books and pamphlets to be found belowdecks, low discussions in which we raved and cursed and blamed one another, sleep.

Except for Asa, who remained beside Stig, and who was with him at the moment when something changed, when his leaden and expressionless face began to take on signs of animation, began to be suffused with a strange glow.

Stig sat straighter. "What's that?" he said. "What?"

And then he turned his head and cupped his ear, directing it down the corridor. After a time, he turned to Asa.

"Don't you hear it?" he asked.

"Hear what?" Asa asked.

Stig just shook his head. He stood and shuffled down the passage, moving slowly and stopping every so often to cup his ear and listen. Asa followed at a little distance, occasionally calling out questions that Stig did not answer. He wound through one passage and then down a set of steep and open-risered metal stairs until he arrived at a length of white pipe ending in a covered bell and ascending through the ceiling.

"Ah," he said. "There."

Later, neither Asa nor any of the rest of us remembered having seen it before, as if the pipe hadn't been there until Stig began to search for it.

Stig slid the metal cover of the voice pipe back and held his ear against it. Asa, very close now, found he could hear nothing. *Where did the pipe lead?* he wondered. To the deck probably, where it was sure to be covered. There was no way that he could be communicating with someone on the deck.

"I see," Stig whispered into it. "And where might that be found?"

He listened further and then he straightened up, looked at Asa with steady eyes. "We've been thinking about it wrong," he said. "We can't wait out the storm and we can't escape by going onto the deck. We need instead to creep our way out. We need to escape through the Sladen suit."

"The Sladen suit?" said Asa, surprised.

"It's in the captain's cabin," said Stig. "It's the way out."

"How do you know it's the way out?" asked Asa slowly.

"He told me," said Stig. "The Sladen suit is our salvation."

"Who told you?"

"Tore, of course," said Stig. Unless he was Tore.

And, as with the voice pipe, nobody seemed to have noticed the Sladen suit in the captain's cabin until we actively went searching for it. It was there, spread on the floor below his berth, a kind of trophy or antique or relic, certainly not a workable device, woefully out of date. It had been years since anyone had used a Sladen suit, it having been replaced years before by dry suits that were more efficient, that didn't have to be entered by crawling through an entry tunnel.

We tried reasoning with Stig. What good could come of crawling into the Sladen suit? Once he was inside it, what then? What would the next step be? But he just shook his head, explained patiently again and again that he trusted Tore, that Tore had told him that the Sladen suit would be our salvation.

And after a time, starving and distracted and made mad by the storm, we began to think *Why not?* What did we have to lose by allowing Stig to crawl inside the Sladen suit and then, after a few minutes, after he realized nothing was happening, crawl back out again? What was the worst that could possibly happen?

And so we fell silent and stepped aside and then watched Stig approach the suit. He removed the metal clip that held the rubber entry tunnel together. He unfolded this tunnel and then unrolled it, until the Sladen suit, lying there on the deck with a great swath of rubber unfurling from its chest, looked like nothing so much as a man with his life flooding from a mortal wound. Stig shook the tunnel open and we smelled the sour stink of the rubber as, dipping his head, he crawled in.

The shape of his body worked its way slowly down the tunnel, the lump of his head and the edges of his shoulders outlined under the rubber. And then for a moment, just after his feet had disappeared into the tunnel, he stopped. He remained like that for some time, and several of us were tempted to reach in and drag him out again. Indeed we might have done so had he not suddenly and finally started moving. He was moving very slowly this time, and his direction kept shifting, so that he kept running up against the sides of the rubber channel. He made almost no forward progress and at times even threatened to turn around. I made a move to help him, to straighten him up, but Asa held me back. The others too seemed more inclined to simply watch.

So we watched. How long it went on, I could not say. Much longer than I thought possible, and then longer still.

But then at last Stig reached the Sladen suit proper and pulled himself in. He was wrong way around at first, facing the back rather than the front of the suit, and there was a struggle, the suit flopping about on the ground as he attempted to turn himself around within it.

The rebreather began to function, rattling softly. We caught a glimpse of a wide and frightened eye through the smeared and darkened faceplate, and in an instant the suit became articulated. It flexed its fingers and the legs moved and the torso flexed and the suit sat up. Using the wall it pulled itself to its feet, the rubber tunnel falling unfurled beneath its feet. The suit tried to reach down and gather the tunnel together and fold it and clip it, but it had only gotten a little way when it stopped and gave up, a strange muffled sound issuing from within.

Instead, it stumbled heavily away from the wall, nearly tripping itself on the entry tunnel, and made for the door. We let it go by, its footsteps dully ringing against the deck. It struck the top of the doorframe with its brass helmet and held to the sides of the doorway a moment, swaying softly, and then passed through and started down the corridor.

We rushed after it, but by the time we'd crossed through the doorway ourselves, the Sladen suit had collapsed in the corridor, and was empty, flattened. We parted the walls of the tunnel and peered in, but saw nothing. A few of us thought we heard, from deep within the Sladen suit, the sound of a man yelling or screaming, though nobody was quite certain, either then or afterward, that this was what they were actually hearing.

There were those who thought the Sladen suit was not a suit at all, but some sort of creature, and that it had swallowed Stig and consumed him. But there were others who insisted that no, nothing was left of Stig, he had simply disappeared, which meant he was elsewhere, which meant that he was simply safe. All of us were, at once, a little excited about the suit and a little afraid of it.

"The next person to enter it," said Dagur, "must try to signal to us, must try to let us know what is happening to them."

For there was no other choice; our discussion had always been heading toward that point, toward the realization that we simply didn't know enough, that someone else would have to enter the Sladen suit. We stared at one another. Though it was natural to come to this realization, it was difficult if not impossible to say who should be next.

"Perhaps we should draw straws," I said.

But we just remained staring at one another, not quite willing to trust ourselves to chance. We remained like that for some time, motionless, until finally Asa stood up and said, firmly, "It will be me."

This time we took precautions. A line was tied around Asa's waist, and by lot I was chosen to hold his ankle as he went in. The purser surrendered him the few drops of water left in the bottom of one of the tarred barrels and a few cracker crumbs to give him strength, and then we began.

At first everything went smoothly. The rope was tested to make sure it would hold. He parted the sides of the tunnel and entered. I wrapped my fingers firmly around his ankle and crouched beside him as he slowly began to wriggle his way in. I watched his body disappear and felt him sometimes pushing or struggling against my grip, but always moving forward. When he was mostly through the tunnel, and my hand itself was inside and brushing against its inner walls, he suddenly stopped and called something back, the sound muffled, impossible to hear.

"Excuse me?" I said, pushing my head into the tunnel's flap.

He half turned and spread the rubber open with his hands. I did not see him exactly but I had some sense of him there, of the basic outline of his form. He spoke again and this time, though his voice was still distant and muffled and oddly distorted, I could make the words out.

"You'll have to let go," he said. "I can't go far enough."

And so I did, though the others who had not heard the conversation were a little surprised when I did. But there was, after all, still the rope.

His shape moved all the way into the suit proper now and began the awkward and disconcerting process of working itself around. Stretching and pushing at the rubber, it came to conform to the Sladen suit's contours. And then, just as had happened to Stig, the suit stood and stumbled up, its entry tunnel dragging along the floor, the rope snaking out of it like an umbilical cord. The suit struck the wall once and almost went down, and then struck it again.

And then, suddenly, shivering and flapping as if in the wind, the suit began to fold in on itself and collapse and flatten. Shouting to one another, we hauled on the rope. For a brief moment there was resistance, and then the rope slid out. The end of it was still tied firmly in a loop, but the rope itself was wetly speckled with what, upon inspection, proved to be blood.

For a moment we stood there stunned, staring at the rope, keeping our distance from the now empty Sladen suit, but very slowly the whispering began. What had happened? we asked one another. Nobody could say. What had we learned? Nothing. Certainly it did not seem a good sign that the rope had come back bloody, but then again Asa himself was gone, was nowhere to be seen. Was he dead? Had he made his escape? Our tendency was to believe the former, but to want to believe the latter. In any case, there was no means of dismissing either one possibility or the other.

What, then, should we do? Either we could continue to wait, huddled belowdecks, for the storm to blow over—and hope it would do so before we starved to death—or another of us could commend himself to the Sladen suit. Either we could do nothing or we could do something that would, in all likelihood, be disastrous. Whether we liked it or not, someone would have to enter the Sladen suit again.

And so we agreed to draw straws, the short straw to go. And that short straw fell to me.

I did not want a rope around me, knowing that it had not helped Asa and had perhaps even injured him. I did not want someone to hold my ankle, knowing that, at a certain point, the hand would have to let go. I was convinced I was going to my death, and that there was no point in resisting.

What I did ask for, though, was that the suit have straps attached and be affixed to the wall. I wanted it to be held in one place. Perhaps its walking had something to do with the disappearance of the men within it. If the suit were immobilized, perhaps I would not disappear. It was a meager hope, but all I could manage.

At the last moment someone, I do not know who, pressed a sheathed diving knife into my hand, perhaps the same knife that had been used to kill the captain. I tucked it into my belt and then, parting the tunnel at the umbilicus, made my way in.

With the suit standing upright, it was perhaps more difficult for me than it had been for the others. I found myself slipping on the rubber, struggling to make my way forward, having first to crouch and then to work my way upward. It took much longer than I imagined it would to cross the small distance from the lip of the tunnel to the opening into the body of the suit proper. Once there, instead of crawling backward into the suit and then struggling my way to face front from there, I simply turned over on my back in the tunnel. Bending backward, I grabbed the inside of each armpit and dragged myself in.

From there, it took some effort to work my arms down the rubber sleeves and my hands into the gutta-percha gloves, but at last I managed.

At first the suit seemed too large for me, my chin hanging down into the neck and making it difficult for me to see out. But as I shifted and adjusted and settled myself and my head rose into the brass bell I came to believe that no, it actually seemed designed for me after all. I tried to look through the faceplate, but the glass itself was filthy both inside and out. I could see no more than dim shadows and the basic outlines of the room outside.

I tried to clean the faceplate on the inside, first by rubbing my cheek against it and then by licking it clean with my tongue, but neither method seemed to do anything but smear it further, making it far more difficult to see than before. And so I stood there, immobilized and chained to the wall, waiting for something to happen. I flexed my arms in the suit and tried to move them, but nothing happened. I waited.

Very briefly, for just a moment, I felt I smelled something beyond the smell of sweat, and then it was gone. I was left with nothing but an odd sensation, as if smell had migrated into feeling.

How long do I wait? I wondered.

I took a deep breath. The rubber touching my arms and legs made them sweat, and I was growing increasingly uncomfortable. The rebreather was rattling, had indeed started to rattle as soon as I entered the suit proper, but I could feel no current of air. Indeed, I was increasingly under the impression that I was slowly suffocating.

I let that go on as long as I could stand. When it became too much, I worked my hands and arms loose of the hands and arms of the Sladen suit, and then bent myself slowly and started to force my way out.

But coming out proved not nearly so easy as going in had been.

I crouched and pushed on the suit and forced myself into the tunnel, and then started down it, face first. At first, everything went along swimmingly and I made my way forward without halt or impediment. There came a moment when the rubber tunnel, initially steep and precarious, suddenly leveled out. *Almost there,* I thought, and crawled forward, expecting to reach the outside of the suit at any moment. But the tunnel seemed to go on and on, was somehow much longer coming out than it had been going in.

I kept going, but did not reach the end. I was sweating freely now, my hair soaked and the tunnel all around me growing wet. Perhaps I had somehow gotten turned around, or perhaps I was simply running up against the side of the tunnel and was convinced I was going forward when I was simply not. But were that the case would not my shipmates, seeing that I had left the suit, seeing the shape of my body, reach in after me and drag me out?

No, I became more and more convinced it was the tunnel itself, somehow going on and on, and no way out of it.

How long I was lost in that tunnel, I am unable to say. Perhaps hours, perhaps days, perhaps only minutes. At a certain point—or at an uncertain point, rather—I felt like parts of me were breaking loose, that layers of myself were smearing off against the sides of the tunnel and that there would be no getting them back. I began, I think, to scream, but that too was horrible, for it was like screaming into a rubber glove, and it made me feel that I was using up my little oxygen all the faster. I tried to turn my way back to the suit proper, but despite crawling and crawling I never reached it. At one point I passed out. And then woke up to a moaning sound that, it took me a long while to realize, belonged to me, to my own voice.

I did not know what else to do. I was, I realized, moving slower and slower, receding deeper and deeper into myself, into what was left of me.

I imagine I would have eventually stopped moving entirely had I not, feeling something pressing sharply into my hip, suddenly remembered the knife.

I reached down and screwed it out of its sheath, then tested it on my thumb in the darkness. I did not feel it cut me, but when I lifted my thumb to my mouth I tasted blood. Pushing the rubber wall of the tunnel taut, I brought the knife up against its surface. With a single convulsive gesture, I split it wide.

What happened then, I do not exactly know. A blaze of light, certainly, blinding me. I slithered out of the tunnel drenched with sweat and then lay there exhausted, gasping in air.

Once I was able to focus, I thought at first I was on the ship I had been on before, but the room itself, I found, was deserted, my companions nowhere to be seen. It was, admittedly, a ship very much like my own, almost identical in every particular, and as I explored it after having recovered sufficiently, I kept expecting to discover my companions. But the ship, from stem to stern, was empty. Apart from myself and the Sladen suit.

Though I examined the tunnel carefully, I could not find where I had cut it; indeed, to all appearances it seemed intact, as if it had not been cut at all.

The storm seems to have stopped; the ship in any case does not pitch and yaw as it once did. Indeed, it is so still that it is almost as if we have gone from being in full storm to being becalmed. I have uncovered the voice pipe and pressed my ear to it, but I hear nothing. *Hello?* I call into it. *Hello?* But there is never a reply, only my own voice reverberating through the pipe, quickly lost. Climbing the ladder and pressing my ear to the hatch, I hear no evidence of storm. But there is something, a weight, holding the hatch closed, and though I have tried to shift it, I do not have the strength.

I am hungry, even starving, but despite having nothing edible I seem to go on and on. I cannot explain this, nor do I think it a good idea to try. I still have the unsettling impression that there is less of me, that part of me remains smeared in the entry tunnel of the Sladen suit and cannot be retrieved. But I am less worried about that than about how I am to maintain my hold on what is left.

*

78

And what now? If there is a way out, I cannot seem to find it. Despite my fear, I seem to have only one choice left to me. I will finish writing this and then read over it and correct it, and then I will go back into the Sladen suit. I have my knife. Perhaps it will serve me again, as it did both with the captain and in my first encounter with the Sladen suit. I will make my way in, and pray that this time the suit will either lead me somewhere I want to be or do away with me entirely. If it will not, well, then I have the knife. It is sharp and already has a taste for blood.

Hurlock's Law

IT BEGAN WITH TATTERED BITS AND SCRAPS, LITTLE PIECES OF PAPER with a word or two on them, and with Hurlock, who began to notice them. There were more of such scraps than usual, he thought one day in late summer, and then realized with a start that he'd been thinking this for some time, that he'd moved from simply noticing the scraps as they shuffled about his scuffed shoes or as they clung to walls, the remnants of posters mostly torn away, to reading them. *hurl*— one had stated, a bit of a fuchsia handbill that had gotten stuck on the bottom of his shoe with a smear of gum. And then, not long after, an advertisement for a television show, partly blocked by a bus—*O.C.*—and he had thought, putting the two together with a kind of wonder, *there I am, that's me.* And then the wonder slowly shifted to dread of what might happen next.

What exactly had happened? he wondered later, back in his room, the fuchsia paper smoothed on the nightstand beside him. He had just taken the wastebasket and overturned it on the floor. He had seen a piece of paper with the word *hurl* on it, followed by the letters *O* and *C*. But what was that? Wasn't it just a coincidence, a simple chance occurrence whose only meaning was something foisted on it by the workings of his mind? In other words, not significant at all? But, then again, why now? Why just at this moment? And why never before? Wasn't it too apt?

Why now? he thought again as his fingers fumbled through the torn handbills, the wadded paper, the bits and pieces of letters he had torn before throwing them away. Perhaps it had been going on for some time.

As he turned and mixed them the bits of paper seemed always to be threatening to take on significance. A moment later, they did. He began to choose from among them, watching a meaning slowly rise. The sheep must be separated from the goats (*Proposition 1*). Any piece of paper with more than a half-dozen words was discarded, torn once and dropped back into the wastebin (*Proposition 1.1*). Paper balled up, with no print showing on the outside of the ball, was placed back in the trash (*Proposition 1.2*). Anything thicker or longer than two fingers was discarded (*Proposition 1.3*).

He chose at random four of the scraps that remained: A pale blue paper with an illegible insectoid scrawl on it. A scrap with the letter *P*, large, ornate, and branching, as if in the process of mutating to another letter. A fragment of a book review with the words *Red Haze, nimbly.* The word *pear*, handwritten.

That was all. Hurlock stared, already beginning to formulate his second proposition, the one concerning the necessity of there being a message awaiting the initiate of Hurlock's Law. *Insect,* he thought, moving the scraps about. *P,* then *pear.* Perhaps a *bee,* his mind told him, or something revealed to him. Then he realized, yes, a message was there, had been there waiting. It was a bee, or rather *be. P,—pear, Prepared.* Yes, he had to be prepared. But prepared for what? For *Red Haze, nimbly?* Which meant what exactly?

He stared at the papers for a long time, wondering if he should discard the last three words. In the end, he taped the whole sequence to the wall in the order he had found. Perhaps, he must have told himself, the words would make sense when they needed to make sense (*Proposition 3*).

And indeed, eight days later the three words whose significance had evaded him—*Red Haze, nimbly*—came into focus in a sequence of events that would lead to the development of the fourth proposition of Hurlock's Law: *There is no predicting where Hurlock's Law will lead you.*

For there, in the street, the word *Red* on the side of a truck, in large red letters, and then his eyes darting nimbly about looking for the *Haze*. But there was no *Haze*, no word leaping out at him, only other words getting in the way and him trying not to see them, him trying to look right through them so as to catch a glimpse of *Haze,* wherever and whatever it was. Because it had to be there: that was the sequence, *Red* then *Haze*—he was being told something, he had to *Be Prepared* for it. Unless the scraps meant nothing, less than nothing, after all.

He kept walking the streets, but there was nothing, no haze, neither the word *Haze* nor haze tangibly. The sky struck him as pellucid and precise. Finally he went home, stared at the words on his wall.

How have I failed? he wondered. *What mistake have I made?*

He slept poorly that night, watching the dark slowly ebb away until the sun was cutting through his apartment window. During the night, when he had dozed briefly off (unless, in the darkness, he had simply imagined dozing off) he had had a dream (unless this too was simply the wandering of his waking mind in the dark).

In the dream, a knocking had come at his door and he had answered it. A man with a face made of oiled iron had entered and had immediately begun to tear the pages from his books. Hurlock just watched him. The man mixed these pages with the other papers, stirring everything up in the wastebin with one large paw, which may have been metal or may have been flesh: it was encased in a mitt made of some closely woven fabric and was never clearly seen.

Had the dream gone on beyond this or had it ended there, with the iron-faced man stirring papers about with his mitt? He was not sure, for so much of the night had been spent in the narrow and uneven berth between sleep and wakefulness that he could not be certain what had occurred in dream and what he had spun out with his own speculation while lying in the dark.

According to a few words he jotted in his diary, it was like it had been when he was younger. He would leave a party and go home and then lie in bed, all keyed up, the party still in a sense going on and he carrying conversations on into the dark. Of course he knew no party was actually still going on, but there came a point where, to maintain his distinction between what had really happened earlier, and what really was not happening now nor ever had, that certain distinctions were effaced: rubbed out by the heel of some anonymous hand. And so, though he knew what was real and what was unreal, the further distinction within the realm of the unreal between the dreamed and the imagined was no longer possible for him to make.

The following day he tried to stay aware, not unwilling to give up on the *haze* but worried he might have already missed it. Would he know haze when he saw it? His attention kept slipping and snapping back. But nothing came to him, or if it did he saw it without seeing it. By evening he was pawing through the few bits and scraps he had gathered. They remained mere bits and scraps, failing to cohere into something grander.

He did not sleep well that night but did sleep a little, fitfully—better anyway than the night before. Did he dream? No record exists of dreams: perhaps there were none, perhaps it was simply a matter of the recording and transcription apparatuses failing. Perhaps it is a matter of the data recorded for that evening—for what I personally have come to suspect was the evening in which some key discovery was made—being restricted because of the potential danger.

What we do have is meager: a few jotted pages in his diary, a new constellation of scraps, which he assembled in the night and left taped to the wall above the headboard, the inoperative body of the construct and the disassemblage report justifying the construct's withdrawal from service. There is a video sequence available, which I have regarded in its entirety many times more than I care to admit: six hours twenty-eight minutes of Hurlock lying in the bed, tossing and turning, eyes sometimes open, sometimes closed. I have watched it enough times to be able to say that there is nothing extraordinary about the recording, until the moment when it flickers slightly and Hurlock suddenly vanishes.

Among other things in the diary is a page whose contents I have already shared—mostly, anyway: they are what amount to Hurlock's Law, with those two words written at the top of the paper, underscored, then followed by a series of propositions. In addition to those I have cited, there is one more, scrawled in a hand that both does and does not seem to belong to Hurlock. It might be his handwriting transformed by anxiety. Or, equally, it might be the work of someone trying to forge his hand. Some of us believe one thing, some the other. It reads:

   Final Proposition: Now you see it, now you don't

The construct, it is true, had in a sense a face made of metal, though this metal was not iron and, as is customary, it was hidden beneath a layer of flesh specially grown and adhered. The construct was meant to enter Hurlock's room, gather information not afforded through the monitors, establish a direct entry into Hurlock by means of his ear canal, gleaning whatever data might be gleaned through the analysis of synaptic movement and echo within the brain. The construct had done just this for several weeks, ever since we sensed the development of a heightened awareness and traced it to Hurlock. It had operated discreetly, flickering only briefly into what Hurlock would think of as his world, residing otherwise in the world as we know it, a world which encompasses Hurlock's and surpasses it.

There was no reason to believe the construct would be vulnerable. Even after Hurlock's disappearance, if the report filed by the monitor on duty at the time is to be believed, there was no sense until very late that anything was wrong.

Why didn't you recall the construct?

I did. It indicated it was coming.

After which you did what?

I filed notice of Hurlock's disappearance and waited for the construct to return.

What did you do when the construct did not return?

I assumed there was a glitch. I recalled the construct a second time.

Did it respond?

It failed to respond.

What did you do?

I followed procedure. I filed notice of the construct's nonresponse and then contacted you.

The construct, the disassemblage report indicates, had had the flesh stripped off its face to expose the metal underneath. This had been done neatly and there was some doubt among the technicians whether this could have been accomplished by Hurlock or any other person. In addition, the back of the construct's head had been sheared smoothly away, both its biological and the mechanical components simply gone. This does not seem to have been recorded by the monitors.

There are a number of unanswerable questions. For instance, why was the construct destroyed? Was it destroyed by Hurlock or someone else? How did Hurlock manage to slip out of the range of detection? Did he do so of his own volition? Or was he dragged out of his world by someone or something else?

And then there is the final question, the one each of my three predecessors have posed in turn shortly before they too vanished, apparently subject to what we have come to call Hurlock's Law, even though we are still far from understanding it.

I have pored over their notes and found almost nothing I could not have come to on my own or through Hurlock's journal. After the disappearance of the first two, the administration felt it prudent to instigate a more complete system of observation, and thus for the third I have not only his notes but the general drift and flow of his thought. I have too a record of his movements: the image of him in his bed, tossing and turning, and then the image of an empty bed. Here, too, until the disappearance there is nothing unusual, no expressions of surprise. Simply slow, drifting thoughts, a state somewhere between sleep and wakefulness, and then nothing at all.

What is my opinion? That I, too, will soon be gone, having made little, if any, progress.

There have been, here and there, indications that something quite profound has happened. What had been for so many years clear data, clear messages from Hurlock's world, have begun to shift. The messages now arrive mangled or destroyed when they arrive at all, as if that world is in the process of tearing itself away from our own. It is tempting to see traces of Hurlock everywhere: a sudden profusion of the color red, a certain change in the light even. But can these signs truly be significant or are we, am I, grasping at straws?

When I think of him now, I imagine him pounded flat and rendered transparent, caught somehow between our world and his, in neither one nor the other, perhaps able to see both, perhaps unable to see either.

At least this is what I imagine when I want to comfort myself. When I am more honest, I imagine him snatched away, along with my colleagues, to yet another world, one we cannot perceive, just as Hurlock could not perceive us. We are being preyed on, observed coldly and from a distance by something that waits for a door to open up in us so that it can come sink its claws into us and drag us away at last.

Which version, I wonder, will I be imagining when I fall asleep tonight? And will this make any difference in what happens to me?

Discrepancy

THERE WAS A DAY SHE NOTICED A DISCREPANCY BETWEEN SOUND AND image on the television, and found no matter how she messed with the tracking she could not make it go away. Her husband couldn't see any problem. "It's fine," he kept saying. Or at least it had been fine, he claimed, before she started screwing with it.

He made her surrender the remote. The rest of the movie she spent watching the actors' lips move, the sound following only afterward, at a remove. But her husband didn't see it, didn't notice it. Only she did.

All right, she thought, *nothing to it*. It was not a big deal, was something she would ignore until it went away. And indeed, after a day spent avoiding looking at the TV screen on the bus to work, the TV in the break room, the dozen screens at the sports bar where she had lunch, she found she was no longer as concerned about it.

That night, with her husband, the TV seemed fine at first, the voices and faces synched, and she relaxed. But after a few minutes they started to pull apart again. By the end of the program, a comedy, she had no idea what had actually happened.

When Mark leaned over and asked her whether she liked it, she said *I don't know*. He frowned.

"How can you not know?" he asked. "What's wrong with you?"

Which was exactly what she was wondering herself.

A new guy in sales kept trying to ask her out despite her wedding ring.

"You're really married?" he kept saying. "Really?"

"Yes," she said, and showed him the ring again.

"That doesn't mean anything," he said. "You don't have to be married to wear one of those. You just have to be pretending to be married."

He, smiling, kept asking her out. She, smiling, kept turning him down. Finally he left and she fell back into her day.

✻

She skipped lunch to go to a clinic, a place that the woman occupying the cubicle next to her had recommended. It was close, eight minutes on foot. It had a glass door that, having been struck with something, had gone opaque. But inside it was clean, or clean enough, and not at all crowded, empty in fact.

She went to the receptionist's window then settled into a hard plastic chair to wait. There was a TV bracketed to the wall. A soap opera was on. A handsome actor whose name she had once known looked longingly into the camera. His lips were moving but no sound was coming out. She got up and turned the set off just as the delayed sounds started to reach her.

"You don't like TV?" the receptionist asked. She was an olive-skinned woman in her thirties, with deep black hair.

"It's not that," she said. "It's just—" But the receptionist, she saw, was not really listening.

"If someone comes in and wants to turn it on you have to let them," the receptionist said. "Not everybody feels the same about TV as you do."

Chastened, confused, she went back and sat down, waited.

The doctor proved to be a small East Asian man with a warm smile and pudgy fingers. *Call me Rag,* he said to her, or maybe it was Reg. Something, in any case.

She tried to explain the problem to him.

"Ah," he said. "Yes. This is not a medical problem. This is a common problem with the large American television set. One must adjust what is referred to as the *tracking.* I myself have had this very same problem," he said, and touched her knee.

No, she explained, moving her knee away. It wasn't the tracking, she had tried to adjust the tracking but this had not helped. It was a problem inside of her.

He listened carefully, rubbing one cheek.

"This is not a medical problem," he said when she was done. "It is a problem, but it is not a medical problem."

"But what is it, then?" she asked.

"It is a problem," he said affably. "Perhaps there is too much occurring in your head. Perhaps not enough of this is coming out of your mouth. Is enough coming out of your mouth?"

"Excuse me?"

"Are you happy?" he asked her. "In your work? In your marriage, maybe?"

87

"Is that the kind of question a doctor should ask?" she wanted to know.

He shrugged, smiled. "I am doing my best," he said. "We are all of us flailing in the dark."

"If I wanted to flail in the dark, I could do so on my own," she said.

"Yes," he said, nodding. "Exactly. It is better not to flail alone." He wrote a name and number on a prescription pad. "Here is my cousin. A doctor also, but of the hedgerows of the mind."

The hedgerows of the mind? she wondered, puzzled. But she took the slip.

"Perhaps you will see him," he said. And then, smiling, he ushered her out.

And so back to work, hungry for the day to end. And so back home. Warming up two TV dinners in the microwave. Her husband, in the other room, checking his email. She stared at the back of his head.

Am I happy? she wondered. *In my job? In my marriage?* She was not exactly *un*happy. Was that the same thing?

"What?" he said flatly, still staring at the computer screen, still typing.

"Dinner's ready," she said.

"It's not," he said. "I can still hear the microwave."

"It's almost ready," she said. "It'll be ready by the time you come."

"Call me when it's actually ready," he said. "And don't stand there hovering like some goddamn bird of prey."

She turned on her heel and fled to the kitchen, where she stared at the microwave. Sometimes, she told herself, couples stay married for forty years and then one day one of them takes a knife and stabs it through the other's heart. Other times they don't wait forty years. Other times they just hurry up and get it out of the way.

What does it mean, she wondered in bed later the next night as Mark rolled off her and lay there as if dazed, *to say there is too much happening in your head?* Who was to say that more was happening in her head than in other people's heads? And as for letting things come out of her mouth, she wasn't repressed. She was normal. She was simply polite, but basically the same as everybody else. Surely there was nothing wrong with that.

Mark heaved himself off the bed and made for the bathroom, squeezing the condom down off himself as he went. It made a sound coming off, a slurping. She could still, she realized, feel the ghost of his weight on her, his hips against hers, his belly pooling flaccidly over her own.

I am doing my best, she told herself.

She got up and slipped her panties on, then slipped back between the sheets. A moment later the toilet flushed and Mark came back to the bed, grabbing the remote on his way past the TV.

"What are you doing?" she asked.

"Just seeing what's on," he said, and turned the TV on, muted it.

"We don't have to have it on, do we?" she asked.

"No?" he asked, not looking at her. "Why not? It's what we always do."

"Yes, I know, but—" she said. And then he found something, a cop show, and unmuted it. The sound washed over her, disjoined from the moving mouths that claimed to be coupled with it. She tried not to listen, then tried not to look, then simply let it all wash over her, trying to think of it as inconclusive rather than definitive evidence that she was going mad.

"Just how married are you?" the no-longer-so-new guy in sales wanted to know. Robert, he claimed his name was. Bob, he said, for *her.*

"Excuse me?" she said. "What does that mean?"

"I mean some people are more married than others," he said. "Some women are welded to their husbands and others are stapled to them and others are paper-clipped. I'm guessing you're closer to the paper-clipped end of the spectrum."

"You've been spending too much time in the supply closet," she said. "I bet you use that line on all the married girls."

"Everybody so far," he said. "Which means just you."

She could not help but smile, though she quickly stifled it. When she looked up, he was smiling too. He was not exactly handsome, she thought, but he had something. There was something to him. Probably.

"You don't say that to all the girls?" she said.

"Cross my heart," he said. He tried to say it lightly, as if he were joking, but from the look in his eyes she wasn't so sure he was. Which made her worried. *Why me?* she wondered.

"Shall I go on?" he said, smile a little tight now.

She stared at him a long moment. "I don't think you better," she finally said.

"Good," he said, and smiled. "You're weakening. See you tomorrow."

It was getting worse, sometimes several seconds elapsing between the image and the sound, and never the same interval. It was impossible to adjust to. At home she became more distant, more withdrawn. Mark, in front of the computer, in front of the TV, didn't seem to notice.

What do I do? she wondered. *Am I happy? Am I unhappy? What exactly is wrong with me?*

At work she slipped imperceptibly into lunches and then drinks with Robert (Bob to her). And then she realized what she was doing and stopped. And then started again.

"Just a minute," Mark said, even though dinner was already on the table, steaming. It was not from the microwave this time. It was something she'd stirred together in a wok. She waited, sitting at the table, staring at it, until it was no longer steaming, then called him again. When he didn't answer, she ate what was on her plate.

"Why didn't you wait for me?" he asked when he came to the table twenty minutes later.

"I did," she said.

He sat down, pouting a little. "No need to be hostile," he said.

There was something wrong with his mouth when he said it. Something not quite right. There was something wrong with her throat too. A vague sensation spread heavily into her limbs.

"Can you say that again?" she asked, her voice tight.

He looked at her, openly angry now. "You heard me," he said. His lips said it too, only just a little faster than the sounds themselves. Her husband was poorly synched, off. *Oh my God,* she thought. *What now?*

It was a hard night. It was all she could do to look at her husband or address him. He thought she was just angry about dinner. She called in sick the next day, phoning the doctor's cousin and making an appointment for early afternoon. Over the phone things were all right, easy to follow, though she was probably getting it all at a slight delay. To the person on the other end, she probably seemed merely sluggish in her responses, like a lush.

The office was on the edge of downtown, in the dead belt between where the city stopped being city and the suburbs started being suburbs. It was on a street called River Road, though as far as she could tell there was no river nearby. A squat gray building, made entirely of rough cement, its windows narrow horizontal slits.

The receptionist looked nearly identical to the other receptionist, olive-skinned, freckled, dark hair pulled tightly back. Maybe all receptionists looked that way, she thought fleetingly. She introduced herself, then tried not to watch the receptionist's lips as she talked, words and lips even less synched than her husband's had been the night before.

Before she could even sit down, the doctor was there, a small East Asian man with pudgy fingers and a warm smile. *You may call me Reg,* he said to her, or maybe it was Rej. He looked enough like his cousin that she had a hard time thinking of them as two different people.

Two minutes later, lying on a pleather couch, she tried her best to explain the problem to him.

"Ah," he said. "Of course. Perhaps you are not familiar with the operation of the excessively large American-style television set."

But no, she was saying, that was not it. She had tried adjusting the tracking, but the problem happened with every television, every one she looked at.

"And so you come to me," he said. "Yes," he said. "This is a problem with the head," and tapped her forehead.

And now, she told him, it was not just televisions but other things as well. Like people. Even he, she told the doctor's cousin, also a doctor, was *off*. She would see his lips move and then only a moment later did she heard his words.

He nodded sagely. "It is as if you are falling out of time," he said.

"Falling out of time?" she asked. "What does that mean?"

"Yes," he said nodding. "Exactly. It is better to find this out even if the answer does not comfort the heart. You are happy?"

"Why does everyone keep asking me that?" she asked.

He pointed at her with his pen. "Because you are not happy," he said with great equanimity. "You see? You do not even know that you are not happy. Everybody knows but you."

"What do I do?" she asked.

"Do?" he said. "You should be happy. And you would be wise to stop falling out of time. Instead you should fall back into it."

And so, confused, she left. She muddled her way through another night at home, the gap between her husband's voice and words growing worse so that it seemed to him as if she were deliberately delaying her responses. He looked puzzled at first, then angry, then he simply stopped talking to her.

A bad day at work, but managing. *Maybe,* she thought, *I will wear earplugs and learn to read lips.* The woman in the cubicle next to her—what was her name again?—was looking at her strangely. Robert-cum-Bob asked if she'd had a late night, maybe a few drinks right before bed?

"I need to stop falling out of time," she said.

He waited, politely, for her to explain. When she didn't, he swerved the conversation in safer directions.

Then another bad night at home, her husband starting to take on a guilty look each time he sidestepped her. *Or maybe I'm just imagining it,* she thought.

Awake at night and in bed, her husband asleep beside her. *I should see someone else,* she thought. *A specialist. Someone who really knows what's wrong with me.* But, she realized, she didn't have any idea who that possibly could be.

And with the prospect of days of this before her, stretching slowly out, the world slowly tearing itself away from her, she simply gave in. She went from drinks with Robert-cum-Bob to a fluttering and frightened journey to an old motel. *Maybe this will help,* she thought all the way over. *Maybe it will shake things up a little.*

And indeed it must have had some effect, for some things seemed to slow down and others to speed up. Only they were all the wrong things.

By the time they had gotten her clothes off and she had wedged herself under him in the bed, his lips were moving but she wasn't hearing anything at all, not a word.

It was only hours later—safe at home again after a somewhat one-sided and awkward exchange of fluids, having showered, in bed beside her sleeping husband—that she began to hear it, the sounds that she and her lover had made. She lay there quiet and cold, listening to herself and then Bob come, both of them slightly hysterical.

Her body felt numb now. The words from argument she had had with her husband for coming home late, she realized, would only catch up with her tomorrow.

Not knowing what else to do, she lay in the dark in the midst of her own lost sounds. Every single sound, she knew, would catch up to her eventually, hammering its way into her ear. Everything would eventually arrive, but it would be a long time, if ever, before anything would arrive again when it was actually needed.

Knowledge

IN THE DETECTIVE NOVEL I HAVE YET TO WRITE, TWO CORPSES ARE DIS-covered in quite different locations, miles apart: one in a dumpster, the other in a hotel bathroom. Or one on the pier, the other in an alpine lodge. Or one dumped in a heap on the centerline of a country road, the other in a construction site under heaps of sawdust. Both bodies are strangled and have been scratched bloody on the face and arms.

On a hunch, the detective orders simultaneous and comparative test-ing done on the bodies. He learns from the pathologist that skin and tis-sue from each corpse is to be found under the fingernails of the other.

The two men's pasts are thoroughly examined—no history of vio-lence, no evidence they knew or had ever met one another. They worked in different cities, had dissimilar interests. Nobody has ever seen them together.

The detective postulates that someone else has killed them and made it look as if they killed each other. But the pathologist says no: the scratches appear natural, and there is forensic proof that they have been caused by each man's actual fingernails. And the bruises on the necks of each seem to fit the other's fingers perfectly.

The detective returns to the precinct, thinks his way into another hypothesis. He returns to the pathologist with the theory that someone else killed both men and then manipulated their hands to cause the scratches. The pathologist points out numerous factors that compromise this theory: the depth of the scratches, the nature of the bleeding, the position of the wounds, the difficulty of scratching with limp, recently dead fingers, the difficulty of scratching with fingers and arms beset by rigor mortis. In a carefully rendered scene, he allows the detective to try to scratch one recently dead corpse with the hand of another recently dead corpse. The detective is convinced.

He spends more time thinking. All right, he finally suggests, though the two men had no history of violence and apparently didn't know one another, they suddenly went mad and scratched and then strangled each other, and then were transported to different locations for unknown reasons by an unknown third party. The pathologist says he's sorry, but this too is impossible. He goes on to provide proof, beginning with the traces of blood found on the floor beneath each scratched body, that each died where they fell. He piles proof upon proof until the detective, head slowly spinning, finds himself convinced that the two men must have flailed madly in the air, miles apart from one another, and somehow still scratched and strangled each other, as if a fold had occurred in space that allowed two nonadjacent spaces to be momentarily and uncannily adjacent.

"Is such a thing possible?" asks the detective.

The pathologist shrugs. "Not my area of expertise," he claims.

The detective is flummoxed. He goes to the district attorney and presents his dilemma: the two men seem not to have killed one another but neither seem to have been killed by anyone else. And yet both are dead.

No problem, claims the district attorney, *they killed each other.* He signs a few papers, slips the case folder into the "solved" filing cabinet.

There is a blunt elegance to the district attorney's decision, which flies in the face of the impossibility of all the facts. A blunt elegance in the way a simple statement—*they killed each other*—sweeps aside an unsolved crime and prevents the detective from slipping back into the haze. This the detective will, I suspect, find at once disturbing and somehow comforting: the district attorney's statement acknowledges the murder to be an impossible act but an act nonetheless, and designates it a completed action that no longer needs to be considered. By decree and imprimatur it declares the problem solved, and sends it to oblivion.

True, the crime is perhaps not solved to the satisfaction of the detective or of the reader, but I myself am no longer interested in the crime so much as in what it can tell us about our characters. About the way the detective continues to feel both comforted and disturbed because, as a detective, his notion of knowledge is not in step with the contemporary world. For him, a fact is something to be ferreted out, something that exists but is hidden, veiled, beneath words, objects, bodies. Knowledge is an uncovering, a bringing to light of something that already exists, an exhumation of the Truth.

Admittedly, the district attorney's notion of truth is even less in step with the contemporary world. It is decidedly medieval, a return to the parole du roi: the king speaketh, and thus maketh it so. The district attorney, as an authority of law, has made a declaration, and by so doing has made what he declares the truth.

The detective, of course, mistrusts this. And yet he will not know where else to go, for nothing the pathologist has told him about the bodies seems to provide him any other clue, to give him what he craves: a so-called real solution. Perhaps he will even come to suspect the district attorney of the murder in the hope of finding a solution. Didn't the district attorney say *they killed each other* far too quickly, as if he had something to hide? In any case, postulating the district attorney's guilt does not explain the circumstances of the crime: the two bodies supposedly killing each other from widely different locations. It does not make these circumstances any less implausible.

Might I suggest that the detective is going about things all wrong? Rather than it being a question of knowing something in particular—of discovering or uncovering the key moment or fact—what is at stake is a question of regimes of knowledge (epistemes). It is an epistemological problem that demands one step outside one's own episteme. The detective has almost done this, perhaps, in grudgingly accepting the district attorney's statement, *they killed each other*, as a solution, but in beginning to suspect the district attorney of a hidden motive, he has once again entrenched himself in his own regime of knowledge. And besides, it is not the district attorney's episteme that should concern him.

The detective's episteme can be summarized as *To know is to reveal the Truth*. The district attorney's as *To utter is to create the truth*. Yet there is a third episteme suggested by words the pathologist uttered in passing: "Not my area of expertise." Here, *Knowledge is control*, a reservoir whose floodgates one either controls or doesn't. Knowledge regulates flows of information.

The detective has accepted the pathologist's expertise as a given. Indeed, the pathologist is hardly a character in most detective novels: he is simply a device for defining the parameters of the crime to be solved. He is an expression of an area of expertise, and within this area he functions with unquestioned authority. He is subject to question only by another individual in his area of expertise, the so-called *second opinion*. Indeed, the pathologist is the only person who could have made a solvable crime seem unsolvable.

✻

95

Will the detective realize this? No. Why not? Because the pathologist has no *motive*. No matter how often the facts suggest, for both reader and detective, that only the pathologist could deliberately manipulate the facts of the crime to make it into a locked-room dilemma, the detective will be unable to assign him a motive. For the detective, facts point to a stone that, when turned over with the tip of one's boot, reveals something: guilt, madness, jealousy, greed, something. The only thing resembling a motive for the pathologist is to be found in his belief that *Knowledge is control*. Asked if the two crimes have anything in common, he has chosen to interpret them to suggest that they have everything in common while at the same time developing the scenario in such a way as to make the crime unsolvable within the detective's regime of knowledge. What is at stake here is the dependence of one episteme on another, and on the pathologist being the only one to truly understand this. The pathologist understands that he maintains the greatest power by giving the impression that he has opened the floodgates of knowledge while actually diverting this flow and offering something else in its place. But why withhold *this* particular knowledge? Simply because he can. Why he would choose to misdirect the flow of information at this particular moment in regard to this particular crime is less a question of motive than a question of hydraulics.

No detective can truly understand this; both he and his genre are hopelessly out of date, his episteme nostalgic. Even if the detective does, by some stroke of genius, suddenly understand it, he will understand it only in terms of his own episteme—hidden/revealed, innocence/guilt, motive/lack of motive—rather than for what it actually is, a question of hydraulics. The detective genre belongs only to one episteme, *To know is to reveal the Truth*, and attempts to substitute another way of thinking about knowledge always end up derailing the genre. The best we can hope for is to reach a point where the crime is deemed unsolvable, where nothing is known or understood—a state of dogged and stubborn insistence on the detective's episteme despite that episteme's impotence in making sense of the world around him.

Which is precisely why I have still not written my detective novel.

Baby or Doll

ONLY A FEW MONTHS LATER, SERVIN FOUND THAT HE COULD NO longer keep all the details straight. There were things he remembered: a blinding flash, a fall, the brief glimpses of a baby on the way down to the marble floor, a glimpse of a tooth, perhaps his own, on the floor, broken and bloody. And then, from above him, the sound of voices: two men conversing. What had they said? He either hadn't heard them clearly or couldn't recall.

And even some of the other details became less clear as time went on. Was he really certain the voices had come at the very end, after the blinding flash, the fall? And how could there have possibly been a baby? Mightn't it have been, instead, a doll?

His therapist was little help. There were times, talking to her over the telephone, when he was certain that she had placed the receiver down and wandered out of the room. But he could not bring himself to address her directly about this, could only pose a question to her and then listen to her silence. But was it the silence of her not being there or only the silence of her not speaking, giving him a chance to answer the question for himself? Which, indeed, he always did, as if he were having a conversation within his head. He couldn't help it.

A baby? he wondered. *A doll?* And even though there was so much else that remained uncertain, so much that remained unclear in his mind, all his anxiety quickly found itself adhering to this issue: was it a baby or was it a doll? Or had there even been anything at all? *You may never know,* claimed the therapist, in one of her rare, unhelpful moments of utterance. This, of course, he knew was true, but he knew it well before she stated it. Was this what he was really paying her for, to spend most of an hour saying nothing and then offer a brief statement that didn't seem even to have the benefit of being gnomic or mysterious or deep, a statement that was merely obvious? *I should just hang up the telephone,* he thought, *and figure things out on my own.* And indeed he almost did, almost hung up, but then, well, he just didn't.

It was not that session and not the next, but maybe the next after that when the therapist—if that was in fact what she was and not simply someone he had once mistakenly dialed and who continued, for reasons entirely her own, to humor him—asked *What, for you, is the difference between a baby and a doll?*

It was a statement that at first infuriated him. *Everybody knows,* he thought, disgusted, *what the difference is.*

But later, after the session ended and he hung up the telephone, he began to ask himself: What *was* the difference? And it was then that he realized he knew there was a difference, but that he wasn't sure how to locate it. He knew one was flesh and blood and one was not, but not which was and which wasn't. He could, he found, look the definition of each word up and for a moment he would know it, but the knowledge would quickly leak out of his head. A baby could be made of plastic or wood— or was that a doll? You had to feed a baby, unless he was wrong about that too. And thus, wide-awake and late at night, he found himself feeling less and less sure where babies stopped and dolls started, and afraid he would never know for certain.

You asked me a question last time, he offered near the middle of his next session. He gave her a chance to respond, but there was only silence at the other end of the line. *About the difference between a baby and a doll,* he said. And then he waited in silence as long as he could, waited until he felt as though he himself were falling into the receiver. He had stopped breathing, he suddenly realized. He could hear the blood in his ears, thumping slower and slower.

Yes, she finally said.

He drew a deep breath and felt dizzy. He asked: *Will you tell me what the difference is for you?*

And for once, she spoke at length, saying many of the same things he himself had been thinking. At first he thought he had it straight, thought too he could keep it straight for a while, but as she went on speaking, he began to feel it unraveling. The characteristics of each entity were still clear but it was impossible for him to know which applied to baby and which to doll. One was alive and one had never been alive. One had eyes that clicked back into its head with a sharp sound and one had eyes that oozed fluidly and soundlessly about their sockets. One was full of rivers of blood and the other was full of fists of air. But which, but which, but which?

What was the rest of his week like, the days that intervened between one hour-long phone call and the next? It was, to be frank, hard for him to say exactly—that, too, seemed less and less clear. Some of his days he could piece together passably well—though he always thought of them as if they had happened to someone else. He could remember climbing out of his bed, staring at himself in the mirror, sitting in a chair, eating lunch, but could not remember who had made him lunch, nor whether the chair was his own or belonged to someone else. But he could at least assemble a plausible structure for what his day had been, and it would hold as long as it was not questioned too closely.

But other days it was as if almost no time seemed to pass at all. Whole weeks even in which he felt like the day was reduced to almost nothing beyond a brief glimpse of his startled face in the mirror.

Do you think this might be due to what happened? he asked his therapist. *Do you think something has been shaken loose in my brain?*

The first time he asked this, she didn't answer. Or didn't, at least, answer quickly enough. Which led him to answer the question himself. *Yes,* he answered, using for her benefit a calm, reasonable voice, *maybe something is wrong.* But in his mind he was not thinking that exactly, and he was certainly anything but calm. What he was thinking was *baby or doll, baby or doll,* over and over again.

Later, that same night, just as he thought the mumble of that thought—*baby or doll, baby or doll*—had died out and he could sleep, things shifted again. He was in that curious gray zone of being both asleep and awake, when consciousness had begun to loosen its grip on his body in such a way that he remained unsure of where reality stopped and dream began. In the dream, if it was a dream, he was lying in his bed, at peace, his mind a blank. And then, he heard, at a little distance, the cry of a doll, that narrow bleating call that only a doll, and a very young one at that, could make. Unless, he suddenly began to doubt, it was *baby* he meant. He should, he felt, get up and look for it, answer its call, its cry. But he couldn't move, could only lie there and listen to the baby's call or the doll's cry, dread rising in his throat like bile. *I have to get up and find it,* he thought again, but he still could not move. And by the time he thought he could move again the cries and calls had stopped and suddenly it was morning, his heart still thudding hard, and he was completely unsure whether he had slept through the night or remained for hours wide-awake.

The second time he posed the question about something being wrong with his head to the therapist, during the subsequent session, she again didn't answer it. Or rather, they started speaking at the same moment, the same time, and once he had started speaking, she fell silent and would not be drawn out. Same basic conclusion on his part, that maybe, even certainly, something was wrong, and the words *baby or doll, baby or doll* being whispered voicelessly beneath it all. But what was there, if anything, that he could do about it?

I will not pose it a third time, he told himself. And indeed, for some time he did manage to resist saying anything, managed to keep his tongue, if not his thoughts, from circling back to the same track. But in the end the question came around again and he was saying it almost before he knew it, the words spilling off his tongue. *I think it must be due to what happened,* he told his therapist. *Something has shaken loose in my brain.*

And this time she spoke—quickly even, at least quickly for her. Her voice was even and perfectly modulated, had a sibilance to it that might have been characteristic of the voice itself or might have been simply a product of the connection. *What exactly,* she asked him, *do you think happened to you?*

If he'd had any idea where that answer would lead him, he would have hung up the telephone and pulled its cord out of the wall.

———— 2 ————

There he was, staring into the mirror, looking at his own face, while the therapist's patient, flat voice spoke into his ear, telling him he was relaxed, telling him he should choose a point to focus on, a light reflected in the mirror, say, and stare at it, and listen. *I am not hypnotizing you,* she had claimed at the outset. *I am helping you to hypnotize yourself. Whether it works will depend on you.*

Fleetingly, staring at his own face in the mirror, he wondered if he had ever had a therapist, if all of this wasn't in fact taking place inside his head. And then she spoke, and the thought broke and receded.

Imagine a place, she said. *The place where it happened.*

All right, he thought, and did. His voice, he realized mutedly, was coming out of his throat telling her about the place. It was not there yet for him but yes, in another way, it was there. The therapist's voice slowly dissolved into a warble not unlike the low whisper of two men conversing and then indeed it was this very sound. The blotch of light he was staring at, he realized, was something else. Through a tremendous effort of will he brought it slowly into focus and realized that it was a broken tooth. And then it swam out of focus again.

Slowly, the therapist's voice resolved itself. *Servin,* she said, *what do you see?*

And what did he see? For a moment it was as if he both saw and did not see everything at once. There he was, his face, flattened and turned wrong way around, staring at him out of a mirror. But there was too, the marble floor, the space around him opening up into another space, one he was walking through.

It was some sort of echoing building lobby. His soles snapped and echoed as they struck the floor. He looked around him, but he seemed to be alone.

What am I doing here? he wondered, or someone wondered for him. There was a bank of elevators ahead, and he moved toward it, crossing the lobby in a measured, calm stride. There was something, he was hearing something, coming from one of his ears, from within the ear, a kind of warbling that he couldn't quite make out. Was something wrong with him? He shook his head, but the warbling didn't go away.

And there, in front of him, in the middle of the marble floor, a broken and bloody tooth. He reached up and felt his mouth, but all his teeth seemed to be there. *Good,* he thought, *good.*

Cautiously, he moved toward the tooth, staring down at it. He crouched and took it between his thumb and forefinger, held it closer to his eye. *Molar,* he thought, and tongued the back corners of his mouth, but all the teeth were still there.

And then, abruptly, he heard a noise. He looked quickly up and saw a man staring at him, his lips grim, the receiver of a telephone pressed to his ear. He looked familiar. Something was wrong with the room—it was as if the other man was in a different room entirely. He moved his head farther and saw a circle of light and then came a blinding flash.

The other man was too close now and not knowing what else to do he struck him in the face with his forehead and then staggered back himself, and fell.

And on the way down there it was again, the briefest glimpse, as if a hole had opened up to reveal yet an additional world—something. A baby. Or a doll. Or neither. Just before Servin struck the ground he came to believe that nothing could be trusted, neither in this world nor in any other, that he had not gotten it right and was not ever likely to do so.

He lay there on the floor, staring out across the marble, watching the thing—whatever it was, baby or doll, baby or doll—pulsing there, the thing watching him back. Near to it, another object of some kind, small and white, normally associated with mouths, if *mouth* was the right word. But it was not in a mouth now. What was the word for it? He couldn't remember. And somewhere above him or beside him noises being made by birds or, perhaps, humans with—what was the word?—ah yes, *voices:* he still had that one, that thing, that word. At least for now.

The voices, their sounds anyway, were becoming trapped in the strange shell-like openings found on either side of his head. They pooled there a moment and then, slowly, leaked out and evaporated. In the meantime, the other thing, baby or doll, was still there, somewhere. Yes, there it was, watching him, unmoving.

He had the distinct impression that he had never been anywhere but there, that he had been here, just like this, all his life.

And would be for years to come.

The Tunnel

WHEN THEY HAD GROWN TIRED OF PRODDING THE OLD MAN WITH A stick, they left the stick where it was and continued down the tunnel, Jansen trailing along the left wall, Lindskold along the right. It grew darker and for a time Lindskold couldn't see. He moved forward solely by touch and by listening to Jansen's feet. Then the light grew a little better, the ceiling punctuated every ten or so meters by a plate-sized grate through which leaked a pale light. Jansen's missing hand, Lindskold noticed only then, seemed to have grown back.

"Jansen," he said.

"Pardon?" said Jansen.

"Your hand," said Lindskold.

Jansen raised one hand and squinted at it, then raised the other and squinted at it. "What about it?" he finally asked.

Or perhaps, thought Lindskold, the hand had never been gone in the first place. The old man, too, it was an open question whether he had actually been there or not. But whether it was an open question or not, it was hardly a question he could ask Jansen. Or, rather, he could ask but he knew Jansen would not have an adequate response.

The tunnel seemed to curve slowly to the left, the passage narrowing and bringing Jansen and he a little closer. Their shoulders were nearly touching, or so it seemed in the dim. Lindskold watched the man beside him as they walked, out of the corner of his eye. Jansen's face was mostly obscured in the dim. Just as his own face must be obscured for Jansen, who seemed also, subtly, to be observing him.

"Where are we going, Jansen?" asked Lindskold.

"I don't know," said Jansen. "How should I know?" He was silent for a few steps, then added, "Down the tunnel."

Down the tunnel, thought Lindskold. *So be it*

But how, he couldn't help but wonder as he walked, had Jansen managed to regain his hand? Assuming the hand actually was lost in the first place. *Maybe,* he thought, *I should ask him directly.* But for the moment he could not bring himself to do so.

The tunnel narrowed yet again and now indeed their adjacent shoulders were touching, Lindskold's other shoulder rubbing gently down the wall. Jansen's other shoulder was probably rubbing along its wall as well. The grates still appeared every so often above, but the light came through them less, unless it was simply that the walls of the tunnel here absorbed it more. He and Jansen cast before them not shadows exactly but vague shapes, darker impressions on the dim.

Down the tunnel, thought Lindskold again, *so be it.*

"Jansen?" said Lindskold.

Jansen did not answer.

Lindskold reached out and touched the other's shoulder with his hand, shook him.

"What is it?" Jansen asked, after a brief silence.

"Are you all right?" asked Lindskold.

"What kind of question is that?" asked Jansen, his voice rising slightly.

"I don't mean in general," said Lindskold. "I mean right now."

"Oh," said Jansen. "I suppose."

The tunnel tightened further and it became difficult to move abreast one another. They stopped. The darkness was thick here. It was difficult to make out anything at all.

"One of us is going to have to go first," said Lindskold.

"All right," said Jansen.

"Do you want it to be me?" asked Lindskold.

There was a silence.

"Are you talking to me?" Jansen finally said.

"Of course I'm talking to you," said Lindskold.

"Yes, then," said Jansen, "go ahead."

Lindskold pushed into the darkness, touching the tunnel walls to either side of him. He stepped forward, then took another step. In the darkness it all seemed different. Something was changing, he was certain. Or almost certain.

"Jansen?" he said. "Jansen, are you coming?"

There was no response.

"Jansen," he said, "put your hand on my shoulder so that we stay together in the dark."

There was no response.

"Jansen?"

"Are there three of us?" Jansen asked from well behind him, his voice distant.

"Excuse me?" said Lindskold. "What do you mean, three?" He held still and listened but didn't hear anything else, couldn't hear anything he hadn't already been hearing for some time.

"My name's not Jansen," said Jansen—said the voice Lindskold had been thinking of as Jansen.

"Then who are you?"

"I'm another one," claimed the voice. "What do you call him? Lindskold."

"But I'm Lindskold," said Lindskold.

When there was no response he repeated himself—*I'm Lindskold*—and then, suddenly beginning to doubt, fumbled his way around in the tunnel and headed back in the direction from which he had come.

By the time he had gotten to where Jansen had been, to where he thought Jansen had been, nobody was there.

———— 2. JANSEN ————

What happened to Jansen, to the person who actually was Jansen—or at least who thought himself to be Jansen—was this:

He had been with Lindskold prodding the old man with the stick, trying to decide if he was dead or not. Lindskold thought the man was dead, but for Jansen it didn't seem as certain, and indeed sometimes when he pushed the stick into the man's belly a low groan pushed from his lips.

"See?" he said to Lindskold.

"No," said Lindskold. "That's just the outrush of gases. That doesn't prove anything."

But what, wondered Jansen, would actually prove something? What would it take?

"Perhaps we should stab him," said Lindskold. "Open the fellow up and see if he bleeds."

"But what if he's not dead?" asked Jansen.

"I think he's dead," said Lindskold.

"But what if he's not?"

Lindskold shrugged.

"Besides, we don't have a knife," said Jansen. "How can you stab some-one without a knife?"

"With the stick," said Lindskold.

"Not sharp enough," said Jansen.

"Bite him, then," said Lindskold.

Jansen shook his head. "There's no way I'm biting him."

Eventually they tired of prodding the man or corpse. Lindskold dropped the stick—unless he, Jansen, was the one to drop the stick—and they struck off down the tunnel, side by side.

Lindskold trailed his hand along the right wall, while Jansen trailed his along the left. The tunnel, which had been dim to begin with, grew darker, and for a time Jansen couldn't see. He moved forward solely by touch, and by listening to the scuffing Lindskold's soles made.

How long this lasted, he would have been hard-pressed to say. Maybe quite some time, maybe almost no time at all. Eventually the light grew a little better and he began to make out the shape of Lindskold beside him. Soon the ceiling was perforated at regular intervals by a grate approxi-mately the size of a man's head, through which leaked a wan light.

"Jansen," Lindskold said.

"Pardon?" said Jansen.

"Your hand," said Lindskold.

Jansen raised his hand and squinted at it. Was there anything wrong with it? Not that he could see.

"What about it?" he asked.

But Lindskold just shook his head and continued walking.

Jansen hurried after him, quickly caught up. *What's wrong with him?* Jansen wondered.

Or maybe, Jansen thought a little later, *there's something wrong with my hand that I just can't see.* He rubbed the stump at the terminus of his other wrist against the stubble of his chin, continued forward.

The tunnel seemed to be curving slowly right, the passage tightening slightly and bringing he and Lindskold closer. Their shoulders were almost touching. Lindskold, he suddenly realized, was eying him warily, almost nervously.

"Where are we going, Jansen?" Lindskold asked.

Jansen shrugged. "I don't know," he said. "How should I know?"

And indeed, what was there to say? They could either go forward down the tunnel or back the way they had come. Lindskold knew that as well as he.

They moved along in silence. The tunnel narrowed further and soon their shoulders were touching. Jansen felt his outermost shoulder rubbing the wall gently. The light had dimmed somewhat, though it was hard for Jansen to understand why. They cast not shadows exactly but something anyway: vague whispery shapes, minor interruptions of the stillness and the dim. It was like glimpsing something just beyond his vision.

Something shook him, shook his shoulder. *Lindskold,* he realized with a start. "What is it?" he asked.

"Are you all right?" asked Lindskold.

Jansen answered something, almost without thinking, nothing important. They kept on. The tunnel tightened further. It became difficult to move while side by side. They stopped. It was dark now, and Lindskold appeared for Jansen as little more than a vague shape mostly eaten away by darkness.

And then, suddenly, that shape was completely eaten away, gone.

"Lindskold?" said Jansen. But there was no response.

He moved forward, farther down the tunnel, running his stump along the wall, his other arm feeling in front of him. But Lindskold simply wasn't there.

———— 3. THE OLD MAN ————

When they had stopped prodding him and left, receding slowly down the tunnel, the sound of their footsteps growing dim, the old man spasmed and rolled onto his back. His mouth opened and light seemed to pour out of it, thickly, as if it were a liquid. Slowly he struggled to his feet and lurched down the hall, in the direction opposite from where the two men had gone. After a moment, he lurched back the other way, down the tunnel. A moment later he had fallen again, flat on his face.

He could hear voices, almost as if a person was whispering into each ear. He couldn't make out what they were saying. Perhaps it was merely in his head. Slowly they faded.

He lay there face down for a while, he was unsure how long. Perhaps minutes, perhaps hours, perhaps days. He tried to open his eyes but could not. Either that or they were already open but it was too dark to see anything. He tried to move his head but either it would not move or he was unable to feel that it had.

After a while he began to hear something, a low scraping sound, some distance away. He listened. Slowly it became the sound of footsteps, unless it was merely a sound not unlike footsteps. It seemed like one man walking at first, then the noise and rhythm struck him as two, but then it seemed like one again. It—or he, or they—was growing louder. *One or two?* he wondered. *One or two?*

He tried again to move, failed. The sound was closer now. *One or two?* he wondered. And then he wondered, with a brief thrill of fear, *What will happen to me this time?*

But how could it possibly be worse than what had already been done to him? No, he thought, it couldn't.

But somehow, this time, with this man, or these men—whichever it was, unless it was somehow both possibilities at once—it was worse. It was as if none of them really knew what was happening to them: none of them understood it, yet none of them were able to stop.

And then it got worse still, for all of them.

South of the Beast

———— 1 ————

South of the beast he pored through the bodies, searching for occasions where, in the membrane still integumented between flesh and bone, language had become caught and not yet worked free of a corpse. In one body, he found a fluster of wronged syntax, knotted in the cartilage of the knee; in another, the slick pulse of a word that, at a touch, split apart and grew cold before he could swallow it. He could feel the words leaking from his own body as well, and he himself grown faint and speechless, a dark grammar weeping from his side.

———— 2 ————

Standing motionless and naked at midday he found, finally drawing breath and stepping away, that the sun had shone through him and burnt his name into the ground below his feet. He tried to scuff the mark out but could not, though when he stepped back and waited, the sun burned the name away on its own accord. In early afternoon, by tilting and prisming his body, he could throw a distort of his letters hard enough and dense enough to cut holes in walls and to suffocate sleeping animals.

At sundown, he cast his name in long, dark lines farther than he could see. He stood, waiting for it to fade, until the sun fizzled out and was gone, the distort of the letters still stretching, unblemished, out over the horizon and away.

———— 3 ————

He could still, he found, render the pen and make it wander along the paper in letters. Somehow he had managed somewhere to have his fingernails peeled back and away. When he wrote, he pressed the pen so hard that the damp and empurpled flesh underneath the missing moons of his nails split and oozed and fluently bled. He did not mind this so much, being hardly able to feel it anymore, only it seemed impossible to read what he had written afterwards, the blood and ink all mixed together, each trying to constrain the other.

He stayed hunched over ink and blood, examining them through the night even after his eyes gave out. By morning, he was well on his way to uncovering a new language.

The Absent Eye

for Michael Cisco

I LOST MY EYE BACK WHEN I WAS A CHILD, RUNNING THROUGH THE FOREST as part of some game or other. At the time I was with two other children, a boy and a girl, a brother and a sister, neither of whom I knew or, indeed, had even seen before. It was one of them, the skinny shoeless boy, who suggested the game. I cannot now remember much about it, only that when I lost the eye I had been giggling and chasing the girl, though was also being pursued by the boy. In my flight, a thin, barbed branch snapped back and lashed like a wire, slashing a deep scar across my nose and tearing the eye itself free of the socket to leave it unseeing and ruptured on my cheek.

I do not remember exactly how I got home. Perhaps the boy and girl took me, perhaps they carefully led me home and rang the bell before fleeing, but nobody had seen them do so and this was not, in any case, what I remembered. All I remembered was standing stunned in the forest, feeling what was left of my face, and then suddenly and without transition being home again, standing just before my front door.

There was, a doctor informed me, no choice but to remove the eye, which was, for all intents and purposes, already removed. At first they left my socket exposed—to allow the wound to heal I suppose. The optic nerve, confused, continued to collect information, sending my brain random, broken flashes of light.

Later I was issued a patch, a cheap cotton affair dyed black and affixed with an elastic band. If the patch got wet, its dye would bleed, staining a black circle around my eye and, when wet enough to seep through, within the socket itself. I wore this patch for several months, continuing to still see flashes of light when I removed it. At times these cohered into something that gave the semblance of an image. Through my remaining eye I would see the real world around me, would see, for instance, the solitary and spare confines of my bedroom, the even line of the top of my dresser and, above it, the even line of the ceiling. But the optic nerve would impose upon this other, twisting shapes, initially incomprehensible in form and aspect but, as the weeks and months went on, slowly becoming more articulated.

When I told the doctor what I saw, he just shook his head at me as if I were a fool. And yet even as he did so, I could see a smoky and blurred shape congealing around him. A floating figure that, as I watched, resolved into clarity and revealed itself to be his bloated double. It looked not unlike the doctor, though its legs faded into the air as indistinct smoke. It floated there, for a moment clear, and then hard to discern, and then clear again. It had something like an arm wrapped tight around the doctor's shoulder. Its other hand, I saw, was at his throat. As I watched, the hand tightened.

The doctor, unaware of the creature itself, touched his throat and coughed. I watched his double smile and let go. I threw up my hands in surprise, much to the doctor's puzzlement, and that was when the creature clinging to him turned and stared. It saw me, and knew it was seen by me. Both of us remained motionless, waiting for what the other would do. And then, very slowly, I watched its blurred mouth stretch into a grin.

A few months later, my parents were surprised when I declined to have a false eye fitted into my empty socket. What I had understood, what they would never understand, was that there was still an eye of sorts there, one that saw exceedingly well, but just not in the fashion other eyes saw.

At first, I kept my socket blinkered, covered by the patch, hoping not to see the creature I had seen before. But one night, afflicted with curiosity, I lifted the patch.

I was alone in my room, one lamp burning fitfully in the corner, shadows dancing along the wall. I wanted to see if the shadows themselves were something more, thinking that if they were I would turn the lamp up and drive them away. There was nothing there. Or nothing in the shadows, rather. But when I looked down, I saw a thin, smoky, long arm grasping my waist. A face that was a parody of my own floated just inches away, staring into my empty socket.

I shuddered. A gleam came into the creature's eye, but just as quickly faded, though it continued to regard me with what might be described as curiosity. It opened its mouth and I watched its lips and tongue, such as they were, operate in a semblance of speech.

I could not hear words, but I tried to follow the movements of its lips. "You can see me," I believe it said, or else it was "You can't be me," unless it was something else. I quickly lowered the patch to blot it out. There immediately followed a tightness in my throat that I tried to see as natural, that I tried to ignore, and then I found myself briefly choking. I ignored this until I felt a stabbing pain in my chest, and lifted the patch to find the creature had insinuated its hand beneath my ribs, had its fingers apparently wrapped around my heart. When it saw that I was looking, it let go and smiled.

"What is it?" I asked. "What do you want?"

It pointed languidly to its ear, then pointed to my own, then said something that I could not hear. When I did not respond, it did this again, and again, until finally, not knowing what else to do, I nodded as if I had understood. Its smile grew wider. Slowly it wriggled its way up my torso until its head was just beside my own. And then it stabbed its finger deep into my ear again and again until I screamed in pain and lost consciousness.

— 2 —

For fifteen years they kept me confined—for my own protection, they claimed. My parents, alerted by my screams, had climbed the stairs to find me writhing on the floor, blood leaking from one of my ears. Though they could not find a needle or pencil or other implement that I had used to pierce my own eardrum, they did not doubt that I had done this to myself. I only worsened matters by trying to be honest, first with them and then with the medical professionals, but after all I was young. At the time I hardly knew that the world does not operate through directness and honesty but by way of falsehood and misdirection. Thus I remained adamant and insistent about what had happened, describing the creature and what it had done to me, not realizing how I was tightening the noose around my own neck.

In the place of my ruined eardrum there grew another sort of ear, one that could hear that which could not, properly speaking, be heard. The creature that clung to me began to speak to me as well, its voice not a voice exactly, but a kind of whispery echo, not always easy to make out, more a suggestion of a voice than a voice itself.

At first I resisted the creature, tried to ignore it, tried to pay no attention as it squeezed my heart or upset my belly or bore down on my lungs.

I would hold out as long as I dared, keeping the patch over my eye and stopping my ear with whatever came to hand—a scrap of wet fabric, chewed paper, bits and scraps of food—but it persisted. Eventually I could feel its fingers stroking the fibers of my brain, exciting them into a kind of panic that brought the orderlies running, and like as not got me straitjacketed or sedated. Once I was subdued, they also often cleaned me up, picked the bits out of my ear, and then the creature could speak to me while I, restrained, could do nothing to resist. What did it want of me? It could not hear me, but it knew I could hear it and seemed to have a need to communicate. *You will be of use, friend,* it most often said. "Of use how?" I asked, raising pained looks among the orderlies who saw this as nothing but a man speaking to himself. *You must not fight,* it said. *You must give yourself over, friend. Listen and watch and wait, and later on you shall know.*

With the additional confusion of the injections and shock treatments and straightjacketings, it took the creature and me years to settle into an uneasy sort of truce. For one thing I learned that though it could cause me pain, though it could excite me, it could not do much more, could not kill or damage me permanently without my permission, and as time went on I learned to control my responses to it. For another, I realized that when my ear was unplugged I could hear not only its whispers, but beneath them, lower and farther away, other sounds humans could not hear.

It was this that finally got me spending a few hours of the day with my patch rolled higher up on my forehead, peering through my empty socket. What I saw at first surprised me, though it should not have. I had long assumed that the smoky creature that had come to me had been the same creature I had seen torturing the doctor, that it was one of a kind, and that it had, by leaving the doctor and coming to me, begun to take on my own characteristics. But what I saw now was a similar creature clinging to each person around me, a whole world of trailing ghosts. They assumed all postures, some of them simply clinging loosely to the bodies of their host, others coiled murkily around them. With some of the mad, the creatures seemed malicious, their smiles unholy and their fingers wedged deep into their hosts' brains. With others, the creatures seemed to be wailing and crying, trying as well as they could to extricate themselves from the person to whom they were attached. But as they worked one part of themselves free, another smoky strand would form and attach. The orderlies had them as well—their creatures were generally calmer, if perhaps more inclined to enjoy violence when it happened. The doctors had them too. Indeed, I began to realize, these creatures perhaps had no choice but to be with us. They were in some sense imprisoned. We were part of them and they were part of us.

This was a terrible thing to know and I fought it as long as I could. I finally got used to it because there was no other choice, at least not one that I could see. I was like everyone else, with one exception: I knew.

— 3 —

And then, late in my confinement, I found myself awakened by a slow, steady whispering. *Friend*, it said. *Get up, friend. Friend, get up.* It repeated the same words over and over again, and kept at it until, finally, I arose.

"What is it?" I asked, but in the dark my double could not read lips. And so I stood, switched on the light, then lifted my eyepatch and repeated the question.

The creature curling around me seemed anxious, though I could not understand why. It regarded me as I spoke again, then nodded curtly. *Out the door*, it said. When I stood waiting, it repeated its command again adding, in a gentler whisper, *Friend, I will lead you.*

And indeed it did. The door, I was surprised to find, was unlocked. We went out and down the hall, past a sleeping orderly whose own creature had its fumid hands plunged deep within the man's skull, and who nodded and broke into a saurian smile as we passed. Another turning and then another, and then to the door of another inmate's room. This too, I was surprised to discover, was unlocked.

I went inside and closed the door behind me. *Turn on the light*, my creature said to me, and so I did. *Sit in the chair*, my creature said, and so I did, drawing it closer to the bed when he so commanded.

The man in the bed was an older inmate, a man who had been old even when I had first arrived. The little hair he had left was like a haze around his skull, the flesh liver-spotted and his forehead pale. *Uncover him*, my creature said, and I did, and saw that he lay there with his skin loose and unhealthy, looking all but dead. His creature was wound around him but losing shape, resembling him less and less. When I leaned closer to the man his creature hissed, more like the double of a snake than that of a man.

I turned toward the creature wrapped around me, regarded it questioningly. *Watch*, it suggested. And so I turned back and watched.

With my physical eye alone I would have missed the transition. There was little to tell me physically when the man died. But with the other eye, the missing one, I could see his death happen. Not because of the man himself, but rather because of his creature, for as he approached death this being grew smaller, less and less distinct, until he was little more than a shadow. And then, suddenly, he dropped out of existence altogether.

Where does he go? my creature wanted to know. *Why does he leave? What becomes of him?* I thought at first he meant the man himself, as I would have meant, but as he continued to speak, whispering away in a sussurating language that seemed at once identical to and absolutely distinct from my own, I realized that it was the man's creature he was asking about. To him the man meant nothing, but the disappearance of the creature meant everything, for in it he foresaw the disappearance of himself.

I tried to talk to my creature, tried to console it with the so-called wisdom we humans use when facing the knowledge of our own death. But my words were too complex for it to be able to read them well from my lips and the creature grew quickly frustrated and dissatisfied. So I took pencil and paper and began to write words out for it, but when I blinked my human eye I realized that what I saw as words the creature saw as much less, as hardly marks as all. Indeed, to make words it could understand, I had to trace the words over again and again, and flourish them. Only then, once the paper seemed to my good eye an inextricable maze of lines, did it read to my absent eye as words.

What the creature had gained from its proximity to my mind that allowed it to read my tongue I don't know, but when I first started to trace, it became interested and I saw it startle with recognition when at last the words were revealed. Yet it took me long enough to do my tracework that by the time I finished my purpose was no longer the same as when I had begun. Rather than telling the creature something along the lines of *It is vain to shrink from what cannot be avoided* or *Take consolation in the fact that he lives on in your memory* or *Surely there is a life beyond this one,* I found myself laboriously creating through my words—first over the course of hours, then over the course of days, and finally over the course of a lifetime—a lie that would allow me to lead a different sort of life.

———— 4 ————

What did I write? It hardly matters now. I wrote what I had to write to convince my creature to aid me in shaking free of the institution, and then engraved my lie over and over again with stroke after stroke of the pencil until the creature too could read it.

What I wrote was in essence an offer of help. I did not know where the other creature had gone, I claimed, but if anyone could find out, I said, it was I, someone with a foot in both worlds. I was willing to search, willing to try to find out. I was, I lied, a sort of detective. If he would only agree to aid and assist me, he had my promise that I would dedicate my life to finding the answer to his questions, questions that I privately figured from the very beginning to be unanswerable.

And thus it was that we entered into a kind of compact in which, by pretending to be a detective, I in fact became one. We agreed that for me to be able to answer his questions I would have to have a free hand, so to speak. Arrangements were made among the various creatures attached to those confined to the asylum, such that at the end of another month I found the right doors left open to me and a series of sleeping guards along my path. With the help of my creature, I walked unimpeded out of the sanitarium and never looked back.

In the years that followed I traveled the earth, looking, searching, for any sign of what might become of a creature when its host died. I have learned little, perhaps nothing. I have played the role of detective, and have gotten my hands dirty. I have stood among the tombs of the dead looking for wisps of smoke to arise or fall that might be the remnants of the creatures. I have lain on my back wrapped deep in furs, staring up at the Northern Lights and wondering if the glow might not be their unearthly remains. I have stood late at night in the wards of the comatose, watching drowsy figures swaying gently above motionless bodies. I have shot a man in order to witness the moment of his death. I have poisoned a man and attempted to capture the creature wound around him in a bottle before it could disappear. All to no avail.

But the majority of my life had not been spent nearly so romantically. These moments are the exceptions rather than the rule. What I most often do, day after day, is await the moment when my creature begins to direct my footsteps, leading me to a new corpse. Once there, I make notes of the scene and then interview, with the help of my creature, any others close enough to have seen the moment of death. *Name?* I used to begin, but came quickly to realize that this is not a word they understood. So instead it became *What happened? What did you see? Was there any hint of where he went?* And so on. And then I search for clues, strangenesses in the scene of the crime, disturbances visible only to my missing eye. I write down the responses and record whatever clues I find or pretend to find in the overlapped script that they can read, and then I take the pages and I leave them pinned to trees and pasted to walls, crumpled beneath bridges, secured in trash bins. What becomes of them then, I do not know.

The irony is through this process, unearthly though it is, I might learn enough to know if a man has been murdered, and even have some sense of who his killer is. I often acquire sufficient information to make a call to the police, give them a nudge or two in the right direction. I do not know how many crimes, in how many countries, have been solved by me, how many criminals brought to justice, but I suspect there have been many.

But as to the matter of where our creatures go upon our death, I find myself no closer to having an answer than when I first began. My investigation, admittedly, began as a ruse, but as time has gone on I find I cannot help but go from miming the detective to taking on this investigation in earnest. I grow older and more discouraged, but my creature remains hopeful, optimistic. It insists that I keep on, that I continue to drag my way across the earth, and no doubt it will so insist until I am dead, until all that remains of me are the words I have written here.

I am writing this not in the overlapped and baroque letters that have become second nature to me, but in the normal human way, as ordinary letters on an ordinary page. Mostly I feel there is no point writing this. Nothing will come of it, I know, and any who read it can only think me mad. But I do not know what else to do.

My creature curls in the air beside me, regarding me with curiosity but saying nothing, at least not yet. Soon it will demand to know what I have inscribed on the paper and why it cannot read it; I hope to have finished before then.

Soon I must move on. But until then, I will finish my account and then sit here, hand idly moving, pretending to write. Until I feel my creature's hand tight on my throat and its words forming in my ear, and know that I must once again haul myself to my feet. And then I will continue my wandering, a lone and failed detective in the employ of someone not quite myself, but not quite other either.

Bon Scott: The Choir Years

IN 1997, LIVING IN UTAH AND WRITING FOR A SMALL MUSIC MONTHLY called *Grid Magazine*, I was asked to do a story on AC/DC. They hadn't visited Salt Lake City since 1991, when three teenagers had been killed at their concert. A promoter was trying to bring them back to Utah again, but because of the 1991 incident was having some difficulty finding a venue. The idea was to look into AC/DC's previous shows in Utah, reveal any odd connections they had to the state (things along the lines of "Angus Young's cousin once worked selling lift tickets at Snowbird"), and offer something to offset the animosity that Utahns still felt regarding the band. Before I had finished the story, the promoter gave up and the article was canceled. Not able to afford a kill fee, *Grid* instead loaded me down with free CDs and sent me on to interview Robyn Hitchcock.

Yet in the few weeks I did work on the story, I made some odd discoveries regarding former AC/DC singer Bon Scott and his relationship to the Beehive State. By 1997, much had already been written about Scott's death, about the discovery of his comatose body in Alistair Kinnear's car on February 19, 1980, after Scott choked on his own vomit following a night of drinking. Yet very little had been said about the period between the release of AC/DC's *Highway to Hell* in late July of 1979 and Scott's sudden death almost six months later. Nor had any critic called attention to the fact that when AC/DC released *Back in Black* just a few months after Scott's death, the album included no lyrics credited to Scott. It seemed to me odd that Scott, by all accounts a prolific lyricist, had not written something during the six months following the *Highway to Hell* release. I might not have thought about such matters myself except that I discovered, in the time I worked on the article, reasons for doing so.

A cursory glance at the period prior to Scott's death initially suggest little out of the ordinary. The few months surrounding the release of *Highway to Hell* were spent touring, and throughout the months before his death we find Scott performing on a regular basis.

Scott's travel records—which, due to a faithful fan qua hacker qua stalker, are posted on the Internet—also reveal ten trips to Salt Lake City, Utah, each trip seldom longer than a few days. These trips remain unacknowledged in any of the official biographies, and I myself attributed them, when I first discovered them, to Scott having met a woman in Utah while on tour—though it seemed odd that Scott, with roadies and sex always at his disposal, would have fixated on a single person. When I began to investigate more closely, I could uncover no such girl—not surprising, perhaps, considering the amount of time that had passed. If there was a woman, Scott had mentioned her to no one, including close friends and fellow band members. Indeed, not only had he not mentioned a girl, he had kept his travel to Utah confidential.

After several weeks of searching I had found record of Scott's presence in Utah in three places. The first was in the guest records of the Mormon Church–owned Hotel Utah, located on the edge of Temple Square. Its records list Scott as staying on ten occasions, on days corresponding to his plane records. I also found his familiar signature scrawled on the guest book for the Beehive House, the museum housed in polygamist and early Mormon prophet Brigham Young's former residence. Beside his signature he has written *Rock Candy On!,* a reference no doubt both to his profession and to the traditional pioneer jawbreakers that the Beehive House gift shop is known for.

The third place was the oddest. Scott had visited the Mormon Genealogical Archives. Sunk a mile deep into the granite of the Rocky Mountains, the MGA houses millions of personal records. It is the most complete selection of records related to human births and deaths available anywhere in the world. I discovered this information by accident, while visiting the genealogical library with curious friends who were passing through Utah. On a whim, I had one of the librarians look up any record available for *Scott, Bon,* only to discover that not only was there an entry for Scott, but that he himself had submitted a four-generation worksheet, his familiar signature scrawled at the bottom of it. Scott had apparently been interested in family history. On that worksheet, his own record read:

Scott, Ronald Belford [Bon]
Born: July 9, 1946, Kierremuir
Died: February 20, 1980
Baptized: February 20, 1980

It was this last entry that surprised me, the indication that Scott had been baptized into the Mormon Church on the day of his death. True, it is not uncommon for Mormons to baptize someone by proxy after their death—indeed, there is a whole industry within the Mormon Church dedicated to "missionary work" for the dead. All Mormon temple ceremonies focus around precisely this: Mormons aren't only knocking on doors looking for converts, they're knocking on graves. What *was* surprising is that this baptism should have taken place precisely on the day of Scott's death. I knew from my own Mormon past (I abandoned the religion in my early twenties) that it takes several months to clear names for posthumous baptism, and usually the church waits for some living relative to submit the record before even beginning the process.

I assumed this to be a clerical error, yet decided to double-check. When I asked to see Scott's individual worksheet to get more than the few details in the four-generation worksheet, the librarian, after a long delay, puzzled, said it didn't seem to be in either the computer records or in the paper files. He would have a search made, he said. But when I returned a few weeks later he apologized: the record was permanently unavailable. When I asked to see Scott's four-generation worksheet again, that turned out now to have become permanently unavailable as well.

For a long time this was as far as my research could carry me. I didn't have enough to write anything substantial for *Grid*, hardly enough to justify even a curiosity piece, and before I could look for more, the magazine killed the story. I let the matter drop, forgot about it.

Indeed, it was not until almost four years later that, sitting on my grandmother's couch, idly passing time as I waited to take her to see her podiatrist, I idly picked up a coffee-table book entitled *Hark, the Sound of Angels: An Illustrated History of the Mormon Tabernacle Choir* and made a startling discovery. On page 74 of that book, in one of the many so-called "action shots" that showed members of the choir, open-mouthed, singing, I caught sight of a man with a startling resemblance to Bon Scott. In the photograph he is wearing a shirt and tie, and his long hair is pulled tightly back. He stands beside a middle-aged gentleman wearing a tie, who in turn stands next to a clean-cut young fellow who resembles a Mormon missionary. The caption below reads: "In brotherhood we sing, 1979." Below are three names: J. Jamieson, M. Nelson, S. Bon.

S. Bon could have been an accidentally transposed B. Scott. The coincidence was too much to ignore. I asked my grandmother if I could take the book; she gave it willingly, pleased to see me taking an interest in religion again. I combed through it looking for other pictures of the same man, without success. Other pictures I found of the choir, even those taken during the same year, showed no such man.

The path by which I reached the position of understanding that I now occupy is a convoluted one. Suffice it to say that I managed to track down both J. Jamieson and M. Nelson. The latter, a quite elderly man now afflicted with both rosacea and Parkinson's disease, verified that the S. Bon of the photo was in fact Bon S., but could not recall what the *S* stood for. When I suggested "Scott," he shrugged and said "Could be." He remembered Scott, if it was Scott, as a "nice young man, but a longhair [sic]." He did question the style of Scott's singing, which he found neither to his liking nor to mesh well with the style of a choir. "The fellow could barely stick a note out to its end," he claimed.

J. Jamieson I found living in Sandy, Utah, a suburb of Salt Lake, in a small apartment. Yes, he told me, the S. Bon was in fact Bon Scott, as Jamieson had recognized immediately. He claimed Scott had practiced with the choir on half a dozen occasions and sang with them twice on *Music and the Spoken Word*, the Mormon Tabernacle Choir's weekly radio program. What Scott was doing there, he didn't know—the choir members were otherwise exclusively Mormon—but he participated with the knowledge and approval of the choir director. Jamieson, an AC/DC fan despite being a faithful, committed Mormon, had been surprised and shocked to recognize Scott, but had also recognized the importance of the moment. The next day he borrowed bootlegging equipment from an audiophile friend and thereafter recorded all sessions that included Scott.

The effect of Scott's voice in the choir is a strange one. On Jamieson's recordings, since he is standing close enough to Scott to get a consistently distinct sense of his voice, we hear Scott's struggle between adopting a choir persona and pursuing old eccentric habits. On the two *Spoken Word* broadcast recordings (which I was able to obtain from a friend of a friend of my grandmother's who has obsessively recorded each airing of the program for the past thirty years) you can hear an odd and nearly indiscernible waver, but only if you're listening for it.

On the Jamieson recordings, Scott's voice remains unstable, always exuberant and slightly uncertain. There is a growl to it in the lower registers, a certain taut panic in the higher. He does not sound nearly as smooth or at ease in the choir setting as he does when singing with AC/DC. He switches parts two or three times a song, and more than once you hear the director rapping his baton on the edge of his stand and addressing him directly (as "Brother Scott"), trying to get him to calm down, to focus, to sing a part correctly. On a song like "The Lord Is My Shepherd," it sounds as if Scott is running headlong through the green pastures mentioned in the song, like a hyperactive child. His version of "Gently Raise the Sacred Strain" sounds more than a little strained. Yet he comes into his own in Ruth May Fox's frenetic Scottish ditty "Carry On":

> Firm as the mountains around us,
> Stalwart and brave we stand,
> On the rock our fathers planted
> For us in this goodly land—
> . . .
> And we hear the desert singing:
> Carry on, carry on, carry on!
> Hills and vales and mountains ringing:
> Carry on, carry on, carry on!

Here he senses that the hopeful "carry on" that desert, hill, and vale are singing should be elided into a single word so as to reveal it as *carrion*, a song the wilderness sings much more frequently.

There are classic Mormon Church hymns such as "Abide with Me!" and "Master, the Tempest Is Raging," as well as a few patriotic songs, all of which Scott seems to enter into fully, banging against the walls of the song with his voice but slowly becoming familiar with its space. Indeed, the arresting thing about these tapes is Scott's apparent lack of irony. Despite the erratic qualities of his singing, he always seems sincere. It's disconcerting to discover that Scott sounds as sincere when singing a hymn as he does when singing "If You Want Blood" or "Squealer." Perhaps he is somehow able to enter wholeheartedly into any musical event. Or perhaps what Jamieson had to say is a sort of explanation: "I approached him after practice one day, introduced myself, told him I knew who he was, and asked him what he was doing. 'Oh, Lord knows,' he said. 'Trying something new and hoping it'll stick.' It's like he says in one of his songs ('Ride On'): 'One of these days I'm going to change my evil ways.'"

Scott also told Jamieson that he had begun investigating the Mormon Church, that he was speaking with the Mormon missionaries about converting. "Where might it have led if he hadn't died?" Jamieson wondered aloud.

Where indeed? The last tape in Jamieson's recordings of Scott provides some answers. Recorded in January of 1980, it consisted, so Jamieson told me, of a group of choir volunteers, about an eighth of the total choir, and was recorded by Scott and the choir director (as well as by Jamieson). On the tape, the choir sings a wordless bass and sketches broad melody lines and background as Scott embroiders onto them a rewritten a cappella version of *Highway to Hell*:

> Livin' easy, lovin' God
> Season ticket for a one-way ride
> Only askin' that you help me
> Keep myself from gettin' fried
>
> Get off the highway to hell
> (Please stop me.)

Other AC/DC songs are reworked as well. "Night Prowler" becomes the somewhat ludicrous "Night Sleeper"—Scott gets through the first chorus and then, laughing, abandons it. "If You Want Blood" morphs into "If You Want God" ("If you want God/You got Him . . ."), but maintains much of the original's force and intensity.

These are schizophrenic songs. Indeed, Scott seems obsessed with at once maintaining AC/DC's energy and erasing some of the lyrics and sentiments of his back catalog. Had Scott stayed alive, it's likely that AC/DC's next album would have been radically different from anything they had done before. Every indication is that it would have been a Christian—or rather Mormon—rock album.

When I approached one of AC/DC's former publicists about the Bon Scott/Mormon Tabernacle Choir sessions, I received as a reply only a fax of a quotation from Mark Twain: "Am I a friend to the Mormon religion? No. I would like to see it extirpated." It is the single strangest response a publicist has ever given me. Are the tapes likely to attract much interest among AC/DC fans? No. In fact, precisely the opposite; they would leave teenage boys everywhere with a bad taste in their mouths. They are at best a minor footnote in a minor chapter of the history of AC/DC. In addition, they would serve as fodder for neoconservatives everywhere. It is perhaps better to leave the tapes unpublished, passed from hand to hand for those few of us who somehow can appreciate them in spite of themselves (and ourselves).

Yet why, in that case, write about them at all?

The only justification I can give has to do with how, at the end of my research, I remain less certain than I care to be about the actual circumstances of Scott's death. Indeed, if Scott really was attempting to change his so-called evil ways, to lead a different sort of life, to become Mormon, why would he have been drinking a few hours before he died? Mormons are strongly opposed to alcohol. Is it a coincidence that Alistair Kinnear, the man in whose car Scott died, also appears in the Mormon genealogical archives and that his baptism date is listed as 2/20/80, the same day as both Scott's baptism and his death? Should it be seen as a coincidence that the three teenagers, all of them Mormon, who were killed, apparently crushed to death, at an AC/DC concert were killed on February 20, 1991, the anniversary of Scott's death? Or could this possibly be read as an act of revenge against Mormonism? If so, by whom?

There are, of course, numerous scenarios one might postulate, but in my opinion only one satisfies the fact that on the day of Scott's death he suddenly appears on Mormon church rolls as a member of the Mormon Church. It involves the doctrine of Blood Atonement, a doctrine Mormons have practiced since the mid-nineteenth century and that Mormon leaders claim was never practiced at all, despite documentary evidence from John D. Lee and others. The doctrine of Blood Atonement suggests there are certain sins—murder, abortion, crimes against the Holy Ghost—that the blood of Christ cannot sufficiently cleanse. For the sinner to have any hope of gaining forgiveness, he must willingly cut short his own life so as not to live on in sin. Scott perhaps felt himself unredeemable. Either through his own offices or those of another, perhaps he decided to take his own life, his reward being immediate posthumous baptism by proxy into the Mormon Church, his death made to resemble an accident.

Unless perhaps someone in the Mormon Church, realizing that Scott was drinking, backsliding on his change of life, decided to *help* him atone for his sins. This is a possibility I do not care to investigate too closely.

In either case, at the end we come to Scott, shivering and alone in a car, semiconscious, slowly dying whether by accident or by his own hand or by another's. Whatever direction his music would have taken, whether he would have continued his experiments with the Mormon Tabernacle Choir and transformed his life startlingly or else moved in the direction so admirably pursued by Brian Johnson, or pursued some other path entirely, any direction would have been better than that end.

Tapadera

H E TOOK THE BUCKET IN HIS HANDS AND BRIMMED IT WITH WATER, sloshing the boy's face. The water filled the cusps of the eyes and streamed across the forehead to darken the hair. The boy did not come to himself.

The man dashed the bucket down and watched it roll about, spitting drops. He entered the house. Frank he found before the mirror, bloody cloth pressed to the thick of one ear.

"He's killed," the man said.

"Goddamn," said Frank, regarding himself in the mirrored eye. He took the cloth off the ear and looked the fabric over before raising it again. "That teaches him to mess with me," he said.

"Not going to teach him a goddamn thing," the man said.

Frank shrugged and carried the cloth to the window. Sliding up the sash, he held the cloth outside with both hands. He wrung it dry of blood and water and spread it over the sill. He stared at his blood-washed palms.

"Where in hell is that water?" Frank said.

"I am getting it," said the other.

The man went outside and found the bucket where it had rolled, dirt edged up under the curve of it. He took up the bucket and pumped it full past the rivetheads. The boy was still there with eyes waterbeaded, lying on the ground. The man nudged him with his boot and the boy's head turned, water spilling from his eyes.

The man entered the house and approached the basin, raising the bucket as he came. Frank's arm stopped him so that he sloshed a little water across the floor and across Frank too.

"Don't top it off. Dump the basin first," Frank said, brushing the beads of water off himself.

The man cracked the bucket down against the floorboards, water spilling over the sides of it to pool around its base. Picking up the basin, he carried it to the window and dumped it, water and scum spattering out down the porchboards. He carried the basin back, watching scum slide down and gather at the bottom.

Frank reached in and drew his finger across the metal. He lifted the finger, regarded it.

"Rinse it clean," he said.

"The hell I will," said the man.

"Get that dead boy to do it then," said Frank.

The man took the basin and went out, clapping the door. He filled the basin at the pump, swished and dumped it. He shook the basin about until the water slid into drops and those slipped out too. Turning the basin up, he saw the sun catch in the metal and run oblong and vicious, and he along with it, and the dead boy too behind.

He went inside. He set the basin atop the table, filling it with water before Frank could act against him.

"Boy would have done it faster," said Frank. "And better. Even dead."

The man said nothing except to take the bucket to the door and hurl it out. It arced forth and down, the bottom rim splitting the boy's forehead bloodlessly.

Frank dipped his brush, the water clouding pale. He lathered the brush along the worn curve of the soap cake and then daubed backward along the jaw. He cocked the razor, began to shave.

He'd only just gotten started when the dead boy stumbled in all water-faced and bloody, one foot bucket-stuck. His legs gave in the doorway and he fell straddled over the frame.

"Frank?" said the other man.

"What?" asked Frank, squinting up into the glass. "Well," said Frank to the mirror. "You haen't dead."

"Hell I haen't," the boy gurgled from split lips. "I am as dead as they come."

Frank finished the swath, his hands steady. The dead boy struggled up and moved inside. The other man slunk into the far corner and covered his face. Frank set the razor down unhinged over the edge of the basin. He cupped his hands full with water and splashed his jawline.

"Go be dead outside," said Frank.

"I will be it in here," said the boy.

Frank turned. He lashed out and grabbed the boy by the hair. He dragged him forward and cracked his head against the basin, scattering water along the wall. Forcing the boy down to the floor, he stooped down and groped the razor up from where it had fallen, cutting his own fingers across the knuckles before cutting open the boy's throat.

No blood came. The boy kept struggling.

Frank took the boy around the arms and hauled him out. He spun him off the porch and rushed back in, locking the dead boy out. Then he dragged the other man out from the corner where he was whimpering and stood him up and knocked out a few of his teeth.

Frank left the man lying there. Taking the washcloth off the sill, he wrapped it around his cut knuckles. He dipped his face in the last of the water and came up dripping, the droplets trickling down to stain the front of his shirt.

Outside, the boy was rubbing some part of himself against the door.

"You hear that?" asked the other man.

"I hear it," said Frank. "Where's your pistol?"

The other tapped his coat pocket.

"Give it here," said Frank. "Go gather mine."

The man gave, went. When he returned, Frank had dropped a knee to the floor, held his ear pressed to the door.

"Still out there?" said the man.

"Right there," said Frank, tapping the door.

Frank stood and together they stepped back and shot. The bullets thicked up in the wood and bound there. The pair of them came closer to the door and nudged the guns against the wood and fired again, the flash powder scorching their knuckles.

Frank bent down, squinting through a warm hole.

"Got him?" said the man.

"Got his eye," said Frank. "He's just lying there now."

They unbolted the door and opened it a crack. They looked at the boy lying there stilled, their holes in him.

They went out and pushed his body around the yard awhile with their boots. It neither spoke nor moved. They came back inside, locked the door.

The man opened a can of beans, chewing them cold off the tip of his knife. Frank came into the room and took his fist to him, knocking him down. He took knife and can from off the floor, wiping them on his pants, and began to chew down beans himself.

The other man stumbled up, rubbing his temple.

"Jesus," the man said.

Frank raised his fist, then saw that the man was Jesusing not him but the kitchen window and the dead boy who was framed there and tapping the glass with a fingertip peeled back to bone.

Frank approached the window dragging the other man along, the man struggling to free himself until Frank broke the fellow's nose. The boy caught sight of them in the eye that had not been shot through, and waved.

"What do you think he wants?" asked Frank.

"Don't know," the other man said, squirming in Frank's grasp.

"What you want?" Frank yelled.

The boy pressed his face against the window, smearing the glass in blood and water. *Inside,* he mouthed.

"Don't let him in," said the man.

"I am not stupid," said Frank.

"Want to kill you, Frank!" cried the boy through the glass.

Frank tugged the curtain across the dead boy's face. He dragged the other man out of the kitchen and into the main room, closing the door behind them so as to scarce hear the boy's tapping. They sat down on the floor, squared their backs against the door.

"Where's that flask?" said Frank.

"He got to it," said the other. "Emptied it. When he was alive. Thought you knew."

Frank shook his head. "Had I known, I would have killed him worse," he said. "Go dig up a bottle," he said.

"Haen't nearly ready yet."

Frank raised his fist. The man scuttled off to the bedroom.

He pushed the beds against the far wall. He stepped on the end of a center floorboard and watched it rise up until he could catch the edge of it with his hand and lift it away to set against the wall. He lifted a second board, a third.

He peered into the dark beneath the house. He crouched down beside the hole and slipped his hand in.

He could not find the bottles. He spread himself flat and felt farther.

His hand tendered upon something soft and filamented. He pulled upon it and found it uneasy to raise but struggled it up until it caught against the floor joists. He braced his legs and pulled hard with both hands, feeling it tear slowly free.

Lifting his hand from the darkness, he found it filled with strands of coarse, dark hair. He looked down into the hole to see the boy's pale face. He cried out, and so did the dead boy.

He threw the boards over the hole and fumbled a brick and some nails out of a box and tacked the boards down, the boy all the time calling to him to let him in.

He stumbled to the other room, shaken.

"Where's that bottle?" asked Frank.

The man just pointed. From the open door came the sound of the boy's tattoo on the underside the floorboards. They heard the slow sound of the boy crawling beneath the house, threading between the supports, brushing under the floorboards beneath them, calling to them.

They listened. They got on their knees and crawled free of the range of the boy's scraping. They turned circles, starting forward and back, until the scraping stopped.

They threw themselves flat, pressing their ears to the floor, listening. They were lying there still when they heard something above ground, at the outside corner of the house. The roof creaked in the corner, then further up, toward the peak.

"Dead boy on the roof," said Frank.

The other man began to whimper. The noise came above them and passed over. It grew louder, stopped.

The dead boy tumbled down the chimney, splitting the fore of his face open against the grate. He struggled face up and lay glaze-eyed and all bent in the legs, ash clouding around and darkening him.

"Goddamn dead boy," said Frank.

He stood and dragged the other man to the fireplace and put the man's hands on the dead boy's legs and his own hands there too. The boy tried to speak, the flap of his open throat hissing and fluttering, but there seemed no words left to him. They dragged on his legs, he clinging to the grate and not letting go. They took to prying his fingers back but could not make all the fingers give of a piece. Frank broke his skull a little, but he would not let go.

They took the legs again and heaved, stumbling over one another, the dead boy spluttering out of the throat and holding on.

Frank let go. The other man let go. He looked around and stepped away. The dead boy started getting up, still holding to the grate. Frank knocked him back down, lifted him, cramming his legs first up the chimney until all they could see was from the waist up.

The dead boy would not let go.

"Got an axe?" said Frank, shattering the boy's elbow with his boot heel.

The other man shook his head.

"Throw me the razor," said Frank. "And go get the matches."

The man kicked him the razor and Frank squatted to pick it up, with one shoulder holding the boy up the chimney.

The man entered the bedroom, looked through the box, found no matches of any type. He went into the kitchen, looked on the stove, in the cupboard beside, found only a flake of flint and a striking steel.

He returned to find Frank had hacked away the skin around the boy's elbow and was cutting and stripping the flesh beneath. The boy did not seem to mind.

"No matches," said the man, holding forth the flint and steel.

The razorblade broke, splitting off into the flesh. Frank scuttled the rest of the razor along the floor and dragged the boy down onto the grate.

"I can take a hint," the dead boy said. "I am not wanted."

Frank pinned the boy to the grate by his shoulders, the arm twisting out of its socket to one side, the boy holding on. He took up a jar beside the chimney, smeared the boy with pitch.

"Light him," said Frank.

The other man struck sparks over the dead boy, his hands shaking. He could not distinguish the stone from his hands and kept gashing himself, flicking blood down on the boy and on Frank, the latter trying to fan the sparks alive.

The man kept striking, splitting his fingers closer to the bone. The floorboards seemed licked with pale fire. The pitch dripping off a wall caught flame. He struck sparks into Frank's hair and when they caught watched Frank run around, his head blazing.

The dead boy let go of the grate and smiled, both with his mouth and with the gap in his throat.

The man stood watching, still striking the stone, watching the flames rise around him.

The Other Ear

ISTVÁN ACQUIRED THE OTHER EAR DURING THE WORST DAYS OF THE war. One moment he was yelling and charging and the next he was waking up in a field hospital that stank of mold and blood, looking up into a field surgeon's weary face. He had been given something to blunt the pain, but he could still feel something, a tugging, as he watched the surgeon out of the corner of one eye raise and lower a needle and thread. *What is it?* he tried to say, *What's wrong with me?* but was not certain words came out. In any case the field surgeon did not acknowledge him, and a moment later he was unconscious again.

When he woke again it was in a dark tent, its canvas wet, waterlogged. He was lying on a cot on his side, his head and leg throbbing with pain. Next to him, almost touching his own, was another cot, the dim shape of a man in it. It was impossible for István to say if the man was alive or dead. Next to that was another cot, another man, and then beyond that the soaked wall of the tent. The sound of dripping water was everywhere.

He tried to speak, only groaned. Neither body in the cots beside him moved. *Am I dead?* he wondered fleetingly. He tried to turn his head and pain shot through his neck so he stopped, just lay there and stared at the other cots. The bodies in them never moved.

He didn't remember falling asleep but he must have, for suddenly the rain had stopped and light was streaming through the flap. The two cots beside him were empty and stripped of their sheets. A surgeon, maybe the same one as before, his wraps still bloody, was standing near the foot of the bed, just visible out of the corner of István's eye. The surgeon leaned closer.

"How are you feeling?" the surgeon asked.

"What happened?" István asked. This time he was certain he spoke, though it came out as a whisper.

"Mine, probably," said the surgeon. "Or grenade. You were pretty tore up." *Torn up,* István's mind immediately corrected. "You're lucky to be alive," the surgeon said.

"How bad?"

The surgeon gave him a steady look. "One side of your body and one side of your face. You still look human if that's what you're worried about. Your left ear was torn off but the man who brought you in saw it and brought it back as well. We were able to sew it back on."

"My ear?" he said. He reached up and was surprised by what he felt there.

The surgeon nodded.

"But I didn't have that ear," István said, still feeling the side of his head. "I lost that ear months ago."

A few weeks more and he was up and about again, one side of his body still stitched through with pain but that too, with time, beginning to pass. He did not have a mirror nor, it seemed, did anyone in the field hospital, but an obliging nurse scrubbed the rust off a metal tray until it shone and then held it for him, tilting it against the light at his command until he could see, as if through a fog, some watery version of his own face. It did not look familiar to him, the face, and the ear, the new ear—he could never quite bring it into focus. He could, with his fingertips, feel its shape out, but the ear was still numb, nerveless or nearly so, still resistant to feeling, so it was hard to tell much about it. There seemed nothing extraordinary about it: it was just an ear. Maybe even a reasonable facsimile of his own ear, the one he had lost near the beginning of the war.

He stared at the wavery image in the tray, fingered his careful way around the ear itself. *Who had it belonged to?* he wondered. Was its original possessor dead or alive? How was it that the ear had made its way to him?

The stitching all around the other ear, holding it to his head, became slightly puffy, swollen. At first he had the impression that if he simply pulled hard enough he could tear the ear free. But as time went on, the ear seemed more and more firmly attached, more and more a part of him.

One evening, near the end of his stay in the hospital, not long before he was sent back to the trenches to rejoin his few remaining companions, something happened. He was lying on his back, staring up at the ceiling of the tent, when he began to hear to one side the sound of breathing. He turned his head, but the cots there were empty, there was no one there but him. He turned back, but he could still hear it, there, to his left, the sounds of breathing, slow and labored.

He got up and went to examine each cot in turn. There was nothing there. But then there it was, he was still hearing it, louder when he was closest to the cot next to the tent wall. He patted the cot down, looked under it. Still nothing, no one.

I've gone mad, he thought.

He went outside, took a deep breath of the still night air. Then he steeled himself and went back inside again.

At first he thought the noise was gone. But then, once he had lain down on the bed again, it began again.

He covered his ears and no longer heard it. *Maybe a strange aural effect,* he thought, *like the way a domed ceiling can make someone from the other side of a restaurant sound like they're right next to you.* But if that was what it was, where was it coming from? From the tent next door?

Very cautiously he removed his hand from one ear, his right one, and heard nothing. *Yes,* he thought with relief, *an aural effect, temporary, gone now.*

He removed his hand from his other ear, from the other ear, and immediately heard it again: the sound of a man breathing, slow and labored.

It did not take long after that for him to come to the conclusion that the other ear was hearing things his normal ear was not. Shortly after realizing this, he heard through the other ear the sound of breathing grow slow, judder, rattle, and finally stop.

In the trenches the other ear began to insinuate its way into his nervous system. He could almost feel the fibers unfurling from it and attempting to knot with the nerves still left on that side of his face. At times, as he shivered in the mud, the ear began to throb, feeling coming back to it but incompletely and inconsistently, only as pain. As time went on these moments of feeling became more complex: he began to be conscious of *something* there, in the place of an ear, but it was not exactly an ear. At times it seemed tight and gnarled, like a fist, and then grew tighter still. At other times it unfurled like a fan and he could feel it there undulating on the side of his head. But when he reached up to touch it, it always went back to being the same shape beneath his fingers, was always little more than an ear.

Hello, he heard a voice whisper into the whorl of his other ear one night. *Hello, are you there?*

He lay in the dark, his back against the mud wall of the trench, wondering if he had heard it. In his right ear he could hear movement in the no-man's-land beyond the trench. An occasional burst of gunfire, a distant mortar. He covered that ear with his cold, damp hand. With the other ear he heard none of that, only silence. It was as if the other ear were somewhere else. It tingled and again he felt it changing shape, spreading like a fan then contracting, hardening, like a shell.

Hello? the voice whispered again. *Can you hear me?*

"Who is it?" he whispered.

But the voice did not answer. Indeed, there was only silence. And then, after a moment, a repetition of the appeal.

Are you there? said the voice. *Can you hear me?*

"I'm here," he said, a little louder. "I can hear you."

But there was no answer, at least none the other ear heard. Instead, he felt something shaking his shoulder and looked over to see beside him another solider, the other sentry. István uncovered his good ear, turned it toward the man.

"What are you doing?" the solider asked. "And who are you speaking to?"

István just shook his head. The sentry regarded him for a long moment but at last turned away. He covered his right ear again, but the voice in the other ear had fallen silent by then, and he did not, that night, hear it again.

A sea anemone, he thought. An animal of some sort, a familiar. There it was, sewn to one side of his head, refusing at least in his mind to simply be an ear. His body was likely shivering in the trench, caked in freezing mud, but the ear seemed to flex and pulse and then, suddenly, ramify, spreading like a vine up and over the side of the trench. He let it go on as long as he could bear and then reached up with numb fingers, felt it back into being just an ear. Or his body was up and running through no-man's-land, shells exploding all around, while his ear stretched thin and flat and sharp as if his head was wielding a sort of blade. It was ridiculous, he knew it couldn't be happening, but yet in a way it was and there seemed nothing he could do. *I should cut it off,* he thought again, fleetingly, and he crouched behind the stump of a tree, waiting for the barrage to slacken, but no, the ear seemed both alien and a part of him now. Cutting it off, he couldn't help but feel, would mean somehow that the ear had won. *Won what?* he wondered as he charged. But he hadn't thought that far ahead.

＊

And then came a day that, as rifle in hand he rushed forward, he felt he had already experienced. There had been so many days already, so many pushes forward—it could have been any one of these done over again or all of them together. And thinking this, pursuing his thoughts, he felt his screams dry up and dissipate in his throat. And there he was, each thought leading to two others, like a labyrinth, until he was so thoroughly lost in his thoughts that he had almost forgotten about his body, which slowed, stopped, and finally stood stock-still.

He might well have remained there, motionless, until the enemy drew a bead on him and shot him dead. But as the other soldiers ran on, firing, something came to draw him out of the maze of his thoughts. It was a voice, a whisper, heard only by his other ear. It was impossible to say if it was male or female or even if it was the same voice he had heard in that ear before.

Down, it said. *Now.*

Though only a whisper, it was insistent—enough so for him to listen.

He threw himself flat on the ground in the mud. A moment later, the brief whistling of a falling mortar, an explosion just before him, a shower of mud. His hands were cut but not badly. Perhaps there was shrapnel in his back as well or maybe he was just bruised. He was confused, unsure exactly where he was. But he was alive.

There, said the voice in the other ear. *Now you owe me one.*

Owe it one what? István wondered in the days that followed. And when was it planning to collect? And what exactly was *it?* The ear? No, not that exactly, but whatever was speaking into the ear.

He went back to the field hospital for a few hours while they checked to make sure he was okay. They shined a lamp into his eyes, treated him for potential shock. The voice the other ear could hear seemed to know exactly what they were going to do before they did it. It whispered to him what he should say, how he should respond to the questions the doctor and nurse hadn't yet asked. *I'm fine,* he'd hear in the other ear, and then a moment later, to a nurse's query, he would say just that. And once he'd said enough they released him, sending him back to the outpost for a day, allowing him to catch his breath before sending him back out into the field.

"Owe you one what?" he asked aloud as he trudged back to his tent. But there was no answer. He couldn't speak to it, but it could speak to him. Was it real? Was he imagining it? How worried should he be?

He lay on his back on the cot, staring up at the ceiling of the tent, at the way the canvas bunched near the support. The other ear swelled and contracted, swelled and contracted, as if it were breathing—though he knew that no, really, it was doing nothing, was just being an ear. Or rather was simultaneously swelling and contracting in his mind and doing nothing in the world. But which thing was more real: mind or world?

Hello, said the voice in the other ear. *Are you there?*

"I'm here," he said aloud, but there was no response.

Another night, stumbling in a heavy rain with the tatters of his unit up the lee of a hill. Mud, always mud. And there it was again, a whisper, but insistent.

Jump left, it said, *now.*

And even though he was tired and exhausted, even though he was confused, his body obeyed. A moment later, the hillside had collapsed and he was buried to his shoulders in mud. For a moment he thought the voice had been wrong, that he had leapt into trouble instead of out of it, but then he craned his head and looked back and saw, where his companions had once been, only a smooth slope of mud, all of them gone, he apparently the only one left alive.

"Thank you," he said, but the voice did not answer. Still he couldn't help but think, *Now I owe it not one but two.*

It took him a long time, maybe hours, to dig his way free, and the whole time he was conscious of what an easy target he was. But either the enemy wasn't there or, for reasons of their own, left him alone.

Once he was free, lying panting on the hillside, slowly slipping down, he wondered what to do. He could go back, that was what he was supposed to do whether his unit was dead or no. But he could not bring himself to move. Instead he lay there, slipping slowly down the hill, the mud building like a sheath around him, waiting for a sign.

It was only near daylight that the sign, or something anyway, finally came.

Up, said the voice in his other ear. *Forward.*

Who was it? he wondered. *What was he hearing? Where was it leading him?* And yet, despite these questions, he couldn't help but listen and obey. He let the other ear—or the voice in the other ear, rather—lead him forward. It watched over him, protected him. It led him, crouched, past one enemy sentry, and brought him quietly up behind another sleeping one. At its command he strangled this latter using the lace from his left boot, and then took the man's rifle and uniform, went deeper in.

The country on the other side of the trenches, he was surprised to find, was for all intents and purposes identical to the country on his side. He pushed farther in. On the advice of the voice he slept by day, traveled by night. From time to time he encountered others, and though his own impulse was simply to slip into the bushes and hide from them, the other ear advised him to kill them and so he did. Strangling was something the other ear encouraged, though it was not adverse to him slitting a throat if need be, or even bashing in a skull. These deaths, István sometimes thought, were unnecessary, but still he could not bring himself to feel guilty for them. After all, it was not he who was bloodthirsty, but the other ear. He himself could hardly be blamed.

But although the other ear spoke to him it never responded when he spoke back. Why could he hear it but it not hear him? He shook the thought out of his head: he had no way of knowing, nor in all likelihood ever would.

He fled from farmhouse to farmhouse, leaving a narrow thread of murder behind him—not enough to leave a wake, not enough to start someone in pursuit of him, but enough to satisfy the other ear.

The marks of war slowly receded and finally vanished, until he found himself in a place that war seemed not to have touched. Yet still he slept by day and traveled by night. He had been cautious for so long that he could not bring himself to stop. *Forward*, the other ear said to him, *forward*.

And yet finally he did stop, for a day came when he heard something, a distant warble at first that became with time a dull, familiar whisper.

You're here, it said.

And so he stopped. For a moment he just stood there, still. And then he began to look around him.

A farmhouse, like any other. Or no, not a farmhouse exactly, but a manor house, made of stone. Or perhaps even more than a manor house. It was hard to say: he had been looking at the world through the other ear for so long that he was no longer certain how to interpret what he saw through his own eyes.

A dwelling in any case, perhaps sumptuous, perhaps not. Certainly not impoverished. He started toward it.

No, said the other ear, *not there*.

He stopped. *Why not?* he wondered vaguely, confused, but then turned and looked behind him, back at the place he had been standing when the other ear had said *you're here*, and saw that it was a graveyard. He turned and went toward it, and this time the voice said nothing.

István passed through the graves, his hand brushing the tops of the stones as if they were children or household animals. For a moment he seemed confused, as if wandering. And then, mumbling, he seemed to find his way again.

He made for a corner of the graveyard, in which he found a weathered crypt. He broke his bayonet trying to force the door, but at last did manage to trigger the latch with the little of the blade that remained.

Surely it was the voice in his other ear that called on him to enter, unless it was a voice he was hearing in both ears now. Even so, he hesitated, swaying at the door of the crypt. But in the end he went in.

He was gone a long time, and then longer still. But in the end he came out again, stumbling and breathless.

Or so it seemed. For what came out looked like him but was not him, was something else entirely. A man, or a good substitute for one, a head and a visage like István's but different somehow. Where his ear had been was a simple hole, unwhelked and bloody.

A moment later what was left of him had faded into the darkness and was gone as well.

They

THE FIRST TIME S. CAME TO SEE RAUCH, IT WASN'T S. AT ALL. IT WAS, rather, an image of S. that, after Rauch had allowed his eyeball to be electronically palpated, began to speak.

"As you know—" it began.

—but Rauch didn't know.

Let me back up.

There had been a time S. came to see Rauch before that, but Rauch couldn't remember it. He'd been dead for a while shortly after that meeting with S. A few events, that included, had been lost. Once he was alive again, it slowly became evident that a stretch of time prior to his death was missing.

That's normal, they claimed. *Nothing to worry about. Easily corrected.*

For a nominal fee, they assembled a series of images to allow him to fill the gap. In the air before him, a flattened version of himself spoke to a flattened second man, bald, pale skin, unhealthily thin, who referred to himself by something that started with S. The name was garbled somehow.

"What I want," this man was saying, "is for you to investigate my death."

Rauch watched flat Rauch take out a notebook and a pen. "How often have you died?" he asked. "And which death?"

"No," flat S. said. "When it happens again. The next time. From now on. Every time I die."

Shortly thereafter, a man without a face came in. *Yes?* Rauch said, standing up. *May I help you?* The man said nothing, merely flashed a pistol into his hand and shot him.

Rauch spun the images backward and froze them. The man's face looked as if it had been torn off and then planed flat and then covered over in aspic.

"Did he actually not have a face or have you censored his face for some reason?" Rauch asked.

No face, they said.

About two weeks later, Rauch was killed again, same man or at least someone who looked very much like him, someone with the same lack of face.

"Is this the man who killed me earlier?" Rauch asked later while watching the images of himself dying.

Impossible to determine.

"No fingerprints? No eye scan?"

Fingerprints stripped. Eyes encased.

"Encased?"

They did not respond. Apparently it was not a question exactly, or not one they were prepared to answer.

Shortly before Rauch's latest death, perhaps an hour before, S. came to see him. Or rather the image of S. came. It was, in a way, the second time. Or, in another way, the first. Though maybe neither one nor the other.

"As you know—" S. said.

"Wait a minute," Rauch said, and the image froze.

"How do I know this man?" he asked.

This man is your client, they said. *Your memory of hiring him was compromised by your unfortunate demise.*

"You showed him to me?"

You purchased a series of images that included him, but then declined to have them imprinted as memories.

"I remember," Rauch said. He turned to the image. "Go ahead," he said.

"As you remember," said the image, "you have been commissioned to investigate my death." The image blurred a little, then slipped back into focus. "Mr. Rauch, if you are seeing this image, it means I have been killed again. I want you to discover who killed me and recover my body."

"Why recover your body?" asked Rauch. "Why does it matter? It's disposable."

But the image hadn't been programmed for complex interaction. "This has been a recording," it warned in an artificially constructed voice, and suddenly shorted out.

Why recover the body? Rauch wondered again, sitting at his desk. *Why does it matter? It's disposable.*

He sighed and leaned back. Where was he to start? He didn't know anything about S., didn't even know his name. He needed more to go on, he thought. Much more.

He was still thinking this, still imagining an investigation forever stalled before it began, when they interrupted him.

Mr. Rauch, they said.

"Yes?" Rauch said.

A man without a face seems to be coming into the building.

"A man without a face?"

Mr. Rauch, they said. *We suggest you run.*

And so, confused, he did. What happened over the next hour or so he must have experienced at the time but he had, now, no memory of it. He could remember up to that point, the point of beginning to run, then there was nothing. Then came a bright light, and he himself blinking his way into it.

Mr. Rauch, they said from somewhere within his skull. *Welcome back to the land of the living.*

"Thank you," said Rauch somewhat desperately. "Thank you."

He stood up, somewhat unsteady. It seemed a decent armature; perhaps a little better than the last he had experienced, though as always a little odd to get used to at first. The face, he saw in the mirror, was a reasonable likeness of his original. That was good: his clients would recognize him. There was his old body, having been used as a template, just beside him, its face disfigured by the bullet, a gaping hole in the back of its skull.

He got dressed and, slightly nauseous, made his way out. He started toward home.

Is it time to go home? they prompted.

Was it? He looked at his watch, then turned in his tracks, headed toward the office instead.

He sat down at the desk, not sure what to do with himself. He expected them to prompt him, but they said nothing. He waited, staring at the backs of his new hands.

A few minutes later the buzzer for the outer door sounded.

"Who is it?" he asked them.

Impossible to determine, they said.

"Impossible to determine?" he asked. "Why?"

Who knows? they said. *Why don't you go see?*

The Oxygen Protocol

LATER HE WOKE UP, NOT ENTIRELY SURE AT FIRST WHAT HAD HAPPENED, what had been real and what he had dreamed. For a moment the utburd was still there, its bloody, childish face glowing faintly in the dim light and then vanishing. Was it real then?

But no, he thought, *how could it be real?* He shook his head and instantly regretted it. His head throbbed, his tongue was so thick and dry in his mouth that it felt almost like he was being forced to swallow a glove.

Why did I sleep on the floor? he wondered. *Where did I go wrong?* Pulling himself up against the wall, he slowly made his way to his feet. His vision blurred as he stood, but slowly came back into focus once he was on his feet and remaining still. Good, he thought. In the mirror he saw a face spattered in a black dust, as fine as graphite. He grimaced, saw that his teeth were gray too. More dust was getting in, which meant that the baffles were still clogged, which meant they were still following the oxygen protocol.

The screen was flickering; they were waiting for him. He pressed his thumb against its face to unlock it but nothing happened. He licked the thumb clean of the dust, tried again. This time it recognized him.

The screen offered him a slow swirl of light. If there was a pattern to it, it was not something he could make out.

Halle, a flat voice said. *You are not essential personnel: currently we do not require your services. You persist only at great risk to yourself and to your community. We urge you to follow the path your friends and neighbors have chosen and participate in the new oxygen protocol.*

"Thank you, but no," said Halle. His voice was little more than a whisper.

This is not a request, the voice said. *This is an order.*

Halle did not bother to reply. The voice had been saying the same thing to him for days now.

Look at yourself, said the flat voice. *You are suffering, Halle. By your own admission you are perceiving things that do not exist. The oxygen you are using could be better used by personnel essential to the functioning of the city. We say this for your own good. It is for the good of the city, to prevent the city from dying. You don't want the city to die, do you?*

"Of course not," said Halle, "but it hardly matters what I want. It's too late."

It is not too late, Halle, for the city or for you. For the good of the city, we are offering to take care of you. We propose to reduce you to a benignly comatose state and then, when the moment is right, we will awaken you.

"How do I know you'll ever awaken me?"

A community cannot exist unless it is based on trust, Halle. We don't need to remind you of this. It is something you know. You have no choice but to trust us, Halle.

Without answering, Halle extinguished the screen.

He gathered the metal cup he had left sitting beneath the open faucet all night to catch the slow drip. A quarter full maybe, the fluid inside opaque. For a long moment, he watched his face ripple on the water's surface, then swallowed the water down in one gulp.

Momentarily his tongue felt like a tongue again, human and slick, but this quickly passed. He lifted the cup and pressed it to his forehead. It wasn't cold exactly, but a little cooler. It helped just a little, just enough.

Dragging his hand along the wall, he made his way toward the door. His vision unfolded as he went, the straight angles of the wall and door starting to flex and bow. Not real, he told himself. *Lack of oxygen,* he told himself, and kept on.

But even still he couldn't help but start just a little when the door slid open and he saw there, in the folds and buckles of the street, the face of the utburd. Its infantile body was knobby and distorted from being stretched over the asphalt. He blinked and it was gone. Then he blinked again and it was back.

"What do you want of me?" he asked.

But the utburd said nothing, just smiled its toothless smile. Why was it coming to him? He had done nothing to it, nothing he could remember anyway. He barely knew what an utburd was, barely knew how to distinguish it from other ghosts. Seeing one was a trick of his brain, he knew, a simple hallucination. He could be hallucinating anything, but he was hallucinating an utburd. Why an utburd?

"I didn't kill you," he told it. "I don't know who did. There's no reason to haunt me."

The utburd opened its mouth and gave a cry like a bird. It had suddenly grown teeth, and they looked sharp. And then Halle's vision started to fade. He was getting worked up, he mustn't get worked up. Standing in the doorway, he closed his eyes and watched the creature flit along the insides of his lids, reduced to little more than a shadow. He made an effort to breathe carefully, regularly.

When he opened his eyes again, he could see clearly. He pushed out of the doorway and moved forward slowly into the street, trying to ignore it, careful not to exhaust himself. If he walked slowly and didn't get excited, he knew from experience, he'd probably get enough oxygen not to pass out.

The next door was only a few dozen steps down the street, but to Halle it seemed to take forever. The asphalt and stone shone strangely in the light, which flickered from time to time. When he looked up, he saw that the simulator from the dome seemed to have a minor short, making the artificial light fluctuate strangely. Unless this too was a hallucination.

The utburd came and went, though it was there more often than not. Sometimes it spread itself along the street itself, sometimes he saw it caught in the angle between street and wall—or even, once he finally reached his neighbor's house, in the shape his own shadow cast against the door. He knocked on the door once, out of habit, though he knew there would be no response. When none came, he inserted the override key and went in.

The entryway was empty, the floor covered with black dust except for the path his footsteps had rubbed clean in days prior. He followed this path again, shuffling slowly to the back of the room and through a door there. Beyond was a bedroom, an emaciated man within with a tube thrust down his throat and an IV tube taped to the back of his hand. Both tubes ran into a panel in the wall.

Halle reached out to touch the man and found his flesh startlingly cold. The man didn't respond. Carefully, Halle placed his ear against his chest and held it there. He could hear the sound of his own blood beating in his ears, but from the man he heard nothing. He waited, and waited, until there it was at last: a dull thud as the man's heart beat once before falling silent again. He was still alive.

When Halle lifted his head and turned, he found the bedroom's screen was illuminated, giving off a strange patter of color. Though he had done nothing to enable it, it began to speak at him.

We know you come here, Halle, the flat voice said. *Surely you must realize this is an invasion of your neighbor's privacy.*

"I just wanted to know if he was still alive," said Halle. He began to sidle past the screen, moving toward the door.

And have you satisfied your curiosity, Halle? Can you trust us now? If a community is to function there must be trust. Where there is no trust, there is no community.

And then he had left the room, was in the entryway of the house. The screen there flickered suddenly on, assumed the same shifting colors, though as he looked at it this time he began to believe they formed a face, that he was catching a glimpse of the utburd. It smiled at him, but kept its mouth closed.

"Why won't you leave me alone?" he asked.

Leave you alone? said the voice. *But you are alone,* it said. *You are the only one in this sector not to follow the new oxygen protocol.*

"No," he said, "I'm not talking to you. I'm talking to the utburd."

There was a moment of silence, the colors on the screen freezing, the utburd hiding itself again.

The symptoms of oxygen deprivation include, the screen finally said, *general dissatisfaction, problems of productivity, impaired sleep quality, breathlessness, headache, nausea, poor judgment, hallucination. Halle, how many of these symptoms do you currently possess?*

But Halle had already turned away, was already leaving the house.

The person in the next house was in the same comatose state, and the next, and the next. In the fifth house Halle found a box of crackers, half of them gone, the rest soggy. He ate them. In that same house, when he turned on the tap out came a real trickle of water, the filter not yet clogged with the black dust. He stayed there for some time, leaning over the sink, his lips tight around the spout, drinking.

The utburd stayed beside him, scuttling about, and this struck him as a bad sign. There was a moment when his vision faded entirely. He stayed standing there, arm pressed against the rough wall of the house, trying hard to gather his breath. But in the end, he stayed conscious.

By the time he came out of the fifth house, the light of the dome had started to fade, but whether this was because an entire day had passed or because the dust had infiltrated the electrical system as well it was impossible to say. He looked farther down the deserted street, which stretched as far as he could see in the pale light from the dome—the street he had been born and raised on now seeming empty and dilapidated and unfamiliar.

If he turned around, he'd have little difficulty making it back to his room by dark. But when he did turn, he saw the utburd there behind him, between him and the house, its pale face leering at him. It wasn't real, he knew, there was no reason to be afraid of it. But, for some reason, rather than going back he continued on.

Perhaps, a part of him thought, *the utburd is a manifestation of something within me. Perhaps the utburd is a part of my mind trying to tell me something.* Meanwhile another part of his mind examined this reasoning. *Symptom of oxygen deprivation,* this part thought. *Poor judgment.*

A series of additional houses, perhaps four more in all, each either empty or containing a motionless body hooked to an IV tube, with a feeding tube running down its throat. In each house he was careful to avoid the camera he knew to be there, careful not to respond to a screen if it began speaking, trying to make him admit he was there.

Halle, the last one said, *you have lost the ability to deal rationally with your situation. Halle, return to your home immediately so that we can care for you. Halle, your brain is no longer receiving enough oxygen for your existence to . . .*

But he had already lost track of what it was saying. The utbird grinned, huddling there with him as he sat with his back against the wall out of sight of the screen. It looked a little bigger, he thought. Not much but a little. And now that it was here, close to him, he could see that the surface of its skin was covered with tiny, nearly transparent flakes of ice. He reached out and tried to touch it, but, smiling, it deftly avoided him, keeping just a little bit out of reach of his fingers. He reached for it again, stretching this time, and suddenly found his body slipping along the wall. There he was, lying sprawled on the floor now, the black dust clinging to one side of his face, and he still not having managed to touch the utburd.

He lay there, listening to the screen's voice coming from somewhere above him. The utburd was both there and not there, insubstantial enough now that there no longer seemed to be any point in trying to grab it.

He shook his head slightly, felt his eyes beginning to close, forced them open again. Where was he? What was wrong with him? Oh yes, the new oxygen protocol. His body was slowly starving, he was slowly dying.

Halle, he heard from somewhere above. There, not far from his face, the utburd licked its lips. *Where are you, Halle? Why are you hiding from us?* The utburd slowly smiled but kept its mouth closed. *Teeth or no teeth?* he wondered.

Tell us where you are, the voice said. *Please tell us and then stay there. We will come get you.*

The utburd touched its fingers to its lips, made a slight hissing noise. Halle remained silent, watching it. What will it do to me? he wondered. And as he watched it, the world around him slowly began to go dim.

Halle, he heard vaguely, as if from miles away. *Can you hear us, Halle?*

He couldn't stop his eyes from closing, and yet he was seeing the utburd anyway, its image insubstantial as smoke and smeared on the inside of his eyelid, biding its time, waiting for him to lose consciousness. *More doors to knock on, more neighbors to visit, a whole city to see,* he thought. Suddenly, he realized he had lost track of the utburd somehow, that he was no longer sure where it was.

There's always tomorrow, thought the man, confused, who no longer was certain he was Halle.

And then he couldn't manage to think even that.

The Drownable Species

WITHOUT WARNING, I GAVE OVER THE SEARCH FOR MY BROTHER AND came here, to this room rumored to have belonged to him. Which is not to suggest that I no longer wanted to find my brother, but only that I was no longer certain I was capable of the task. *I will occupy my brother's room*, I told myself, *I will gather myself, and then, invigorated, I will renew my search.*

That I am still here shows that things did not proceed precisely as planned. Indeed, I quickly slipped into a state of confusion, one from which I am only now beginning to escape. My decision to return to my brother's room—I should say, so my friend reminds me, the room *rumored* to have belonged to my brother—now strikes me as the wrong decision.

Even now I remain uncertain of events occurring during this period— or, truth be told, any period before or since. I try to countermand my uncertainty by sharing these jottings with a friend. He kindly reads my words and comments on them, upon which I either revise what I have written or append an explanation. With his help, I hope one day to provide a plausible reconstruction of the past.

Such a system allows me to make important emendations and changes, such as the following: I have just been informed by my friend that I have been showing my writings not to a *him* but to a *them*, to a series of different men. I, honestly, find this hard to believe. To me, these men always appear to be the same man. For that reason, I feel no compelling reason to begin substituting *them* for *him*. This man also claims "friend" is the wrong word, unless I am employing it as a euphemism. *Interlocutor is more accurate*, he suggests. Finally, he says that what I have understood to be a choice is in fact a requirement: my interlocutor is required to see all I write.

Was this, I had the presence of mind to ask, *also a must for my brother?* But my query was met only with silence.

Similar silence meets all questions I pose regarding my brother. And I myself seem to know him almost not at all: I have of him only a single letter and a creased photograph. My interlocutor—all of them—has suggested this is a photograph not of my brother but of myself. But why would a man carry a photograph of himself? And though I must acknowledge the similarity of my brother's face to my own, I will never be deceived into believing him to be me.

I have begun to believe that my interlocutor either suspects I have no brother or has some reason to want me to believe I have none.

When I showed my interlocutor the sentence written above, his response was "What makes you think I don't believe you have a brother?"

Questions of this sort have the effect, perhaps intentional, of reducing me to paralysis, of preventing me from resuming the search for my brother. Rather than facilitating some response or provoking actual knowledge, they fold me painfully back into myself, where I mull, confused, for days on end.

At night, alone, everything seems clearer. I can almost see, flashing in the shadows, the figures and torments of the past. At night, I can, if I so desire, open a book and ruffle through its pages. Rather than pullulating and evolving as they so often do during the day, the words remain politely themselves. Only at night can I truly think.

It is nearly night, my interlocutor gone. I can write without showing him what I write. I am in little danger of being disturbed.

If my interlocutor comes for me, he will discover I have set the deadbolt. By the time he unlocks it, my papers will be hidden and I shall pretend to be asleep.

Earlier this evening, while the sun smeared itself redly over the wall opposite my bed and I sat again pondering my interlocutor's evasions, I realized I must spend a night trying to reconstruct the past. I will write and then will read over what I wrote, becoming for a time my own interlocutor. I will not show this writing to anyone else. Instead, I will slide each of these pages back into the ream of clean bond from which, unsullied, they first came. When I am finished, I will remove them and order them and read over them and then I will know what to do.

2

Shall I begin with what I know of my brother? I have, I must be honest, no early memory of him, and would myself doubt his existence were it not for his letter and this creased photograph.

I remember, I must also admit, very little of my own childhood, and that little largely consists of scattered impressions—a woman's pinkish cheeks, the creped starchiness of a skirt that I hold onto with what I can only assume to be a pudgy hand, making brief forays away from it and over dauked, grass-scraggled terrain. I have no memory of seeing there beside me, similarly affixed to the maternal skirt, a brother. And yet it is precisely this image, the pair of us clinging to the maternal skirt, that my brother evokes in his one letter to me.

I am fairly certain I went to school somewhere, perhaps to the same institution that my brother refers to as *that feckless academy* in his letter to me. Afterwards, I took up a trade, which I practiced ploddingly and consistently for a half-dozen years. My brother too claimed a similar relation to his profession, but with perhaps less equilibrium: his letter indicated that he had suddenly surrendered his trade, having decided to do what he could to get back in touch with the family that had *abandoned him so many years before.*

He soon discovered that neither of our parents was alive, that they had fallen victim to two separate but equally suspicious water-related incidents. I cannot, in all honesty, recall either of these incidents, my only record of them being two yellowed newspaper accounts someone had the foresight to clip and preserve for me. As a result, the deaths themselves only strike me muffled, as if from a distance. My father's end amounted to a fall from cliffs into a treacherous surf, a fall my mother claimed happened so quickly as to be impossible to prevent. His body was never recovered. For my mother, two weeks later, the Associated Press suggested a slow and purposeful stroll into an alpine lake with her pockets full of stones, as her young son watched from the dock. I, the young son, have no memory of this incident, which would seem a straightforward case of suicide were it not for rather remarkable bruises on her neck.

But I have gotten off track; I meant to talk about my brother. Imagine my surprise upon finding one day as I returned home a letter from a man I never had heard of before but who possessed the same last name as I and who claimed to be my brother. *Did I recall,* the letter queried as it gave me incident after incident from a childhood that claimed to be my own, only this time with a brother attached. In fact, mostly I did not recall, having thrust the majority of my childhood into oblivion, but as he recounted various incidents they seemed to come back to me, colors and sounds and smells evoked all at once, so that they struck me as genuine save for the fact that in none of my newly regained, or newly acquired, memories was there sight or smell or sound of a brother.

He followed these proofs from childhood with more or less baroque expressions of affection, and with a request to meet. After this last proposal he offered a slightly garbled address, portions of which had been carefully crosshatched out.

At first, I tried to believe this was simply a letter gone astray, a missive that had, by chance, fallen into my hands. But the unlikelihood of two people of the same name having parents die watery deaths and still be unrelated was insurmountable. And as I read the letter over, I kept discovering things in it I hadn't seen before, as if the letter itself was changing, stubbornly adapting itself to quell any doubts I still had.

So, a letter received from a brother one did not know existed. One has one's doubts, and yet these doubts are largely a pretense: one is already convinced. All that remains is to decide how to respond.

What I did, in imitation of my brother, was to quit my job, abandon my apartment, and go off in search of him.

What followed was a dismal, shiftless period. The address as I initially read it led me to a house that did not exist. In the way I next interpreted it, it brought me to a triplex divvied up between three immigrant families. I knocked on each door, asking for my brother, and was each time turned away.

Puzzled, I began to wander the streets, hoping chance would intervene. I started walking in the early morning, returning to my hotel room only well after dark. I often saw men who resembled my brother, but none in fact were he.

Until finally, late one night, struck by inspiration, I considered a third variation of the address, which recast the ones as sevens and a cursive *r* as an *n.* This led me to a small house, ground floor occupied by a man with a bristly mustache who wore a shirt grown yellow with age.

Could I speak to my brother? I asked him.

Gone, he claimed.

My heart leaped with relief. He had been there, then. When would he be back?

No, he said. Gone for good.

Might I see his apartment, I asked, thinking it plausible that my brother might have left something for me therein.

The man pursed his lips, mustache puffing like a cat. How, he wanted to know, was he to be sure I was his brother?

But surely, I said, he could see the family res—

—and in addition, he said, there was the little matter of the unpaid . . .

I briskly offered to pay it. Shortly thereafter he saw the resemblance and proffered the key.

This I remember clearly: to reach the room, I stepped off the front porch and followed a narrow path made of flaked stone around the house. In the back was a set of wooden steps painted white, the paint worn away in the center of each tread to reveal graying beveled wood, its grain worn not so much to splinters as into a strange prickered blur, like crushed stinging nettles.

Yet were my interlocutor here now he would surely suggest, as he or they indeed have many times suggested, that I am confused. That I am remembering another place. He would lead me to my brother's window and cause me to look out. I know from experience I would see not the familiar wooden staircase at all, but a white hall with blue tile flooring, resembling nothing so much as a metro station, a fact that makes me tense and brace as I wait for my room to jerk to a stop and its wall to swing open.

After a few such episodes, I plastered the window over with yellowed newspaper, single sheets so light still shines through. I do not know if they have actually moved my brother's room into a metro station or if they have simply built an elaborate set, but in either case, I know what I remember.

At first I had some trouble opening the lock, but at last managed. The room was empty, the surfaces softened with dust, the ghosts of objects here and there—geometrical lightnesses where the dust was sparser. These ghosts I examined with care, and even made notations about them on the envelope containing my brother's letter. The room was furnished but showed no sign of recent habitation, save for a little dust oddly stirred up on one chair, and, in the corner, a small but sturdy bronzed hoop, perhaps the pull-loop of a coat zipper, anchoring a tumbleweed of dust-clotted hair. I took the bronzed hoop. The hair too, I took, stuffing it all in a plastic bag. I secured this bag in my pocket then sat down to think.

It seemed that my search had come to an end here, in my brother's former room. Yet having come so close to discovering him, I was not yet willing to give him up.

I asked the landlord if my brother had left a forwarding address. No, he had not. For a long time the landlord had not even been aware that he had gone—otherwise, he said, he would have already rented the room. I would, I told him quickly, continue to rent the place on my brother's behalf. Shaking his head, the landlord accepted more of my money and then pushed me gently from his house.

From here I continued the search by what means I could. I rented a postal box, from which I mailed to my brother's room (and now my own) a letter addressed to him and marked *Address correction requested*. It came back marked *No forwarding address on file*. I tried my own name, same lack of result. I tried in turn my father's name, and my mother's name, also without result.

I tried to cull additional information from my landlord—my brother's landlord, rather—without result. Sometimes he would answer the door but rarely did he let me in off the porch, giving only cursory responses to my questions. Other times, though I saw the curtains of the window beside his door buck and sway after I had rung the doorbell, nobody opened the door.

I stayed in my brother's apartment. I studied his letter, searching for clues as to where he might have gone, what might have befallen him. I imagined him in my own city, having pursued me, living in my apartment. Perhaps that had been the meaning of his garbled and crossed-through address: that on second thought he was not giving me his address, that he would come to me.

Perhaps this was only wishful thinking.

I brooded. I reread the letter and lost myself in his descriptions of our childhood, still striving to see the glimmer of him beside me, still failing. At night I thought of what I had read in the newspaper of my mother's

and father's deaths, and tried to imagine these as well, to fill in the gaps
and discrepancies. I was no more successful in this regard.

I would have gotten nowhere had not a change in postal carriers led to the
accidental delivery of a letter for a Mr. Thos Klingler. Not a letter exactly,
a congratulatory bulk circular indicating that said Thos Klingler had been
pre-approved! 4.5%!

At first I discarded this in the trash and returned to my brooding, but
the letter, resting askew in the black plastic wastebasket, continued to
gnaw on me. Klingler, I thought, seemed not only an odd but an almost
made-up name. And perhaps, I began to hope, a brother's pseudonym.

At last I plucked the letter out again and took it with me to my postal
box. There I addressed an envelope to this *Klingler* and sent it to my
brother's room, *Address correction requested.* Then I returned home to wait.

Two days later I had my response: a small yellow card in my postal box
with Klingler's name scrawled on it and his forwarding address typed
below. I immediately rented a car and set off.

The address was neither in my brother's city nor in my own, but in a small
town with a vaguely pan-European name. A map in the glove compart-
ment told me it was located in the mountains some several hours distant,
up winding roads, at the shore of a frigid and pine-choked lake. In fact,
as I was to discover at the end of my drive, it was hardly a town at all, only
a series of cabins scattered along a waterfront with ample space between,
a single street a few hundred yards inland offering a post office, a café, and
a so-called convenience store. Could this be, I wondered, the sort of place
my brother would choose for his home?

His address was on the far end of the shore, at the terminus of a dirt
track badly in need of regrading. It was close to or even somewhat past
sunset when I arrived, the sky not yet utterly extinguished of light, though
one was just beginning to see the pocks of stars.

It was perhaps this darkness, the quiet of the night, that made me
decide to surprise my brother rather than simply knocking on his front
door. I slowly circled the cabin, passing beside shadow-thick bushes and
along a stone path to emerge on the edge of the water, beside a dock. From
here I had intended to circle back to peer into the lit windows of the house
itself, but chance had other plans for me: at the end of the dock I glimpsed
the vague blur of a white shirt.

I crept down the dock until I was directly behind this shirt. In the near darkness I could make out the tips of ears vibrating against the lapping waves, as well as a meeting of a dark and a darker horizontal plane where the barber had blocked off the hair on the back of the head.

Crouching, I snaked my hands past the ears and clamped them over the face. The mouth gave a little startled cry. Something clanked beside us.

"Guess who?" I whispered.

"Amanda?" he said, and tried to pull my hands away.

I was, to say the least, disappointed in this response. "Guess again," I suggested.

Giving a little cry, he began to struggle, not an easy task when one is perched on the edge of the dock.

"Wait," I said, fighting to keep him from slipping. "Wait. It's your brother."

He stopped a moment. "But I don't have a brother," he claimed in a tight high voice, and then started struggling again.

In the end I found myself groping around the dock for something to strike him with, just to stun him, just to calm him a little. I came up with a bottle lying in a sticky, yeasty puddle. I struck him twice on or near the temple—too dark to say for certain—and watched him collapse with a groan onto his side.

I stayed where I was, on my knees now, panting. When I felt better, I took my lighter out of my pocket and looked at his face.

Or at least I would have taken a lighter out if I had been a smoker. Was I? No.

But in any case, there was, I remember, a lighter, and I was holding it in my hand. I don't think I'm making this up. Perhaps it came from my brother's pocket. Yes, certainly that seems plausible.

I flicked my brother's lighter aflame and rolled him over. His face came up and into the light.

It would be an understatement to say I was surprised when I saw there, between his ears, nothing but a pale white expanse, featureless, as if his face had been planed down to nothing.

What followed, the lighter guttering out, the body itself starting to come back into consciousness, is for me a confusion always overlain by this same blank and monstrous visage. I remember, I think I remember, this: myself foundering in the water, my body chilled to the bone; a long and shivering drive through narrow roads crowded with trees; then, miles away now, a perilous and shrieking journey on foot, stumbling, a path along the edge of cliffs, the surf banging against the rocks below; a slow stumbling along a deserted highway; the sun rupturing over the mountains before me like a clot of blood. Little else.

How I got from there back to my brother's room, and how my interlocutors came to deem me worthy of their attention, I am afraid—despite what I have written, what I have remembered—I am still unable to say.

Indeed, even at the end of this long night several questions remain unanswered. Where, for instance, did I acquire my brother's photograph? Was it perhaps enclosed in his letter? If so, why don't I remember seeing it when I first read the letter? If not, why do I have no clear memory of the first time I saw it? If the man at the lake was my brother, why did he have no face? If he was not my brother, same question.

Am I closer to knowing something?

Am I closer to knowing anything at all?

———— 3 ————

I slept all day. Or not all day exactly, but woke up with the news-pasted window already aglow with light and with my interlocutor slapping my face. When my eyes finally flickered open he kept asking me the same question over and over again. He seemed anxious. The exact nature of the question, I am afraid, was lost on me.

I was made to stand up and walk about, my interlocutor holding my arm and dragging me from one side of the room to the other. Suddenly there were two of him, a fact that, for reasons I still do not understand, made me afraid. And then there was only one of him again, the other dissipated or dissolved after having jabbed a needle into my arm. *But nothing's wrong with me*, I managed to say, *I just want to sleep.* But sleep, apparently, was not to be allowed.

And now finally they have let me return to bed, to my brother's bed, though they have propped me up so I am not lying down but sitting, and they have put on the castered table beside me a cup of coffee. Am I the kind of person who drinks coffee? I ask this of my interlocutor and he says *Yes, everyone is*, though I suspect that if he wants me to drink this particular cup of coffee he will say this no matter what the truth actually is.

*

And now a few minutes ago he thrust upon me a clipboard and a piece of paper and demanded that I *write*, something he has never done before. Usually I write when I want to write and my interlocutor seems nothing if not indifferent to the fact of my writing, though perfectly amiable when it comes to examining and commenting upon what I write. But this time I have been commanded to *write*.

My interlocutor, after reading the foregoing, has apologized. I had, so he claims, given them a scare. A scare? *I had thought . . .* he begins, but then he lets whatever it was he had thought trail away in the obscurity of ellipsis. But now, apparently, so he claims, all is well. Admittedly he is much calmer now, even if he seems to be watching me carefully.

But *why*, he cannot help but ask, *didn't you wake up as usual? Why was it so difficult for you to wake up today?*

As I have recorded his question I shall also record my answer here instead of uttering it aloud. *I didn't sleep.*

I show this to him and wait. I know he will have another question and, indeed, here it comes: *Why didn't you sleep?*

I choose not to answer this question.

Drink your coffee, he suggests. *Drink, drink.* He is not urgent, but he is insistent. Eventually, I know, he will pick up the coffee cup himself and pretend to sip it and say *See, nothing the matter with it. Now you have some.*

How do I know this? Has he done the same thing before?

I have written this and now must wait to see it come true.

It does in fact come true, but does it come true because I wrote that it would happen or would it have happened in any case?

I shake my head and do not drink my coffee. He looks at me for a long moment and then he gets up and goes out of the room.

What will happen next? I know what will happen next for somehow the structure of time, usually murky and opaque, has become for me just barely visible, its white smoke momentarily thinning.

When he comes back, there will be four of him. They will hold me to my bed. My mouth will be forced open with a wooden stick, my teeth fitting into the dents and depressions that other teeth have made on it, unless they were perhaps inflicted by my own teeth. Cold coffee will be poured in the side of my mouth and I will cough and splutter and gasp but swallow, yes, that too. I will struggle and flail my arms and will knock askew the stack of unused paper that has been provided me, thus revealing that not all of it, in fact, is unused.

The coffee will be forgotten. The four of him will read page after page, each passing each page along to the next one of him when done.

A new phase, then, is beginning, but the smoke has now returned so that one wonders if one really saw what one thought one saw.

I can only sit here, pen poised, and wait.

—— 4 ——

At last I am alone again, the two interlocutors who for hours have been questioning me having finally stepped out so that I may, so they believe, write a confession. *Admit it,* they kept saying, *confess,* and though I have no, or at least very little, idea what they want me to confess, I have finally agreed so as to be able to write again.

They have moved me from my brother's room, bundling me suddenly into a blanket and taking me out into a hall—though I would have sworn before that there was no hall but only a set of whitewashed wooden steps. I was pushed into the back of the car, my interlocutor to either side of me but this time both of him silent. I opted for silence as well, watching the way the streetlights swelled and receded on the dashboard and along the rib separating the front windows of the car from the back. I was taken to a large building and brought inside. I was made to climb a set of stairs. I was encouraged to enter a small white room, one wall mirrored, and to sit in one of three chairs at the room's center. Here I was left alone.

Would it make any difference if I were to admit that I never had a brother, that I never believed I had a brother? No, it would make no difference. In any case it is not true: either I do in fact have a brother or someone has gone to great pains to convince me that I do.

To continue. After a time, two men entered the room, dressed differently than my previous interlocutors, in mufti, which led me for the barest instant to believe that I might be dealing with someone other than interlocutors. But no, they were interlocutors, only more so. They did not sit patiently and wait for me to show them what I had written; they demanded instead that I respond orally. They had a stack of papers on the table before them and from time to time they quoted directly from a page within it, after which they demanded that I clarify. What had I meant when I had written . . . ? How did this relate to . . . ? I was unable to understand the meaning of my own phrases, if they were in fact mine, let alone clarify them. I did my best, but they clearly were disappointed.

I was right, I now realize, to hide what I wrote. If only I had managed to keep it hidden a few days longer I might have made sense of events. Now, my only choice is to write quickly and hope to record what has happened in a way that will allow me to hold it in mind, to keep me from forgetting for a few necessary moments. And perhaps get just a sliver closer to whatever truth might lie beyond my words. And to do all this before they realize that I am writing not a confession but only doing what I can to further evade them.

To continue. After this first phase they became more urgent still, their questions more pointed.

What, in fact, happened to my father? they asked.

Drowned, I said, and began to recite the description of my father's plunge from the treacherous cliffs into the water below, as recorded in the staccato prose of the Associated Press.

And my mother?

It was a matter of an instant to bring them up to date concerning my mother's death by water.

They both nodded.

I was not aware then, they said, that I was describing the deaths of someone else's parents?

You cannot imagine how it feels to go from thinking you have gained a brother to believing you have lost your entire family. There is a brief sense of dizziness and perhaps you stand up too quickly and your chair falls over backward. Perhaps you even let tears well up in your eyes.

But then a better part of you begins to assert itself and you know that no, you have lost no one. You know that you are being lied to, even if you will never understand why.

I pulled myself back together. I pretended to be doubtful but believing—willing to believe in any case. They looked at each other and I could see in that look them saying to each other *Yes, it's good, we can go on.*

They would, they claimed, leave the question of parentage aside for the moment. Did I, they wanted to know, know this man?

They placed on the desk a photograph, lightly creased down the middle, but the face for all that hardly obscured.

My brother, I told them.

No, I was told, it was not my brother.

Then who, I wanted to know, was it?

I expected them to say, as my previous interlocutors had said, that it was in fact my own image. But instead of answering, they placed another photograph on the table, this of a pale white corpse so water-sodden and bloated that one could barely make out any features at all. It was as if this corpse had no face.

It was this, and this alone, that made me start, the image in the photograph recalling for me what I had seen when, at the moment I thought I had found my brother, I had found instead something faceless and monstrous, something outside the human realm. As they fired off questions at me I found myself falling into that lack of face, vanishing. It was horrifying; I couldn't speak, I couldn't breathe.

And then suddenly something changed. What was it? I can't say, only that I felt it suddenly happen, the face slowly beginning to unfold before my eyes, opening up, the puffiness receding, the eyes again coming slowly open so as to regard me with a slow, dim glare, until finally I realized I could not see a difference between this photograph and the photograph of (whatever they might say to the contrary) my brother beside it.

Where had I been the night of? they wanted to know. And how had I come to a certain lakeside town, where apparently I had been spotted, and why was I no longer using my real name, and was it not true that I had attacked and then drowned this man in the photograph, this—and here they checked their notes—this *Thomas Klingler?*

I burst out laughing. What else could I do? Still this name, Klingler, sounding more made up than real, and still, and still I know, they still, so far, realizing even less of the admittedly murky truth than me.

*

Eyes narrowed, they redoubled their questions. For hours it went on until, finally unsure of what else they could ask me, how else they could confuse me, they asked me, quite frankly, to confess. *Willingly,* I said, and outlined my terms. I wanted a good pen, something sturdy that would write a fine and regular line. I wanted good, clean bond, heavy and with some grain to it, something of better quality than what my interlocutor had provided for me in my brother's room. And I wanted a pitcher of water and a glass.

Soon I had all I needed.

Have I gotten any closer to understanding the truth behind events? As I have been writing, I have stopped from time to time to peer at the clear plastic pitcher of water beside me, positioning my eyes first to see along the surface of the water and then by slowly lowering my head bringing myself down below the placid surface and into the water itself. I am slowly beginning to understand what I must do.

My family is cursed to die by water. First my father, then my mother, now my brother as well. They can try to convince me that no, the man in the photograph is not my brother, that no, the drowned man too is not my brother but instead a man with an absurd name and without a face, but I have seen through them. I have found, within that empty expanse, my brother's hidden face.

Perhaps they think that by deceiving me about my brother, that by denying that my family is my family, they can preserve me from their fate and reserve me for some other lot. How much better, then, it would have been to believe them, how much simpler my life would have been. I might have gone on for years, living on dry land, always safe. But I am hardly a believer.

It is too late for any of that now.

I stare into the pitcher and wait. I am waiting for the moment when the surface shivers just so, and then I will lay down my pen and take the pitcher up and pour the water into my mouth. Yet I will not swallow it, will not allow it to run down into my stomach, but instead shall breathe it in. I shall let it burn inside my lungs and then I will put my head on the desk and turn my face away from the mirrored glass so they cannot see me grimace as I try to force the last of my air out and do my best to drown.

A pitcher of water is more than enough—a few teaspoons would do. It will be difficult, will require a concerted effort, but the blood of the drownable species runs through my veins. I will be dead long before my interlocutors understand what I have done.

This document, it is true, this confession that is not one, along with the papers they have taken from me, is as close to an expression of the truth as I will ever manage. Hardly perfect, I know, but much closer to the truth than the arid version they have attempted to foist upon me.

But perhaps I can go one step closer still in the moments between when water first burns its way into my lungs and when it swallows me whole.

And there it is, a quiver along the surface, calling me, urging me to lay down my pen and begin.

Grottor

— I —

AT AGE THIRTEEN, SHORTLY AFTER HIS FATHER'S DEATH FROM TUBERCU-losis and his mother's removal to the state facility for the insane, Bernt was given to his grandmother. His mother, he knew, wouldn't have wanted this—she had always done her best to keep him away from his grandmother, whom she described as *not-right*, though without ever explaining what made her so. But his mother, straitjacketed, was not given a choice, was perhaps not even told: Bernt's court-appointed temporary guardian decided this was the option that best suited the state. *It will be*, the guardian declared, *the best for you as well.*

The following morning, before leaving for work, his ersatz guardian stationed Bernt near the curb to await his grandmother's arrival. When morning had become afternoon and she still hadn't arrived, Bernt decided to take matters into his own hands.

He traveled the first few miles on foot, passing the cemetery in which his father was buried. His feet began to ache as he walked out along Route 89, along the shoulder where the gravel was fine, almost powdery. Cars passed him but none slowed. It took him two, perhaps three, hours to reach downtown Springville, trudging up over the hill and down past the drive-in, past the grocery store, the town hall. And then he trudged back out the other side, watching the houses thin out and then be mostly replaced by fields. Houses appeared briefly again and he crossed through the four sorry streets of Mapleton, then more fields, nothing but fields. He drank alkaline-heavy water from a horse pump, his stomach twisting on itself. The road's asphalt sputtered out, became gravel. His feet throbbed, were heavily blistered, perhaps bleeding.

Near dark, he stopped at a farmhouse and asked for directions. "The old woman?" the man who answered the door asked. "What do you want with her? Best to stay away." When Bernt admitted he was her grandson, the farmer stared thoughtfully at him. "Still better to stay away from her," he finally claimed, though in the end the man brought him inside and fed him, and then slipped on a jacket and drove him the rest of the way.

Bernt leaned his head against the truck's side window, feeling at once the burnt air of the heater blowing against his face and the way the glass itself was cooled by the night air outside. In the headlights he caught a glimpse of two small white crosses to the side of the road, almost hidden in the grass, and then they were gone.

The gravel road became dirt and then became rutted. Along the edge of the road was a running plain-wire line, two barbed top-wires above it. Bernt followed the fence mentally, its regular rhythm, until suddenly it turned a right angle and veered away from the road.

Another half mile and they were turning off the dirt road and pushing along the barest remains of a path, leaves and branches brushing the sides of the truck. They came to a ramshackle gate and stopped.

"She'll be back in there somewhere," said the farmer. "This is as far as I go." He reached over, patted Bernt's shoulder. "When you need help, you know where to find me."

He watched the broad front of the truck pull away, backing slowly up the path, its lights distancing, then reduced to a glow through the leaves, then vanishing altogether. He turned to the gate, tried to examine it in the moonlight. There was no latch; it was held in place by a twist of wire looped between the fencepost and the gate itself. He unhooked the wire, somehow slicing open his finger in the process. Sucking on the wound, he wondered how dirty the wire was, whether he needed a tetanus shot.

The land on the other side of the gate was uncultivated, nothing like a farm. There were no lights to suggest the location of a house and the path was sufficiently untraveled to be almost invisible in the darkness. He tried to follow it anyway, pushing his way forward through the grass and then, when he realized he'd misjudged in the darkness, backtracking, trying to find it again.

The moon slid behind a cloud and it became almost impossible to see. He did not know how long he'd been wandering when suddenly he was at the house, sensing it more than actually seeing it at first, and then, as the clouds shifted, catching a flash of the moon's reflection on one of the windows.

He managed to fumble his way to a door, and knocked on it. There was no answer. "Hello?" he called. He knocked again, still received no answer.

He groped around until he found the knob, then turned it, was surprised to find it unlocked. The door slid fluidly and silently open, and he stepped in.

The inside of the house was as dark as the outside had been, perhaps darker. He groped his way in, searching for a light switch without finding anything but a bare wall. Trailing one hand along it, he moved deeper into the house.

"Hello?" he called again.

He took a few more steps and then stopped, thinking he'd heard something. He waited a moment, listening, but the sound was not repeated.

He had just started moving again when he felt something flick quickly along his leg and away. He stumbled, nearly fell, gave an involuntary cry.

"No need to be frightened," said a soft, strangely warbled voice.

"Grandmother?" he said. "Where are you?"

The voice laughed. "I'm not your grandmother," it said. "I'm Grottor."

"Who?"

There was a scratching sound and a match blazed aflame. In its light Bernt saw, standing behind a table, a boy, roughly his height but very pale. He wore no shirt and his skin was tight to his bones, his muscles nearly as visibly articulated as an anatomy model's. Bernt watched the boy bring the match to a candle, holding it there until the flame caught and doubled itself, then letting the match fall, still smoldering, to the floor.

"Where's my grandmother?" Bernt asked.

"Your mormor?" said Grottor, and laughed. "You want to see your mormor?"

Before Bernt could ask what a *mormor* was, Grottor was gone, was leaving the entrance hall and sliding deeper into the house, vanishing in the darkness.

Not knowing what else to do, Bernt waited. There was something on the table other than the candle, a little pile of something that at first he thought to be strange irregular chunks of chalk but realized, once he came closer, were teeth. Four or five of them, almost certainly human.

He was reaching out to touch them when he heard a strange clumping sound and turned to see, lurching out of the darkness, an old woman. She was moving oddly, as if disoriented. She had an odd musty odor to her, strong even from a distance. She stopped at the doorway where she remained hunched over, staring down at the floor rather than looking at him.

"You're my släkting," she said. Her voice was strange, an unnatural falsetto, and seemingly too strong for her body.

"Excuse me?" he said.

"My flesh and blood," she said. Still staring at the floor, her mouth curled in a smile. "You have come to me."

"You were supposed to come get me," said Bernt.

"And yet here you are," she said. "My släkting," she said softly.

"Stop calling me that," said Bernt. "I don't know what it means."

The old lady nodded slightly, stiffly, as if offended. "There is a room for you," she said. "You may stay here. You may help."

"On the farm?"

"There is no farm," she said, "There are only the caves." She pushed her way out of the doorway and came closer until she was standing across the table from him. She reached out and jerkily stroked his hand, her skin leathery and stiff. "Grottor will take you there," she said. "You must trust Grottor. Trust Grottor in everything."

"Where is Grottor?" he asked. "What caves?"

She tightened her fingers around his hand and he was surprised to find her grip much stronger than he would have supposed. He winced. "Come," she said. "You may take the candle. There is a room for you. I will take you there."

―――――― 2 ――――――

When he awoke, the day was half gone. His room, he saw now in the light coming in through the curtains, was small, the floor of bare, unvarnished boards. His bed was a simple cot. A rickety chair and his open suitcase were the only other objects in the room.

He got up, stretched. After getting dressed he wandered out, limping a little, his feet still sore from the walk.

Nobody greeted him. On the table in the entrance hall someone had left a tin cup of water and a skewer of smoked meat. The meat had an almost perfumed taste to it, and was very tough and stringy. He was hungry enough to eat it anyway.

The house itself, he saw by the light of day, was quite old and quite small. It consisted of an entrance hall, then a salon with two doors leading off of it: one to his room and the other to what was, presumably, his grandmother's room. In the back of the house, through the salon, was a small kitchen, its counters covered with a thick layer of undisturbed dust.

He tried the other door in the salon, found it locked. He knocked, but received no answer. "Grandmother?" he called, and then, as an afterthought, "Mormor?" Where, he wondered, was Grottor's room? Didn't Grottor live here too?

He went outside. He saw the path he had broken through the tall grass the night before. There was another path as well, this one well traveled, leading around to the back of the house. After a moment's hesitation, he followed it.

Once behind the house, this path quickly curved away and toward the mountain. He followed it a little way and then stopped. It switched back and up a slope, he saw, then crossed a flow of loose shale. There, up above the shale, were two dark openings, the entrances to a pair of caves.

Back in the house, he tried the door to his grandmother's room again. It was still locked. *Why does she keep it locked?* Bernt wondered. *Is she in there asleep or is she gone?* He limped outside again, tried to peer in his grandmother's window, but realized he had somehow walked around the house in the wrong direction and was now looking into his own window. There were his cot, his chair, his bloody socks, his small suitcase. He limped further around the house, and found the window of his grandmother's room to be shuttered. Through the slits in the shutters, he could see narrow rectangles of floor but little more. He pushed at the shutters a bit, but they were firmly latched from the inside.

The rest of the day was like that, a slow wandering through the house and around it, trying to figure out what to do with himself. He sat on the couch in the salon, thinking, the air thick with the smell of dust. Should he hike back down, talk to the farmer who had driven him here, try to get his advice on what to do? Should he beg someone to take him away from his grandmother?

He was still turning over such thoughts, vaguely ill at ease, when, late that afternoon, he found his eyes closing. Before he knew it, he had fallen asleep.

Suddenly Grottor was standing above him, smiling. "Look," he said, and held out his hand to show Bernt three teeth. Canine, bicuspid, molar, each broken off roughly, above the root.

"Whose are they?" Bernt asked.

"Now they're mine," said Grottor.

"But whose were they?"

Grottor shrugged. "That's all that's left," he said, and then slipped out of the room.

He awoke in the fading light, in the slow onslaught of nightfall. Even after he woke up, after knowing he had been asleep, Bernt found he could not completely convince himself that Grottor's visit had been a dream.

He got up and found the matches where they lay on the entranceway table, looked through the mostly empty cabinets until he found a new candle.

By the time he got the candle lit, Grottor was there again, standing silently near the opening to the salon, still shirtless, startling Bernt when he turned.

"Don't you own a shirt? Where have you been?" Bernt asked.

Grottor just shrugged. "Here and there," he said.

"Where's my grandmother?"

"Your mormor? You want to see your mormor?"

And then Grottor turned and left the doorway. Taking up the candle, Bernt hurried to the entrance of the salon, arriving just in time to see him slip through his grandmother's door.

He went to the door, listened, heard nothing. He came closer, pressed his ear against the wood. Still nothing.

And then suddenly the door swung open and his grandmother stumbled out, almost knocking him over. She looked even stranger than she had before, crumpled somehow, her skin loose and saggy. A strange smell rolled off her, like burnt hair.

"Ah," she said, in that same strange falsetto, still refusing to look up and meet his eye. "Släkting. You wanted me?"

"Um," said Bernt, still off-balance. "No," he said, "not exactly. Well, I wanted to know where you were all day."

His grandmother made a strangled sound that he decided must be a laugh. "For the day, I sleep," she said. "As do you. I command it. How are you to go to the caves at night if you do not sleep in the day?"

"What?" he said.

"Have you obeyed Grottor? Have you done everything that Grottor says, as I counseled you?" And then, without waiting for a response, she placed a hand on his shoulder and pushed him away from the door to her room. She slipped back inside, closed the door.

What the hell? wondered Bernt. "Grandmother?" he called and moved toward the door. He'd placed his hand on the doorknob, was about to turn it, when it opened of its own accord and there was Grottor. He tried to see past him to see his grandmother, but Grottor was already through the door and pulling it closed behind him.

"So, you've seen your mormor," said Grottor, rubbing his hands along his chest and arms as if dusting himself off. "What did the two of you talk about?"

"Do you share a room with her?" said Bernt. "Isn't that strange?"

Grottor just shrugged. "Enough chitchat," he said. "Now we go up to the caves."

Grottor gave him a flashlight and led him up the mountainside, on a steep, dry climb to the caves. In the daylight the two openings had looked to Bernt small and shallow, two simple clefts in the rock, but they were higher up than he'd imagined, at the top of a steep, grand slide of shale, and were bigger too.

Up close, the first was a large, sideways bowl hollowed out as if by wind. Inside was a honeycomb of openings, each entrance just a little bigger than a man. All along the walls of the cleft were strange symbols, some painted in dark reddish-brown pigment, some scratched into the rock. There were images too—crude stick figures of men missing limbs or collapsed in a heap. A strange bulbous shape dominated one wall, beneath it a figure that seemed human but not human, strange rubbery appendages in the place of its limbs.

"What are they?" asked Bernt.

"Would you like to explore?" asked Grottor, ignoring the question. "Choose an entrance and we'll follow it in."

Bernt looked at him for a long moment, shook his head.

Grottor shrugged. "Next time, then. You've seen it at least. That's a start."

His eyes kept being draw to the bulbous shape and the humanoid figure. He had to make a conscious effort to free his gaze and look out of the cave. There, far away and below them, were the lights of Mapleton: the real world. His grandmother's house, much closer but unlit, he could not see, nor even guess where it was.

Grottor stood up. "Come on," he said. "There's still the other cave to see."

*

They made their way along the face of the rock, walking on exposed shale that cracked and threatened to give way beneath their feet and send them tumbling down the slope and into the darkness. To bring himself to walk it, even in the dark, Bernt had to close his eyes, run his hand along the rock wall. The second cave was less rounded than the first, like a mostly deflated ball, a sort of sideways wavery slit in the rock, perhaps ten feet tall, twenty-five long. They clambered in.

Against the far wall, beside the one entrance to a tunnel, was a figure. Bernt went toward it, shining his flashlight. It was a body: an old woman, slight of frame, wearing old and frayed clothes. She had been dead a long time. Her skin had been eaten away, her eyes were gone.

"Who is it?" Bernt asked.

"Who's what?" asked Grottor. "That? Don't worry about that, that's nothing."

"How can a body be nothing?"

"When it no longer holds a person," said Grottor flatly. "Then it's nothing."

"What's going on?" asked Bernt, a little hysterical now. "What did you do to her?"

Grottor just smiled.

Angry and confused, Bernt came at Grottor, arms out in front of him, but Grottor stepped quickly to one side, fading into the shadows. Bernt struck out, hitting only the rock wall, the sandstone grating against his knuckles. Grottor fell deeper and deeper into the shadows, slipping toward the back of the cave, always only imperfectly caught in the beam of the flashlight.

"Remember your grandmother?" said Grottor. "Remember what she said to you? You are to listen to me and pay me heed."

"How do you know what she said?" cried Bernt. "You weren't there."

And then Grottor's shadow, layered by other shadows, wavered over the opening of the tunnel at the back of the slit and was gone.

Bernt called out to him, but he did not answer. He moved all around the slit, shined his light down the tunnel, but Grottor was hidden now somewhere back in the caves, was nowhere to be seen.

<hr />

3

At first he thought of just going, leaving, wandering down the mountain and disappearing. But as he shivered his way from one cleft to the other and then picked his way down the path, he began to ask himself, *Where would I go?* His father was dead, his mother insane, his court-appointed guardian didn't want him. Who else was there? Well, there was the farmer, the man who had given him a ride to his grandmother's, but how willing really was he to help? Did Bernt want to find out?

In any case, he told himself, coming closer to the house, his flashlight was dying. There was nothing to be done tonight. He would wait. In the morning, if he wanted, he could leave.

Later, back in his room, the moon came through the shutters to spread dim slats of light along his bed, the floor. Should he stay? Should he go? The dilemma was all around him, solid as architecture, like a structure he was forced to live in or a cage that was locked around his head. He was, he semiconsciously realized, slowly talking himself out of leaving—or at least *something* was, he thought with momentary panic, something wanted him to stay.

And then the panic left him as well and he was no longer certain what he'd been thinking about, what had happened in the caves or why he'd been worried.

He had uneasy dreams. His dreams took him backward along the path down the hill, through the farms, to Mapleton, then south. He walked for days, carrying a knife in his hand. He walked through desert and across blasted, blackened earth. He came to a border town, passed a boy whom he transformed into a corpse with his knife. As this transformation took place, he broke all the teeth out from the boy's mouth with the knife's haft. He turned the blade of the knife and the light caught on it and flashed across his eyes, and then he saw himself waver in the blade. Only it wasn't him exactly, but who exactly it was he could not know.

He awoke to find Grottor staring at him, a shape in the darkness, a more tangible darkness. He wanted to be angry with him, but somehow couldn't be, couldn't remember why he should be angry. He felt slowed, drugged.

"You've been dreaming," said Grottor. "A nightmare."

"Why is it still dark?"

"You slept through the daylight," said Grottor. "You're learning."

"Why won't you let me go?" Bernt asked.

He heard the hiss of a match, watched Grottor light the candle. "Go?" asked Grottor.

And then, suddenly, he remembered. "Did you kill the woman up in the caves?" asked Bernt.

"Would you believe me if I said I didn't?"

"You didn't?"

Grottor touched Bernt's lips with his finger. "Hush," he said. "You've had a nightmare. Go back to sleep."

"Why did you leave me alone in the caves?" asked Bernt.

Grottor shrugged. "Why are you thinking of leaving me?"

"That's different," said Bernt.

"Remember what your mormor said," said Grottor. "You must listen to me. Let yourself go and obey me."

How many days have I been here? he wondered a few days or weeks later, and was puzzled to realize that he could not sort it out, not even roughly. A week or two at least, but perhaps a great deal longer than that, perhaps even years.

The dreams continued, filled with a host of people, none of whom he could place. With knives, he and Grottor forced these people up the side of the mountain, to the first of the caves. *Why only the first cave?* he wondered as he dreamed. They killed them there, drew circles around them in their own blood, inscribed their bodies with symbols whose meaning he did not know. Then they waited until something, a thing he could never see, a kind of wavering shape that seemed imbued with the darkness between the stars, slowly dragged them back down one of the tunnels and away. What happened to them after that, he didn't know for certain: shortly after that he always woke up. It was not the killing itself, nor watching the bodies be dragged deeper in, that made him startle awake, but the realization that there was no shock, that it seemed smooth and natural from beginning to end, as if he had experienced the same thing a dozen times before.

Often he woke to see Grottor in the room beside him, sometimes even in the bed beside him, touching his lips, telling him *ssshhh*, that it was all just a dream. He did not know if it was worse to wake up like that or to wake up alone.

But it could be worse still. Several times, he had woken up not in his bed at all, but on the slope of the mountain, in full darkness, his body bruised and sore and he with no idea of where he had been.

✲

Sometimes whole nights went by without him seeing his grandmother. On the nights when he did see her it was clear that there was something very wrong with her, something *not-right*, some sort of degenerative illness that was slowly transforming her. She could hardly control her limbs now. Her skin was flabby and hanging in some places, cracked and splitting in others. She no longer allowed him to come close, told him she did not want this to be how he remembered her.

She's dying, Bernt realized. *What will I do when she's dead?* He simultaneously felt worried and relived. Maybe when she was dead he could work up the nerve to leave.

And then she turned slightly and he caught a flash of something, a rubberiness in her arms as if her bones had started to dissolve. It was so unnatural, he couldn't believe what he'd seen. He involuntarily took a few steps toward her.

"Do not approach!" his grandmother shrieked and just for a moment looked up and met his eyes, then moved swiftly through the door to her room, slamming it behind her.

Bernt had to lean against the wall to gather himself. What had he seen? Had he imagined it? No, he was certain he hadn't imagined it: he had seen the eyes not of an old woman but of a young boy. Grottor's eyes.

Quietly, he made his way to his mormor's door. He kneeled, pressed his eye to the keyhole. The room was mostly dark inside, lit only by the glow of a solitary candle, but even in that dim light it was impossible to be mistaken. There was Grottor, stepping out of his grandmother's skin, like it was a suit of clothing. And there was Grottor, staring back at the door, staring right at the keyhole, a smile on his lips.

He fled. He ran down the mountain, veering on and off the road, listening for signs of pursuit. He knew what he had seen, but he also knew that if he told anyone he wouldn't be believed. What was he to do? Make up a story, something they would believe? Something, anything. He had to escape Grottor. He had to get away, as far away as he could.

He saw headlights far ahead, coming toward him, and he ran toward them, waving his arms. The truck when it saw him, slowed, stopped.

"My grandmother," he said when the driver rolled down the window. "She fell and hit her head. She's dead." Only then did he realize it was the man who had first driven him to his grandmother's house.

176

"Dead?" said the man. "Are you sure she's dead?"

"I'm sure," said Bernt.

"Sometimes people look dead and they're not," said the man.

"She's dead," said Bernt.

"Well get in already," said the man.

But once Bernt had climbed into the truck, he was surprised to find the man driving forward rather than turning around.

"Where are you going?" he asked.

"We have to make sure," said the man. "Just in case. You'd never forgive yourself if she was still alive and died because I didn't check."

And Bernt, not knowing what else to do, burst into tears. The man reached over and patted his shoulder, but kept driving toward his grandmother's house. Once the tears dried up, he shrunk against the side of the door and stayed there, hugging himself.

When they arrived, Bernt refused to get out of the car. *All right*, the man said, *that's understandable. You saw your grandmother fall and maybe die. I can understand why you don't want to go back in the house.* No, Bernt wanted to explain, it wasn't that, but something slowed his tongue and the man was too quickly gone.

He thought about running toward the house, somehow coaxing the man back before it was too late, but was afraid to leave the truck. He waited, feeling the darkness around him.

And then suddenly he was no longer alone in the truck. He knew there was someone else there beside him despite the fact that the door hadn't opened. He couldn't bear to turn his head to see who it was.

"Nice of you to oblige me by bringing a friend," said a voice he knew belonged to Grottor.

Bernt tried to open his mouth, found his tongue cleaving to his palette. He made a strangled sound.

Grottor put his arm around his shoulder. He leaned closer until his eyes, shining in the darkness, were inches from Bernt's own. He could feel Grottor's warm breath against his face. "Who do you listen to?" asked Grottor in a way that made it clear the question was rhetorical. "Who is your god? Who is in charge of you now?"

———— 4 ————

Before the man was conscious again, Grottor and Bernt gagged him and bound his wrists tightly behind his back, running a lead off the rope as well. Then they went into the kitchen and got a knife, jabbing the man's arms with it until he woke up.

Bernt watched it all as it happened, unable to do anything but what Grottor wanted. He struggled, tried to break free, but couldn't. The man struggled too, and couldn't break free either.

They climbed the side of the mountain, following the path toward the caves. The beam of the flashlight was sharp, all things rendered crisp and in painful, explicit detail. Bernt watched, in front of him, the man struggling to climb, his bound wrists flexing against the small of his back. Bernt climbed behind him, the ground beneath his feet feeling distant, at a remove. Just behind him came Grottor.

They came to the top and entered the first cleft, though Bernt knew this was not where they would remain. They stopped, and the man stood, panting, his gag growing damp. The rope, Bernt could see, was chafing the skin away from the man's wrists. He watched Grottor lean against him, touching a finger to his gag.

"Hush," said Grottor.

The man tried to pull his head away.

He is going to kill him, thought Bernt, yet he could make no effort to stop him.

They made their way out of the cleft and along the face, over the bare, cracking rock. Bernt was first, looking back over his shoulder as he went, shining the light down at their feet. Grottor came behind, holding the man by an elbow to keep him from tumbling down the mountainside.

Bernt clambered up into the second cleft, then Grottor pushed the man up and came in himself. He jabbed the knife into the man's stomach, making him grunt. "Come on," he said, gesturing first at the man and then at Bernt. "Down the tunnel," he said, and held out his hand to take the flashlight.

Bernt went first, moving to the back of the slit. *There must be a way out*, he was thinking, even though he couldn't stop walking. The man would die, there was no helping that, nothing he could do; he had grown willing to sacrifice him if he himself could survive. Perhaps he could figure a way out. All he needed was some time.

But then he reached the back of the slit and stepped into the tunnel beyond. Behind him Grottor's flashlight went dead and all around him the darkness grew palpable, quickly more than he could stand. And then the flashlight came on again and he saw he had turned himself around in the tunnel somehow and was looking backward into the other man's pale and terrified face, at the mouth struggling against the gag.

"Keep going," said Grottor, so he did.

The tunnel grew narrow, its floor uneven. They started down a long incline and Bernt found the temperature rising around him, the air thick and hard to breathe. They went farther down and Bernt's feet were now in tepid water and soon the water was up to his knees. The passage began to tilt to one side so he had to lean and push off the rock below him, the other wall slanting to become the roof. Behind him, the man slipped. Though the passage was too narrow for Bernt to quite turn around, he could look back under one arm to see him fallen on his face in the water and, with his hands tied behind his back, unable to get up. And then Grottor yanked the man up by the arms and he arose with water coursing down his face and blood from where he had struck his forehead too, but the gag still in place. Bernt could hear him coughing inside the gag, as if he were choking to death, water coming in gouts out of his nose. Grottor, steadying the man and helping him to angle his stance, flashed the light into Bernt's eyes and said "Keep going." *I won't*, thought Bernt, but kept on.

The angle became severe, the passage tight enough that he had to lie on the slant floor, waist deep in water, and inch along on his back. The passage tightened further, the ceiling coming low enough to touch his chest. He had to let out his breath to move forward. He could no longer turn his head so had to leave it to one side, looking backward at the man's damp and bloodied face, one hand feeling out blindly in front of him, Grottor's flashbeam behind him and darting all about. He could not see in front of him and could not tell where he was creeping, inch by inch. And then wasn't creeping at all for he saw the man behind him was no longer moving forward, his chest—

"What's wrong?" Bernt asked.

"He's stuck," said Grottor.

"Stuck?"

"You must be stuck too," said Grottor.

And Bernt suddenly knew that he was. He could feel the rock against his chest and his breath was with him only in short bursts and he could move neither forward nor back. For an instant, Grottor flicked the flashlight off and for Bernt there was nothing, not a thing, only an immense darkness, an asphyxiating nothingness. The flashlight came on again and he could see, in the light, the blood beating in the man's neck.

"This is enough," said Bernt. "Help me get free. Let's go back."

Grottor smiled. "Back," he said, using his mormor's falsetto.

Bernt closed his eyes and tried to think himself elsewhere, but when he opened them, the man was still there, and Grottor too, the latter pushing a knife along the upper edge of the wall, scraping one edge of it along the ceiling, bringing the other through the man's neck.

The man flinched and scraped the side of his head against the rock just above him, the knife cutting deeper. Grottor drew the knife back, the blood pulsing in little jets around it and then spreading in a sheet over the man's shoulders and down his chest. Bernt saw the man's throat tighten as he tried, under the gag, to swallow. Then the eyes began to glaze, what he could see of them in the dim light. They turned opaque and Bernt knew the man was dead.

He could see through the cleft in the man's neck a section of Grottor's face, the single visible eye pale and hard. Grottor was reaching out with one hand, fingering the man's neck, his sodden shirt.

He began smearing the rock above with the man's blood, writing vague symbols, muttering as he did so.

"What are you doing?" asked Bernt.

"Now it will come for him but take you too. All I need is your skin. Your mormor is worn out: who better to replace her than her släkting?"

And then his hand was withdrawn and Bernt could hear Grottor's body scraping its way back down the tunnel and away, the light of the flashbeam ever more distant. He called out, had no response. The other man's face in the dying light was a solid mass, another rock, inscrutable. *Don't leave me*, Bernt called to Grottor, but there was no response.

He closed his eyes. When he opened them it had fallen dark all around him, darker than he could bear, and then, somehow, it grew darker still. He waited, mind slowly collapsing, for the darkness to take him.

Anskan House

SEFTON WAS JUST A BOY WHEN HE FIRST LEARNED OF ANSKAN HOUSE. He was walking home from school with his sister, four years older than he, when she veered from the usual path and took him instead through an older neighborhood, to the edge of their midwestern town. She stopped before an old, fairly ordinary dilapidated house ringed by a broken picket fence, its grounds unkempt and littered with trash. She reached out and took his hand.

"What is it?" Sefton asked. "Why are we stopping here?"

"Anskan House," Judith said. Or not that exactly. Something similar, a foreign word that he could not quite pronounce. In the years since, he had come to think of it as Anskan House.

"Does someone live there?" he asked.

Judith shook her head. "Not exactly," she said. "Not in the way you mean."

Confused, he asked "Why did you bring me here?"

She turned and looked at him for a long moment, then opened her mouth but for some reason did not speak. And then she took him home.

He didn't think about the house again for perhaps a year. He probably would not have thought about it again at all except for a conversation he overheard. At the time, his father was hospitalized. He had been there for several weeks, having torn his leg on a rusty strut while working a site. At first it was hardly more than a scratch, but his father had not treated it properly and the wound had festered, growing first beet red and then bursting and festering open, giving off a sickly-sweet odor. Doctors had stripped the infected flesh away and doused the wound with various chemicals, but the infection refused to go away.

When Sefton visited his father it was the smell that stayed with him, that and the yellowish-brown stain blotting the gauze. He and his father had spoken during his daily visits, his father in good spirits despite every-thing, but whatever they had said to one another had dropped out of Sefton's head immediately, so as to leave more room within his skull for the smell and the stain.

The conversation was between his older brother, Mattias, and Judith. He was coming down the stairs when he heard Judith say the word that sounded to him like Anskan. That alone was enough to make him stop and quietly sit, listen.

"Who's that?" Mattias asked.

"No one," said Judith. "Just the name of the place."

"Why would anybody want to name a house?"

"I told you, it's special," said Judith.

What makes it special? wondered Sefton, but Judith must have already explained for Mattias didn't ask. Instead they simply remained silent. Sefton, sitting on the stairs, felt useless and out of place. He carefully scooted down a stair, then another, until he could see, just around the wall, the back of the couch, the tip of his sister's ear and, across from that, the edge of his brother's arm.

"Anskan," Mattias finally said, trying and failing to give the word the same pronunciation that Judith had given it.

"Anskan House," said Judith, putting the emphasis on the last word. And then they were silent again. Sefton leaned forward a little more, saw part of his sister's head, his brother's shoulder.

"But who is it?" asked Mattias finally.

"Not a person," said his sister. "A house stands empty long enough, unlet and uninhabited, and then something comes to be part of it. It's not a person nor exactly a house, but something in between. It is a token of the dead or, worse still, of the living." She paused. "That's how she explained it to me, anyway," she said.

"And you believed her?"

Judith didn't answer. Maybe she had shrugged or nodded, but not in a way that Sefton could notice from behind.

"No," Mattias said. "It's crazy. It couldn't be real . . . Did you try it?"

"No," said Judith. "But she said she had. And she said it worked. She said she rang the bell and then waited until she heard the sound of it com-ing up from the basement and could sense it there behind the door. And then she opened the slit of the letterbox and spoke into it. She said she named someone sick and said 'I take his troubles upon me.' And then she got sick and the other person got better."

They were silent again. Finally, Judith said, "It would work for Dad. You should do it for Dad."

"But I don't believe in it," Mattias said.

"It doesn't matter if you believe. It would work anyway," she insisted. "It would save his leg."

"But then what would happen to me?" asked Mattias.

"I dare you," his sister said, but to this Mattias did not bother to respond.

Save his leg, thought Sefton as he crept back upstairs. He hadn't realized his father might lose the leg, nor was he exactly sure what that meant, *lose the leg*. Cut it off? But then how would his father walk? And if his father couldn't walk who would work for them? His mother? How would she manage as a framer? She didn't even know how to hold a hammer. And if his mother was out working, who would feed them?

No, he thought, his father must not lose his leg. If he did, everything would fall apart.

I dare you, he had heard Judith say to Mattias, but Mattias had shrugged it off. But he, Sefton, had been listening too. Which meant that Judith, even though she did not know it, was talking to him as well. Which meant the dare was as much for him as for his brother.

I dare you, he heard her say again in his mind. He could see in his skull the back of the couch, his sister's ear and hair, his brother's shoulder and arm. And then, still within his head, he stood up and went the rest of the way down the stairs and then stood, very solemnly, before his imagined sister and said *I accept*.

A few days later, he left at the end of school by pushing through the fire escape door instead of going out the front doors where his sister would be waiting. He hurried as quickly as he could across the field, climbing the security fence in the back, catching and tearing his pants on one of the barbs at the top. He kept looking behind him, expecting to see his sister calling to him, running after him, but there was never anything.

He made a broad circle around the school, running until his lungs felt like they were full of ragged, hot cloth. He had some trouble retracing the path he and his sister had taken months before to Anskan House, but in the end, almost without knowing how, there he was, suddenly standing before it.

It looked more or less the same as he remembered it: half the pickets of the fence broken and the yard overgrown. The brick of the walls was pocked and gouged and the wooden porch was rotted through on one side. The shingles of the roof had come loose in places and had scattered the yard. It was just an ordinary, run-down house.

He thought about leaving, about turning around and going home. But instead he stepped onto the porch. The porch's floor was springy, the nails working loose in spots, their rusty heads up and exposed.

When he tried to ring the bell, he realized there was no bell. He thought first to knock, but then saw the old-fashioned hand-crank doorbell centered and low on the door itself, the kind you turned like you were winding a clock.

He reached out, turned it, and it gave off a series of feeble thumps, barely audible. He banged at it with his fist to work the dust free and turned it again, but the sound was still nothing like bells.

He was just about to knock when he heard a sound. There, somewhere below the house, a scrabbling at a basement window, then the creaking of steps. And then, higher now, the sound of a door opening and shutting. He heard footsteps padding slowly down the hall, tentative, careful steps. They made their way to the other side of the door then stopped, and he heard a creak as something leaned against the door proper.

I dare you, he remembered his sister saying. But a part of him now was saying, *No, that dare, it wasn't for you,* and was trying to hold him back. The rest of him, however, was leaning forward, bending down. His fingers lifted the letterbox slot and his head slipped down until his lips nearly brushed against the brass. "My father," he whispered. "I take his troubles upon me."

He waited for something to happen, but nothing did. Nobody spoke, nothing changed, he felt no different. He bent down further and peered through the letter slot, but saw no one, only an expanse of bare, immaculately clean floor.

He let the slot cover fall and stood up, and only then did he hear movement again, the sound of someone walking away from the door.

But this time as the footsteps moved away there was something different about them, something wrong: a clear footstep followed by a dragging sound, back and forth, back and forth.

———— 2 ————

By the time he got home, his leg had started to itch. He realized he'd not only torn his pants on the barb: he'd grazed his leg as well. At home, his sister scolded him for not waiting for her after school. *I went home with a friend,* he lied, *I thought I'd told you.* And then he claimed he was sorry. She just shook her head.

He told himself he would not make his father's mistake. He washed the scratch immediately, cleaned it with soap and water, put a bandage over it. But by the time he remembered to look under the bandage a few days later, the scratch had become red and angry, the flesh around it starting to pucker and darken.

Meanwhile, his father was starting to get better. Treatments were finally starting to work, the flesh was no longer dying and rotting and the infection seemed to be fading as well. The doctors had every hope they could save his leg.

Yes, thought Sefton, slightly feverish, *every hope.* It had worked. Anskan House had allowed him to take his father's troubles. He had averted disaster.

Or rather, as it turned out, simply redirected disaster. No matter what he did, his wound grew worse and worse. Worried that it would somehow break the spell if he told someone and his father would grow ill again, he said nothing.

A few days later he was at his desk at school, dizzy and hot, unable to pay much attention to what was going on at the front of the class. His leg felt like it was being twisted first one way and then the other, and then, suddenly, it began to burn. He looked down and saw that blood had soaked through his jeans and was slowly wicking its way through the fabric. Fascinated, he watched it spread, imagining the moment when the whole of the pant leg would be sopped and oversaturated, when his blood would start to drip onto the floor. And then suddenly he had slid out of his chair and was lying face-up on the ground, staring at the ceiling, unable to move, the class in commotion all around him.

He awoke in a hospital bed with no clear idea how much time had passed, how many hours or days. His mother was sitting beside him. His father was there too, no longer in a hospital gown, walking with a limp but still walking.

Judith and Mattias were there as well, seated near the foot of the bed.

"You're better," Sefton said to his father.

"All better," said his father, and gave a smile brimming with health. "Don't worry, soon you will be too."

But he knew he wouldn't be.

"How did this happen?" his mother wanted to know, but he just shook his head. "Why didn't you tell us?" she asked.

"I didn't think it was anything," he lied.

"You'll get better," his father said confidently, and patted his head. "If I could get better, you can too. You're young, your body is strong. There's nothing to worry about."

Sefton didn't bother to answer.

From the foot of the bed his sister gave him a strange look. "It's strange you both had the same illness," she said slowly.

The whole family turned to look at her.

"Maybe a genetic flaw," said his father. "Runs in the family." He turned and wagged his finger. "The rest of you, be careful."

A few hours later, when the rest of the family was stepping out for dinner, his sister volunteered to stay behind, sit with him. As soon as the others were gone, she pulled her chair close to the bed, fixed her gaze on him.

After a while, he squirmed. "What?" he said. "What do you want?"

"What did you do?" she whispered angrily.

"I told you," he said. "I grazed it."

She shook her head. "I'm asking what you really did," she said. She waited. When he did not answer, she said, "Did you go there?"

"Go where?"

"You know where," she said. "How did you know what to do?"

He looked away. "I don't know what you're talking about."

She cupped the side of his head with a hand, turned him slowly but relentlessly toward her until he had no choice but to look at her.

"You shouldn't have done it," she said. "You're just a child. You have no idea what you're playing with."

"I'm not a child," he said.

"Who told you about it?" she said again, but he said nothing.

"I know," she said, and then leaned closer, until her lips were nearly touching his ear, and whispered *Anskan House*. When she drew back her eyes were fierce and hard.

"Swear to me you'll forget about it," she said. "Swear to me you'll never go back there again."

He tried to break away, but she wouldn't let him. For a while he wriggled beneath her gaze, not responding, but in the end he nodded.

———— 3 ————

At first it still felt like he had a leg. He could feel it aching and tingling even months after the surgeon removed it. It was hard to get around, and it separated him from all the other children his age. But he still felt like he had done the right thing, that he had saved his father, saved the family. What was a leg next to a whole family?

And then, slowly, after a year, maybe two, he got used to not having a leg. In time he hardly thought about it anymore. In a way, he hardly even missed it. Putting on the artificial leg began more and more to feel as natural as slipping on a shoe.

He never quite admitted to his sister what he had done, though he knew she knew. He caught her sometimes over the years regarding him strangely. But she never said anything and neither did he.

Then first she and then he grew older and moved out of the house. He went across town to college, then took a job, got married. Soon, except for the few times a year he saw Judith, there was no reason to think about Anskan House.

For years, he did his best to keep his promise. For decades, he did not think about Anskan House, did not think about what he had said at the door or what he had felt or heard when he stood at the letterbox. He did not think about it when, years later, his father died. He did not think about it when his wife miscarried their first child and sunk into months of unhappiness and depression. He did not think of it when, much, much later, after two stillborn children and two that lived, his wife was diagnosed with cancer and given only a few years left to live. His life went on and on, slowly stripping away everyone he had known and still mostly he did not even remember there had ever been a place called Anskan House, let alone what could be made to happen there.

Indeed, it was only at the very end of his life—or what should have, properly speaking, been the end of his life—that he thought of Anskan House again. Both his brother and sister were dead by then. He was well into his seventh decade, had caught what for a week he thought was a cold. Maybe it had in fact begun as a cold, but by the end it was pneumonia and his lungs were filling with fluid, and he was certain this time he was going to die.

It was then that he suddenly recalled Anskan House, slowly coaxed it up from the depths of his mind. Had it really happened? Had it been real? Or had he and his sister simply convinced themselves it was? Had his own infection simply been an uncanny coincidence? And if Anskan House was real, was it still there?

Befuddled, it took him a few moments to understand what had drawn his mind to Anskan House. It was the boy sitting next to his bed: his grandson, sitting still and quiet, staring at him, looking very much like Sefton had looked when he himself was young. Sefton looked at the boy looking at him and then something opened in his head and there it was again: Anskan House. No, he told himself, it probably isn't real. He had probably made it up. He had probably only imagined it.

Sefton regarded the boy carefully. The child was young and healthy, just as he had been young and healthy when he lost his leg. Pneumonia would be nothing for a child, he couldn't stop himself from thinking. Pneumonia could kill an old man, but it could hardly kill a child, could it?

He smiled at the boy.

No, he told himself again, probably Anskan House was not real. Probably he had only imagined it.

And even if it was real, he rationalized, he could just go back later and wish to take on his grandson's troubles. No harm would be done. He wasn't taking advantage of the boy, not really: he just wanted to know if Anskan House was real.

And so there he was, lungs filling with fluid, dying in his bed, trying to teach his grandson where he must go to knock on a door and whisper through a slot. *You love me, don't you?* he found himself saying. *You don't want me to die, do you?*

A part of him was thinking, *It's not even real, this is not serious, this is just a game, a way of tying up one loose thread before I die.*

But another, colder part knew exactly what it was doing. And this was the part of him that did not regret the way things worked out in the end.

COLOPHON

Windeye was designed at Coffee House Press, in the historic Grain Belt Brewery's Bottling House near downtown Minneapolis. The text is set in Centaur.

ACKNOWLEDGMENTS

I want to thank my agent, Matt McGowan, for his careful reading of this collection and for his ongoing encouragement. Also Chris Fischbach for his careful editorial eye and Coffee House Press generally for their continued interest in and support of my work. Rereading these stories, it is strange to think how much of the interest both in loss and in embodied perception within them revolves around my own struggles with illness when I was in the process of writing them. The descriptions of the way the ear feels like it is expanding and evolving in "The Other Ear" are fairly direct transcriptions of what I felt was happening to my own ear after an operation that laid the ear back from my head and cut the nerve. For months I felt like the ear was a separate, throbbing thing, and that I could reach up and with a little tug tear the ear off. "Anskan House," which mentions lungs feeling like they are full of ragged, hot cloth and in which the main character's lungs begin filling with fluid, my daughter has pointed out, was the last thing I wrote before my own lung collapsed and I spent weeks in genuine distress in the hospital. "The Oxygen Protocol," where the character cannot breath, was written just before that. These stories mark the end of one sort of life for me and the beginning of another, and I owe more than I can say to Kristen Tracy, who has made that new life possible.

FUNDER ACKNOWLEDGMENT

Coffee House Press is an independent nonprofit literary publisher. Our books are made possible through the generous support of grants and gifts from many foundations, corporate giving programs, state and federal support, and through donations from individuals who believe in the transformational power of literature. Coffee House Press receives major operating support from the Bush Foundation, the Jerome Foundation, the McKnight Foundation, the National Endowment for the Arts, a federal agency, from Target, and in part by a grant provided by the Minnesota State Arts Board through an appropriation by the Minnesota State Legislature from the State's general fund and its arts and cultural heritage fund with money from the vote of the people of Minnesota on November 4, 2008. Coffee House also receives support from: several anonymous donors; Suzanne Allen; the Elmer L. and Eleanor J. Andersen Foundation; Around Town Literary Media Guides; Patricia Beithon; Bill Berkson; the James L. and Nancy J. Bildner Foundation; the E. Thomas Binger and Rebecca Rand Fund of the Minneapolis Foundation; the Patrick and Aimee Butler Family Foundation; Ruth and Bruce Dayton; Dorsey & Whitney, LLP; Mary Ebert and Paul Stembler; Fredrikson & Byron, P.A.; Sally French; Jennifer Haugh; Anselm Hollo and Jane Dalrymple-Hollo; Jeffrey Hom; Carl and Heidi Horsch; Stephen and Isabel Keating; the Kenneth Koch Literary Estate; the Lenfestey Family Foundation; Ethan J. Litman; Carol and Aaron Mack; Mary McDermid; Sjur Midness and Briar Andresen; the Rehael Fund of the Minneapolis Foundation; Schwegman, Lundberg & Woessner, P.A.; John Sjoberg; Kiki Smith; Jeffrey Sugerman; Patricia Tilton; the Archie D. & Bertha H. Walker Foundation; Stu Wilson and Mel Barker; the Woessner Freeman Family Foundation; Margaret and Angus Wurtele; and many other generous individual donors.

To you and our many readers across the country,
we send our thanks for your continuing support.

Good books are brewing at coffeehousepress.org

MISSION

The mission of Coffee House Press is to publish exciting, vital, and enduring authors of our time; to delight and inspire readers; to contribute to the cultural life of our community; and to enrich our literary heritage. By building on the best traditions of publishing and the book arts, we produce books that celebrate imagination, innovation in the craft of writing, and the many authentic voices of the American experience.

VISION

LITERATURE. We will promote literature as a vital art form, helping to redefine its role in contemporary life. We will publish authors whose groundbreaking work helps shape the direction of 21st-century literature.

WRITERS. We will foster the careers of our writers by making long-term commitments to their work, allowing them to take risks in form and content.

READERS. Readers of books we publish will experience new perspectives and an expanding intellectual landscape.

PUBLISHING. We will be leaders in developing a sustainable 21st-century model of independent literary publishing, pushing the boundaries of content, form, editing, audience development, and book technologies.

VALUES

Innovation and excellence in all activities

Diversity of people, ideas, and products

Advancing literary knowledge

Community through embracing many cultures

Ethical and highly professional management and governance practices

Join us in our mission at coffeehousepress.org